Southern Storm

To Susan —
Enjoy!

A sequel to the novel,
Southern Sanctuary

A novel by
Don Pardue

Copyright © 2016

Don Pardue

ISBN 13: 978-1535577533

First printing 2016

Printed in the U.S.A by

G

G J Publishing
515 Cimarron Circle, Suite 323
Loudon Tennessee 37774
865-458-1355
www.neilans.com

To Barbara,
The wind beneath my wings

Cover Design by
Victor Pardue

Editing by
Victor Pardue and Donna Pardue Thompson

Acknowledgments

During the 1950's, the Southern states continued to be a hostile environment for African Americans. They were denied many freedoms, such as voting rights, and dining privileges in public restaurants. Also, black children were not allowed to attend public schools. This became a major cause of illiteracy, for it initiated the establishment of many inferior Negro schools. Black people endured many other denials of human rights that were taken for granted by white citizens. It was only after the passage of the Civil Rights Act of 1964 and the Voting Rights Act of 1965 that conditions began to improve.

Enforcement of these laws has stimulated public recognition of the continuing progress of our Southern states during the last half-century. The Deep South has made great strides in the improvement of race relations, education, and individual opportunity. Although still an imperfect environment, the states south of the Mason Dixon line will always be my home.

Also, I owe a debt of gratitude to my daughter, Donna, who worked many hours in editing this book and also provided continuing encouragement and an inexhaustible supply of creative ideas. In addition, I am indebted to my son, Victor, who not only edited portions of the book and offered helpful advice, but also designed the outstanding cover. And most importantly, as always, to Barbara, my wife of sixty years, whose optimistic and youthful spirit has been my source of inspiration.

Prologue

The flames from the burning cross leaped upward into the hanging boughs of the trees, illuminating the forest and nearby meadow. With no hesitation, the Klan leader stepped forward. From beneath his robe he pulled his revolver and placed the muzzle against the elderly man's forehead. The loud report of the pistol echoed among the trees and faded as it reverberated across the river. With the back of his head gone, the preacher fell limply to the ground. Then, when the Klansman shot Rufus, the force of the blast slammed the black man's face against the tree to which he had been tied prior to his brutal beating.

A wisp of smoke drifted from the barrel of the revolver. The Negro's upper torso fell backward and he hung like a skewered animal from the ropes that bound him to the tree. The scent of gunpowder mingled with the pungent scent of the burning cross.

Nick Parilli was trembling when he suddenly awakened and sat up in bed. His heart was beating so rapidly it felt as if it might leap from his chest. For a long while he sat in his bed reliving the terrible dream, the recurring nightmare that had become so familiar. His recollection of the violent event was even more terrifying than the ghosts that continued to haunt him after the horrors of the Korean War.

He glanced down at his wife, Lauren, who was lying beside him. Upon his first glance at her, his nerves began to calm. She stirred and rolled over onto her back. He watched her as she slept. Strands of disheveled raven hair half-covered her forehead and her open mouth expelled a gentle snore.

With an abrupt snort, she awakened. In an attempt to identify her surroundings, her sleepy blue eyes explored the room before a gradual recognition dawned in her expressive eyes. She brushed away the stray strands of hair from her forehead and turned to face Nick. She was aware of his terrible memories and always tried to help him overcome them. She looked up at him. "What's wrong, Nicky?" she asked. "Can't you sleep?"

"No, I can't sleep." he answered. "I had that horrible dream again—the same nightmare that continues to haunt me…Damn it!"

"Do you mean your memory about the Klan killing?"

"Yeah, that's the dream. It keeps coming back to me. I can't seem to get it out of my mind."

She hugged him tightly. "Would it help if you talked about it?" she asked. "I'll listen if it will help you."

"No, I don't want to talk about it, but thanks for asking. I want to try to forget it and go back to sleep."

She reassuringly hugged him. She told him goodnight and continued to cling to him until she once again fell asleep.

Nick slowly pulled away from her and turned over in bed. Because he was still shaken from his terrible nightmare, he continued to tremble as he lay beneath the covers. Hours of terrifying memories haunted him before he finally slept.

Chapter 1

On the following morning Nick awakened to the sound of the ringing telephone. In his effort to keep from awakening Lauren, who was still asleep beside him, he silently got up and crept to the phone. When he first answered he heard no response. Finally, he detected a familiar voice that sounded like his former friend and Lauren's first cousin, Stan Mullins. "Hello…Is this Nicky?" Nick was surprised, for he hadn't communicated with Stan in months. He noticed that Stan, as well as Lauren were still calling him 'Nicky.'

"Yes, this is Nick," he replied. "Who am I speaking to?"

Stan continued. "This is Stan. Let me speak to Lauren."

"Are you all right, Stan? Is something wrong?"

"Yes, I'm okay. Please…just let me speak to Lauren."

Nick handed her the telephone after she rose from the bed and stood beside him. She yawned and rubbed her sleepy eyes when she answered. "Hello. Who is this? Stan? Well, this is sure a surprise! What did you say about Daddy?" She suddenly turned to face Nick, who was curiously watching her. *"Oh God no! Nicky, Daddy's dead! Stan said he shot himself!"* The telephone fell from her hands and she collapsed into Nick's arms.

Nick gently lifted Lauren onto the bed as she began to sob and uncontrollably moan. As if to blot out the knowledge of the tragedy, she covered her ears with her pillow. Nick picked up the telephone and spoke to Stan. "Damn it, talk to *me*, Stan! Why did you want to speak to Lauren instead of me? What did you say about Lauren's dad? Did you say he shot himself?"

Stan again hesitated before he continued. "Nicky...I was afraid you wouldn't want to talk to me after...after the way our relationship turned out. And I can't really blame you."

"Tell me what happened, damn it!" Nick demanded.

"Are you sure you want to talk to me?" asked Stan.

"It's not a matter of what I *want*. When you have that kind of shocking news, you should tell *me*...not my wife even if she *is* your cousin!" Nick was angry. Because of past events he was still resentful of Stan.

Stan remained calm. "Well, for now, I'll just be brief. Lauren's dad, the county sheriff, is dead. The police believe he shot himself. I didn't get to finish my conversation with Lauren before she became hysterical. You and Lauren will need to come to Cedar Valley for the funeral. It will take place on Monday afternoon. There'll be a lot of people there because Lauren's dad was well-known as the sheriff. I'll explain more when I see you. There's been a lot of changes in Cedar Valley since I last saw you. You and I have a lot to talk about, pal."

"Why can't we just talk about it *now*, Stan?" asked Nick.

"It's too complicated, Nicky. I can explain it better when we meet face-to-face. You're gonna be shocked. Can I depend on you and Lauren to come back here to attend the funeral?"

"What do you mean, *'can you depend on us'*? You know damned well that Lauren will attend her own father's funeral!"

"Well, what about you, Nicky? Will you be there too? You're not too fond of the sheriff, you know." Stan was curious.

"Hell yes! Don't you realize that I intend to always support Lauren?" Nick was becoming angry with him. "When did this happen, Stan? Do you know why he shot himself?"

2

Stan answered, "It happened sometime yesterday. It was a total shock to everybody who knew the sheriff. The police say that he committed suicide. But I don't believe he killed himself. I don't know for sure who shot him, but I have a pretty good idea. I suspect that it was a member of the Klan."

"But why would a member of the Klan shoot him? After all, he also belonged to that hellish group," said Nick.

"I'll explain more about it whenever I see you. Maybe you can help me solve this murder."

"Are you kidding?" asked Nick. "The last time I tried to poke my nose into police business, I almost lost my life."

"That was partly my fault, Nicky. Maybe there's some way I can make it up to you."

"Good luck with that, pal!" said Nick, sarcastically.

"Nicky, I need to give you a word of caution. The police is still trying to find out the whereabouts of the guy under suspicion of committing the Klan killings…Deputy Mike Bronson. Some people think that news of the killing was only a rumor. All of the Klan members know that you witnessed the killing and they may be determined to kill you to keep you from testifying. When you and Lauren left here, I was the only person who knew you were now living in Louisiana. Also, I haven't told the public about the Klan murders. I'm not sure how the news leaked out. Anyway, when you come in for the funeral, be careful. When you arrive in Cedar Valley give me a call and I'll tell you where to meet me. Tell Lauren that her mother will be here with us. She's grieving, but I think she's gonna be okay. When you arrive in town, don't expose yourself to the public. Be careful." He gave Nick his private phone number, and told him goodbye.

"Goodbye, Stan."

Nick slowly walked to the bed and sat beside Lauren, who still had her head buried in the pillow. She continued to cry. He cuddled her and said, "I'm so sorry, Lauren. I know how you loved your daddy. Things will get better—just give it time."

"Oh Nicky, I'm so full of regret! I've written to Mother a few times since we left Cedar Valley, but I never even wrote to Daddy…He was so mixed up. I wish I could see him just once more so I could tell him I forgive him."

"Don't keep blaming yourself, Lauren. I believe your father always knew that you loved him."

She wiped away her tears. "So what do we do now, Nicky?"

"Well, we need to start packing and go back to Cedar Valley, Tennessee. Today is Saturday and they're having the funeral on Monday. I'll have to go to the bank and withdraw some money. We'll need to leave New Orleans this afternoon."

She continued to cry as she rose from the bed. Between sobs she said, "It's a good thing it's early June and I'm on summer break from my teaching job; also, you've already taken your final exams. And just think…Daddy's dead! We were planning to take a short vacation when the school year ended. Some vacation *this* is!" She again began to cry. He took her into his arms and hugged her. Her voice trembled when she said, "Poor Daddy. I already miss him so much."

Nick continued to hold her and spoke softly. "Honey, I've learned that sometimes we just have to accept whatever fate has in store for us. We can't change the past, or wish away unhappy events in our lives."

Lauren was still sobbing when she slipped on her robe and walked into the kitchen. In order to temporarily rid her mind of the terrible news, she tried to immerse herself in some trivial chore. She asked Nick, "Honey, do you want me to make you some breakfast?"

Nick smiled at her. "No Lauren. I'm not hungry and I know you're not either. Just put on a pot of coffee. Maybe it'll help us on our long drive to Tennessee. The funeral is going to be held Monday, so we'll need to get there by tomorrow night. If we get hungry, we can always stop along the way."

When they sat down for coffee, Lauren again began to cry. She finally wiped the tears from her eyes and helplessly

4

looked at Nick. "Nicky, do you think maybe Daddy shot himself because of the way I rejected him?"

"Don't start blaming yourself, Lauren. Stan suspects that he was shot by somebody else. Obviously a sheriff is sure to make some enemies." Nick didn't reveal to her Stan's belief that a member of the Klan had shot her father. In fact, Nick himself was puzzled about Stan's suspicion, for he remembered that Sheriff Mullins was also a Klan member.

She eyed him curiously. "Do you have any idea why Daddy would kill himself?"

"Your guess is as good as mine, Lauren. Stan said he'd explain more about the whole situation when we get there. He said that we're going to be surprised at some of the things that have happened since we left Cedar Valley."

Out of his respect for Lauren's need to privately grieve, he remained quiet as they sipped on their coffee at the kitchen table. Although she occasionally sobbed, she gradually began to regain her composure. In spite of their need to talk and make plans, Nick remained silent. He finished his coffee and left the table.

He walked into the bathroom and peered into the mirror. The image of his bloodshot eyes bore evidence of his near-sleepless night. He also noticed that he had recently lost a bit of weight; however, with his dark hair and Italian demeanor, Nick was still a healthy, handsome man. At six feet in height, he tipped the scales at a muscular 175 pounds.

In order to become more fully awake, he splashed cold water on his face. He then leisurely brushed his teeth as Lauren appeared in the bathroom door. In his effort to comfort her, he smiled and again hugged her. "Honey, I'm going to drive to the bank and withdraw some money. Can you think of anything else we need before we leave for Tennessee?"

"No, not at the moment. I'm still too miserable to think very clearly, Nicky."

Because of their hasty exit from Tennessee, Nick had abandoned his vehicle. As a result, he always drove Lauren's car for transportation. He quickly got dressed and drove to the local bank where he withdrew sufficient cash for their journey to Tennessee. He then returned home where they rarely talked as they packed their necessary clothing. A neighbor agreed to keep an eye on their rented apartment during their absence. After Lauren entered the car, Nick tossed their suitcase into the trunk of Lauren's car and drove away.

It was near noontime when they left the city and drove eastward through the sweltering heat along the Southern Gulf Coast. Although Nick occasionally made attempts to console her, they only engaged in limited conversation as they travelled past Lake Pontchartrain, through the city of Slidell, and then turned northward into Southern Mississippi. Nick drove deeper into the state through Hattiesburg, and Laurel. When they turned northeastward into Alabama, Lauren finally regained some of her composure and began to share limited conversation with Nick. They drove through Birmingham, and then turned northward until finally they stopped for dinner in Chattanooga, Tennessee, where they decided to spend the night. Because of their emotional strain, both Lauren and Nick were exhausted. At dinner they only ate sparingly. It was nearly 9:00 p.m. when they retired in a motel in the eastern suburbs of the city.

After a quick shower both Nick and Lauren retired to bed and dimmed the bedside lamp. Because they were both emotionally distraught, they lay awake until nearly midnight, reflecting on recent events. Lauren finally spoke. "Nicky, I know that you think Daddy was a bad man. After all, he treated you unfairly, and tried to break us up; but he seemed to like you when we first started dating. I wonder why he changed his mind about you."

Nick hugged her. "Lauren, there were several reasons: First of all, he thought that you'd eventually get tired of me and stop dating me. Also, I attacked two of his deputies when they arrested me for nothing. And he found out about my army court martial. But most of all, he didn't want you dating anybody. It wasn't just *me* he didn't like."

"Nicky, do you think Daddy was a bad man?" she asked.

Nick answered, "Lauren, like all of us, he was both good and bad. It's like Preacher Temple once told me—'None of us are righteous, for we are all stained by sin.' Maybe your dad was just a victim of his environment. After all, look at the kinds of people that a small-town county sheriff is constantly associating with: drunks, bootleggers, crooked politicians— people with dubious reputations. He was constantly dealing with bad people."

They cuddled together in the bed, discussing their romance in Cedar Valley, Tennessee, a time that seemed so long ago. He finally said, "Lauren, we'll talk more about this in the morning. Right now, we need to try to get some sleep. The next couple of days are going to be tough for both of us."

She snuggled close to him. "I guess you're right, Nicky. I'll try my best to go to sleep. Goodnight—and I love you."

Because of her physical and emotional exhaustion, she soon fell asleep; however, because of his unsettled nature, Nick lay awake for hours. When he realized that falling sleep was impossible, he began to relive his experiences of the last few months.

He vividly recalled his most recent memories of the past. He remembered the quick exit from Cedar Valley, Tennessee, when both he and Lauren left town after witnessing the killing of the Ku Klux Klan leader who had committed two murders during a Klan gathering. As a result, they feared retaliation from the vigilante group. They immediately left—or rather *escaped* Cedar Valley to arrive the following day in Buras, Louisiana, the home of Nick's Uncle Cataldo. Nick's uncle was childless, for he had never married; as a result, he shared a special connection with Nick, his only living relative. He was delighted to meet Lauren, and welcomed the couple into his home.

For years Cataldo Parilli had made his meager living from his commercial fishing business in the Gulf of Mexico. While Lauren served as housekeeper and cook for them, the two men worked together on Uncle Cataldo's fishing boat. Since Nick and Lauren were still single, Nick's uncle served as best man in their wedding.

Lying in his bed, Nick was saddened when he recalled his final memory of his uncle. In less than a month after the wedding, his Uncle Cataldo had died of a massive heart attack. Nick became haunted by the loss of his last living relative.

He continued to reminisce. He remembered that shortly after his uncle died, he and Lauren left Buras, Louisiana and settled in New Orleans. With the aid of the G.I. Bill he had earned in the U.S. Army, he joined Lauren when both of them enrolled at The University of New Orleans.

Times were hard. They lived in a sleazy apartment near the downtown area while Nick worked part time as a waiter in a restaurant on Bourbon Street. Because Lauren already had a college degree, in only three quarters of study after her enrollment in graduate school she became qualified to teach English in a New Orleans high school. Her teacher's salary and Nick's part-time employment supported the couple while Nick attended college.

Nick restlessly rolled over in bed as his mind again wandered deeper into his distant past. Because of his former combat fatigue and other complexities in his life, his recollections were random and vacillating, and came to him in only fragments. He had difficulty in recalling them in their correct sequence. The Korean War was now behind him; however, the horrible memories lingered in his mind. He felt a smoldering hatred of the conflict. He remembered being court-martialed for showing disrespect to his inexperienced commanding lieutenant during the heat of battle. The officer had issued a stupid order that would have meant almost certain death to Nick and most of his squad members. Although he was hesitant to obey the order, he finally complied, but only to be severely wounded. He never fully recovered from the emotional and physical effects of his injuries. He had previously been awarded the bronze star for bravery; however, because of his display of disrespect of the officer Nick was convicted and reduced in rank from sergeant to private and sentenced to serve three months in the army stockade. He was also haunted by his memory of killing a teen-aged North Korean soldier during one of the fierce battles. Because of his terrifying experiences during the war, he suffered from combat fatigue after his discharge.

Nick had many other sad memories of the distant past. He recalled that his mother and father, Marina and Donato Parilli were originally from a city in the Old Country—Salerno, Italy. They came to America in search of a better lifestyle; however, their success was limited because they never mastered a fluent use of the English language.

Prior to the war, Nick had attended a college in Indiana with his former friend and roommate, Stan Mullins—Lauren's first cousin. However, during his junior year, Nick dropped out of college and joined the U.S. Army after his mother died of cancer. Her death had completely decimated his father; as a result, he became an alcoholic man of the streets at his home in Chicago, Illinois. After his discharge from the army Nick returned to his former home in Chicago, where his father, Donato was currently living in an abandoned apartment building. He later died and was buried as a pauper.

Before The Korean War Nick had always been an idealist, and as a younger man he held a simplistic expectancy that most people would be fair and honest. He detested pretentiousness and dishonesty. It angered him when he thought of the way his father had been treated prior to his death. Because Nick had always harbored a deep feeling of outrage about the injustice and inequities of the world, he had begun to develop a profound cynicism.

He began to reminisce about his former relationship with Stan Mullins that took place during their college years, months before the war. In spite of their strong bond, he realized that they were drastically different in both personality and background. One of their major differences was their opposing beliefs in regard to justice. While Nick believed in adhering to the letter of the law, Stan had adopted the attitude of a maverick. In keeping with the viewpoint of some Southerners, he only believed in '*Southern justice*,' a system in which men sometimes created their own laws.

In college, Stan had been outgoing and popular. With a quick wit and a playful nature, he enjoyed playing pranks, and had a penchant for ridiculous humor. Since he was from an affluent family, he was accustomed to always having money. His membership in a fraternity ensured his popularity with the other students, particularly since he seemed to be consistently in a good mood. Except for his adeptness in playing tennis, he was not particularly skilled in athletics; however, he idolized Nick's boxing skills and his heroics on the football team. Further cementing their strong bond was the fact that they had been roommates, and neither of them had siblings.

In contrast, Nick was a loner. He had a reserved, almost brooding personality. Because his father had always held menial jobs, he grew up in a lower-income neighborhood and never knew the pleasure of having money, a fact that his friend, Stan had never fully realized; however, Nick seemed to harbor no jealousy of his friend for his affluence. His opportunity to attend college had been made possible only as a result of his football credentials from high school, which motivated the college to offer him a partial athletic scholarship. However, because of a knee injury he was forced to quit football in his junior season. Lack of money became a problem and his grades began to suffer. Also, during this time, his mother had died. Ultimately, Nick had to drop out of school while Stan had graduated. Soon afterward, Stan became the manager of his father's lucrative construction business in Tennessee while Nick had joined the army and was sent to Korea.

Damn! I need to go to sleep! Nick realized; however, he was much too restless to sleep, for his mind continued to explore the depressing times after his discharge from the army and the tragic death of his father. After the war he had plunged into deep despair. In search of a location that would help restore his sanity, he decided to abandon big-city life and travel by bus from Chicago to the Deep South. His planned destination was the home of his Uncle Cataldo, in Buras, Louisiana, a small town on the gulf coast. But first, he wanted to make a three or four-day stopover to visit his former college friend, Stan Mullins, who lived with his parents in Cedar Valley, Tennessee, a small town near the city of Knoxville. But this detour, which was intended to last for only a few days, became an extended visit that lasted for months after Stan gave Nick a job in his construction business. The events that occurred in the small community forever changed his life.

Stan was the only son of wealthy parents, and made his home with them in their stately mansion. Nick remembered how Stan had taken him into his home where he had met Stan's parents, Lester and Mary Jane; also he had made the acquaintance of the Negro handyman, Rufus, and Minnie, the Negro maid and housekeeper for the Mullins' home. He had no way of knowing that Rufus, the Mullins' handyman would later become a traumatic part of his life.

After Stan hired Nick, they eventually moved to their own apartment. When Nick thought of his former relationship with his college friend, he remembered how generous Stan had been to him. Most of the pleasant experiences he could attribute to his friend; for it was Stan who had acquainted Nick with the South, and invited him into his home. Since he realized that Nick had little money, Stan had given him a job, a vehicle to drive, clothes, and money. Stan had become his staunchest supporter. They even planned to re-enroll in college together, a decision that would enable Stan to earn a graduate degree. Because of his cynicism about the world's unfairness, Nick decided that he would dedicate his future to making the world a better place by returning to college and studying to become a lawyer. Both men had noble ambitions in their desire to improve the Southern lifestyle.

Nick's extended visit to Cedar City, Tennessee was a mixture of his best and worst experiences, for he made many friends as well as enemies there. When Stan introduced him to his first cousin, Lauren, Nick was surprised that she was the daughter of the county sheriff, Laurence Mullins. It was an unlikely romance, for although Nick was a decorated Korean War veteran, he was also an aimless drifter who was suffering from combat fatigue. In contrast, Lauren was a college graduate with aspirations to become a medical doctor. It was highly unlikely that they would ever establish a lasting relationship; but surprisingly, their romance began to flourish. After a lengthy time, his combat fatigue began to diminish.

When Stan introduced them at a local dance, Nick was impressed by her lovely demeanor. She was a woman of medium height with a stunning figure. Her raven hair flowed to her shoulders, and her bronzed skin contrasted with her white dress and made her perfect teeth appear even whiter when she smiled. She was indeed a beautiful woman. For Nick, it was a case of *love at first sight.*

But the sheriff had always maintained a controlling influence over his daughter. He tried to manage her future by demanding that she become a medical doctor, for she had previously earned a degree in pre-mad; however, her personal ambition was to become a school teacher. Also, he frowned on any involvement she might have with men, and kept her under his closest scrutiny. He even instructed one of his deputies, Mike Bronson to keep a close eye on her whenever she attended social functions. At first, the sheriff disapproved of his daughter and Nick associating with each other. But hidden beneath a veneer of obedience to her father, Lauren had a subtle independent spirit. In fear of her rebellion, the sheriff finally relented and allowed her to date Nick. Besides, she was now a grown woman.

Since he was absorbed in his memories, Nick was still unable to sleep. When he began to sweat, he pulled down the covers and mopped his brow with a handkerchief. He began to realize that he was trapped in his recollection of past events.

His mind again wandered as he recalled the Mullins' Negro handyman, Rufus Headrick who was so fond of Stan that he helped the Mullins parents rear the young lad. He recalled Rufus' daughter, Mary Rose—and her twelve-year old son, Caleb, and the way that he had become friends of the Negro family and sometimes had dinner at their home.

Some of Nick's worst experiences were the times he was unjustly arrested by Deputy Mike Bronson, who Sheriff Mullins had appointed as Lauren's chaperone, or *bodyguard.* Bronson not only had a crush on Lauren, but also hated Nick, whom he unfairly arrested a couple of times. During one of his jailhouse experiences, Nick met Preacher Temple, who had been arrested for public drunkenness. He was a virtuous man who had endured the misfortune of being plagued by the disease of alcoholism.

In the recent past, the sheriff had reluctantly accepted the relationship between his daughter, Lauren and Nick; however, after Nick was arrested without cause by two of the sheriff's deputies, he assaulted both police officers. Upon his release from jail, he was completely taken by surprise when Sheriff Mullins threatened him with additional jail time unless he permanently left Cedar Valley. He also forbade Nick to ever again attempt to date his daughter.

Nick was shocked when he discovered that the sheriff and his band of deputies were involved in a den of corruption: false arrests, payoffs by bootleggers, and the illegal sale of alcohol, in which Stan's father, Lester was also involved. Even more disturbing was the revelation that most of the county police department were members of the Ku Klux Klan.

Nick remembered the many times that Stan had proven his friendship, and had been so generous to him; but when he learned that Stan was also a member of the Ku Klux Klan he felt totally betrayed.

However, the most unforgivable offense committed by Stan was the event that initiated Nick's terrible recurring

13

nightmare: It was the moment during the Klan gathering when Stan, whose membership in the Klan was unknown to Nick at the time, helplessly watched while the Klan leader brutally whipped and eventually murdered the elderly Mullins' handyman, Rufus—the Negro who was a close friend of Stan's and like a second father to him. The incident that brought about the Klan's punishment of Rufus occurred after Nick and Rufus made a routine trip into town. After they parked their vehicle, a little white girl carelessly ran out into the street. When she was almost hit by a car, Rufus immediately dashed into the street and rescued her. When he attempted to release her, she remained terrified, and continued to cling to him. As a result, Rufus was unjustly accused of fondling her, an act that would spell certain doom for a black man. When a prejudiced Southern man witnessed the incident, he harshly reprimanded Rufus. Unfortunately, the angry Southerner was a secret member of the Ku Klux Klan. Nick, who had accompanied Rufus into town, immediately defended his friend. He threatened to attack the Klan member. After making many threats, the man cursed at Rufus as he walked away. Several days later, the Klan kidnapped Rufus and delivered him to a lonely spot by the river, where the Klan members had erected a crude cross that had become a blazing inferno.

Nick vividly recalled the memory. He and Preacher Temple had sneaked to the Klan meeting in an attempt to stop the whipping of Rufus. In order to reason with the hellish group and plead for the Negro, the preacher stepped from his hiding place and revealed his presence. In order to expose the Klansman's identity, he even yanked the hood off the Klan leader, Mike Bronson., the man who had been brutally whipping Rufus. Since following the preacher would be suicidal, Nick remained hidden. He then stared in disbelief as Stan remained silent and did nothing when the Klansman killed both Rufus and the preacher,

But on the day that Nick and Lauren escaped Cedar Valley, they witnessed a moment of poetic justice. In total shock they watched as the twelve-year old Negro boy, Caleb stepped from behind a tree with his shotgun and killed Klan leader Mike Bronson, the murderer of his grandfather, Rufus. Because Nick felt that a certain kind of justice had been served he never reported the slaying to the authorities. Also, he wanted to protect Rufus' young grandson from prosecution. Therefore it had remained unsolved.

Nick experienced mixed feelings about the brutal slaying; but in spite of his recollection of the horror, he felt no regret about not reporting the vengeful killing to the authorities; instead, he experienced a certain measure of comfort when he remembered the final retribution. He relived the grisly but gratifying memory of the event until he gradually became calm and drifted off to sleep.

Chapter 2

It was early morning when Nick finally fell asleep. Lauren awoke much earlier and lay awake beside him for a long while, reflecting on her former relationship with her father. After a family death, surviving members often recall both pleasant and sad memories, the victim's personality, and the way they were perceived by the deceased family member. When she remembered her anger at her father, she was filled with regret; for this wasn't just *an ordinary* father-daughter relationship—this one was different, for it bordered on *obsession.* She began to realize that most of her dad's faults were products of his possessive and smothering love for her; and although such a love isn't normal, it is no less profound.

His happiness was almost totally dependent upon her excellence, for he had always vicariously lived his life through her achievements. She was saddened to remember the intimate details of his controlling influence on her; however, she also experienced a contradicting feeling that she had become a disappointment to him. She felt that he had demanded more of her than she had been able or willing to achieve. In spite of her sadness and mixed feelings, she knew that she would continue to love and remember him always.

Nick finally awakened. He yawned, stretched, and rolled over in the bed, facing Lauren. He gently cuddled her and smiled. "Good morning, honey. Did you sleep well?"

"Not too well, Nicky. I've been lying here awake for hours thinking of Daddy."

"Well, that's only to be expected, Lauren. It's going to take a while for you to recover from the shock of losing him." He reassuringly patted her.

"Nicky, sometimes I feel that I really hurt Daddy. He always wanted me to become a medical doctor, but instead, I became a teacher. I know I must have disappointed him. Are you disappointed in me, Nicky?"

"Am I disappointed in you? Are you kidding? I'm proud of you! You followed the path that God intended for you!"

In preparation of getting ready for travel, Nick rose from the bed and walked into the bathroom, where he removed his underclothing and stepped into the shower. Lauren slowly got out of bed and followed him. She spoke to him through the shower curtain. "Honey, I can't get over the hateful way I talked to Daddy before you and I left Cedar Valley."

Through the curtain, Nick answered, "Lauren, it's only natural that you're going to have some guilt feelings about your father. You'll eventually get over those feelings."

She returned to her bed and took a seat while Nick shaved. She remained silent when he returned to the room and dressed himself. She was quiet and still reminiscing about her father when she left for the bathroom where she dressed herself and applied makeup.

Because they had slept late, it was early afternoon when they packed their clothing and personal items and tossed their suitcase into the car. Then they walked into the small restaurant next door and ordered breakfast. They were only munching on their food when Lauren asked, "Nicky, when we were still in Cedar Valley and Daddy was interrogating you in his office about the time you witnessed the murder of Rufus and the preacher—were you surprised when I walked into the room?"

17

"Was I surprised? That's putting it mildly, Lauren. I was *amazed!* You probably saved my life!" Nick answered.

"A couple of his deputies were escorting you out the door to Daddy's car at the very moment I entered. Remember? I've often wondered where they were taking you. Do you know?" she asked.

"No—I'm not sure. But I hope your father wasn't going to kill me to keep me from telling some higher authority about the Klan killings."

"Nicky, I can forgive Daddy for all of his crooked activities and even for cheating on my mother. But I can never forgive him if he had intentions of killing you to keep you quiet about the Klan killings."

Nick thought for a moment before answering. He was sure that Sheriff Mullins had meant to kill him; however, if Lauren were aware of her father's intentions, it would depress her even more. "Lauren, I'm not sure what your father intended to do, but I hope he wasn't going to kill me. Maybe he just meant to escort me out of town to be rid of me."

"Honey, the memory of that moment has haunted me ever since it happened."

Nick looked at her sadly. "Try not to think about it, Lauren. Living it over and over in your mind is not going to help you, or anybody else."

She ignored Nick's comment. "There's another thing that haunts me, Nicky. It's the moment that I revealed his Klan outfit that proved that he was a member of that awful group. He became so embarrassed and ashamed when everyone in the room realized that I knew the complete truth about him. When I remember that, I feel so sorry for him!"

Nick was sympathetic toward her, but he felt that she was attempting to rationalize some of the most glaring faults of her father. "Lauren! You're getting too sentimental when you're describing all of the negative things that happened! Try to deal with reality! Think of your dad as a man with faults! Accept him, warts and all! Then forgive him and try to move on!" He almost regretted his lecture; however, he felt that she needed the advice in order to return to reality. He realized her need to grieve, but he feared she was only delaying her emotional recovery.

They both remained quiet as they left the small café. Nick backed away from the curb and they drove down Highway 11 toward Cedar Valley. Neither of them spoke as they traveled through Cleveland, and then Athens. They were approaching the town of Sweetwater when she finally said, "Nicky, I'm sorry I've been talking so gloomy. I guess it's just hard for me to face reality about Daddy. But since he has died, I'm even more worried about Mother. What will happen to her now that Daddy can no longer take care of her? She's been in a wheelchair for years, you know—ever since she fell down the stairs years ago. Also, she seems to be in the beginning phase of dementia. Do you think that maybe Stan's father can give her a home? Or could you and I help take care of her?"

"I don't know, Lauren. We'll have to give that situation a little more thought. And speaking of Stan…He said that we'd be surprised about some of the things that have taken place since you and I left Cedar Valley. I wonder what he meant. He said he'd tell me more when we meet him. And by the way…I'm sorry if my little lecture hurt your feelings. It's just that I can hardly bear to see you suffer. I like to see you happy."

"I know, Nicky. I'll try to recover from my misery. I know that you've been unhappy, too. Especially about the way Stan betrayed you by being a member of the Klan and witnessing the murder of Rufus and the preacher. You suggested that I forgive Daddy. Have you been able to forgive Stan?"

"Yeah—I forgave him long ago, but I just don't want him to know it yet. I need to hear him explain his actions before I let him know how I feel toward him."

"Nicky, how did you find out that Stan was a member of the Klan?" she asked. "You never did tell me."

"I discovered it shortly after the preacher and I sneaked into the Klan meeting by the river. When we were watching as Rufus was being beaten, I tried to look at all the identifying

19

features of the Klansmen, but since they were covered with those white sheets, all I could see was their feet. I noticed that one of them had a star on the toe of each of his boots. Several days later, while your daddy was questioning me in his office, Stan and a couple of deputies were also there. I recognized those same stars on the toes of Stan's boots. It completely broke my heart when I realized how he had betrayed me. He also betrayed Rufus, who was like a second father to him."

Lauren said, "Well, how do you think I felt when I learned that my own father was a member of that hellish mob?"

"Well, I suppose you felt devastated." said Nick.

"Why did Stan become a member of the Klan?" she asked.

Nick replied, "Stan always wanted to be a part of something that had a purpose," said Nick, "He wasn't a bad person. He was simply misguided."

They again became silent as they drove until they entered the downtown area of Cedar Valley, Nick parked the car in front of a restaurant where he could make a phone call to Stan. When they entered the café, Lauren welcomed the temporary break after their long drive. She stretched to rid her body of the stiffness of travel before she sat at the counter and ordered a soft drink. Nick walked to a nearby phone booth and dialed the number that Stan had given to him. A female voice answered. "Hello…"

"Hello," Nick answered. "May I speak to Stan Mullins?"

"Yes…. Just a minute, please."

After a moment, Stan answered. "Hello."

"Hello, Stan. This is Nick. Lauren and I just arrived in Cedar Valley."

"Hello, Nicky. I expected you a little earlier. I guess you and Lauren will be here just in time for dinner. We'll talk more when you arrive at our house. I'll see you soon, pal." After he gave Nick directions to his living quarters, Nick and Lauren re-entered the car and drove toward the address.

20

Chapter 3

Nick drove the vehicle until he turned to the right and entered a steep hill toward the highest elevation in the small town. Near the top of the hill he pulled the car over into the parking area that overlooked the entire community. He was deeply saddened when he peered into the misty distance toward the Tennessee River. By sheer coincidence, Stan had moved to his new residence atop Kingston Hill. It was from this nearby overlook that he and Preacher Temple had peered into the distance while searching for the sight of a burning cross. He vividly remembered the Klan meeting beside the distant river where Rufus and the preacher were later murdered.

He turned to Lauren. "Honey, if you don't mind I'd like for you to come with me for a minute. I want you to see something that still haunts me."

She stepped from the car and followed Nick as he walked to the edge of the precipice that overlooked the small town. He pointed into the distance toward the river. "Lauren, Preacher Temple and I stood at this very spot on that terrible night when Rufus and the preacher were later killed by the Klan. We were trying to spot a burning cross somewhere in the distance. I was hoping that I would never again see this place."

"Maybe seeing it again and thinking about the reality of it will help you get over it, Nicky." She hugged him.

"Damn!" he said, "How many times do I have to think about it? It's been on my mind for several months!"

They reentered the car and Nick drove further up the steep incline. They travelled a meandering road through a thick forest until they reached the crest of the hill. They had difficulty locating the house, for it was almost obscured by the wild foliage. A weed-infested, seldom-used lane led further up the hill into a thick grove of trees and vines. Between the main road and the wooded yard was a huge meadow, barren of trees. Although the house was almost hidden from view, the empty field in front enabled the house occupants to see any intruder who might travel the road. The location was probably the most isolated area in the county.

The property was a drastic departure from the stately residences to which Stan was accustomed. The house was a dilapidated, wooden structure that badly needed painting. However, because of its seclusion, Nick understood Stan's reason for choosing the run-down dwelling as his refuge.

Nick pulled into the driveway. He and Lauren got out of the car as Stan immediately appeared on the front porch. Following closely behind him was a pretty blonde woman who looked vaguely familiar to Nick. She grinned and quickly ran down the porch steps to Lauren. The two women then hugged each other.

"I'll swear!" said Lauren, "Why it's Kathy Martin! What are you doing here?"

"Stan and I got married a couple of months ago," she said. "I guess you and Nick also got married."

"Yes, we were married in Louisiana," said Lauren.

Stan stepped forward and immediately hugged Nick, who was only cordial in his response. With an elaborate grin on his face, Stan introduced his wife. "Hi Nicky…This is Kathy Martin. Do you remember the girl you met at the July 4th Dance when you first came to Cedar Valley? Well, she and I got married. There'll be no more pickin' up strange women for you and me Nicky!" His joking demeanor suggested that his friendship with Nick was still intact.

Nick finally remembered Kathy. He smiled and hugged her. "Hi, Kathy," he said, "I can see that you're still as pretty as you were when I last saw you!"

When he released her, Kathy and Lauren continued their conversation. Stan placed his arm around Nick and led him up the porch steps as Lauren and Kathy followed. He smiled and said, "Let's go in and see Lauren's mother, Bonnie Rose. I think she's somewhere in one of the bedrooms."

Once inside the house, Kathy expressed her regret to Lauren about the death of her father. Tears appeared in Lauren's eyes as she asked, "Where's my mother?"

Stan called out, "Aunt Bonnie! Lauren and Nick are here! They came here to see you!!" Stan then whispered to Nick, "Lauren's mother is showing signs of dementia, Nicky. I don't think she realizes that her husband is dead or why we brought her to this house." He moved toward the bedroom. "Excuse me Nick, and I'll bring her in here," he said. He then went into the bedroom. When he returned he was pushing Lauren's mother in her wheelchair.

Lauren immediately began to cry as she ran to her mother and hugged her. She only responded with an expression of bewilderment as she looked at her daughter. Lauren backed away from her. "Mother! It's me! And I brought Nicky with me! It's so good to see you again! And I'm so sorry about Daddy!"

"Why did we move to this place?" her mother asked. "Where is your father, anyway? Why doesn't he come home?"

Lauren expressed shock when she looked at her mother's confused expression and shriveled body. Her gray hair was disheveled and she appeared to be weaker than Lauren had remembered her. Kathy followed as Lauren continued to cry when she pushed the wheelchair with her mother into the kitchen. They avoided talking about the death of Sheriff Mullins and the upcoming funeral as Lauren and Kathy began to prepare dinner.

Stan walked to the couch where both he and Nick took a seat. "Poor woman," said Stan. "Lauren's mother remembers certain things, but she seems to have forgotten about the death of her husband."

Nick hadn't yet begun to trust Stan, for he was still unsure of his sincerity. "That's pretty tragic, Stan," said Nick." If that's true, it's going to make Lauren even sadder." His tone lacked the warmth of their former friendship.

Nick studied his demeanor. Except for a slight weight loss and a longer crop of blonde hair, Stan's physical appearance had remained unchanged since the last time he had seen him. He had the same cheerful personality and muscular physique that Nick remembered.

Stan remarked, "I just hope that Lauren can make it through the funeral. She seems to be taking her dad's death pretty hard."

"Don't worry about Lauren," Nick answered, "She's a strong woman. By the way, when we talked on the phone you said that you and I had a lot to talk about. You said that I was going to be shocked at some of the things that have happened here in Cedar Valley since Lauren and I left here. Okay, tell me about it."

Stan looked directly at Nick. "Well, first of all I want to tell you why the sheriff was killed. I think he was murdered. It was because of his conscience. He had a change of heart, mostly because of Lauren. After she became aware of his sins and abandoned him, he was never the same. You know how he worshipped her. In his desire to lure her back to Cedar Valley he decided to confess to the authorities his membership in the Ku Klux Klan. He wasn't at the scene of the crime when the Klan committed the murders, but he felt partly responsible for the two murders. As a result, before he was killed, he even asked me to persuade you to return to Cedar Valley to prove his accusations about the murders. He even talked of confessing his involvement with bootleggers, and his other crooked dealings while he was sheriff. I don't believe he committed suicide, and I think I know who killed him. I believe it was his deputy, Ernie Galyon. If the sheriff were sentenced to prison, Galyon feared that he'd also serve some time. After all, he not only was deeply involved in the crooked activities of the county police, but he was also a member of the Klan and witnessed the two murders. I think he killed the sheriff too keep him from talking. So the sheriff never really got a chance to confess his crimes before he was killed."

"Ernie Galyon? Is he the guy who's known as 'Cowboy Galyon' to most people?"

"Yeah...he's' the guy!" Stan's face expressed anger.

"If you believe Cowboy Galyon murdered him, where did this crime take place?" Nick asked.

"Galyon killed him at the same location that the Klan murders happened: over in that damned lonely meadow by the river."

Nick appeared to be puzzled. "I wonder what motivated Sheriff Mullins to go to that dismal location. Why would he go there? "

Stan's expression reflected sorrow as if he were reliving the unspeakable event. "Well, as you know, my uncle wasn't there when Rufus and the preacher were murdered. He was at a Knoxville political meeting. But because of his membership in the Klan, I believe he felt partly responsible for the horrible events of that evening. I believe he went there to face the demons that continued to haunt him—the horrible reality of his involvement with the Klan and the location of the murder."

Nick considered Stan's accusation. "Stan, you may be jumping to conclusions about someone murdering the sheriff. He may have committed suicide. After all, he was pretty distraught the last time I saw him."

"You're wrong about that, Nicky. When I last saw him he was in the best of spirits. After all, he was intending to clear his conscience by confessing his crimes," said Stan.

"Well, even if the sheriff hadn't been killed and confessed his crimes, and Lauren came back to him...didn't he know that *I'm part of the package?* And if she came back to Cedar Valley, I'd return with her? You know how he hated me."

"Nick, I had many talks with the sheriff. He didn't hate you at all. As a matter of fact, I believe he liked you."

"Well, he sure acted like he hated me," said Nick.

"I don't believe he hated you, but to be quite honest, he didn't like for anyone to date Lauren." said Stan.

Nick pressed the issue. "Stan, I can't believe the sheriff liked me. If he did, how could he have ordered his deputies to escort me to his car when he finished questioning me? Was he going to take me somewhere and kill me to keep me from testifying about the Klan murders?"

"No Nicky. I talked to the sheriff after that happened. He told me that he was going to escort you out of town and give you some money so you could leave Cedar Valley."

"Well, at least I feel better about him now," said Nick.

Stan frowned. "Hell, Nicky, he wasn't a murderer!"

"Stan, you know that the sheriff was sleeping with his maid, Willie Mae. Did he ever stop doing that?" Nick asked.

"Yeah, he discharged her when he decided to reform," said Stan. "He completely repented of all of his former sins. In fact, he said he had experienced a spiritual conversion."

Nick changed the subject. "Tell me, Stan…Why are you hiding from the Klan? Aren't you a member?"

"You're mistaken about that, Nick. I'm no longer a member of that hellish group. I resigned. When the sheriff decided to come clean about his membership in the Klan and his crooked activities, I admired him so much and felt so guilty that I decided to do the same. You'll never realize how much I've suffered over the death of Rufus. I have never been able to get it out of my mind, Nicky." Tears welled up in his eyes as he spoke of the murder. Nick was emotionally touched. He reached for Stan and placed his arm around him. "But you're still safe, Stan. No one knows that you're going to confess your involvement with the Klan, so you don't need to hide from anybody."

"That's where you're wrong, Nicky. Unfortunately, when the sheriff and I were in his office talking about confessing our involvement.in the Klan I didn't realize that Cowboy Galyon

26

was in the next room and overheard the conversation. I saw him sneaking out the back door as I was leaving. Lucky for me, he's not aware of the fact that I know he overheard me. Galyon knows that if I confess about my involvement, I'll have to tell about the murders, which would incriminate the entire group of Klansmen. So unless I stay hidden, I may be killed by one of the Klan. You also need to hide from them while you're in Cedar Valley, Nicky. So I picked this place that will be almost impossible to find. And even if they find it, because of the broad expanse of vacant field in the front yard, we can spot somebody approaching the house from a hundred yards away. I also have a rifle in my closet."

Nick said, "Stan, maybe you're being too cautious in your concerns about the Klan. We aren't living in Chicago, where people commit murders almost daily. Hell, we're in a little hick town in the South. Do you really think a Klan member would kill one of us to keep us from incriminating them?"

"Are you kidding?" Stan asked. "Somebody killed the sheriff to keep him from talking. Why wouldn't they come after you or me? I've kept quiet about the murders because I wanted to protect myself immediately after it happened. But now I'm going to confess my involvement in the crime. I still believe it was Cowboy Galyon who killed my uncle! He was at that Klan meeting when Bronson murdered two men!"

"But Stan...We don't have any *proof* that Galyon killed the sheriff," Nick protested.

Stan became angry. "I don't need proof! I'd kill that son of a bitch in a minute if I thought I could get away with it!"

Nick carefully studied him. "Stan, tell me something. Why did you join the Klan, anyway?"

"I was stupid, Nick. I originally thought that the Klan had a noble purpose. I've never had a grudge against Negroes; besides, they're not always the only target of the Klan. Most Negroes can't cause much trouble in this little town. After all, they're confined to their own territory at night—Bucktown. At first, I really admired the Klan because they punished the slime of our society: child abusers, men who are too lazy to work, wife beaters, and cheating men who sleep with other men's wives. I just never realized that the renegade group was so evil until they committed murder."

Nick looked accusingly at him. "Stan, I only blame you for one thing. You just stood there as Mike Bronson whipped Rufus and then shot him and the preacher. Hell, Rufus even helped raise you! How could you have overlooked that?"

Stan hung his head. "Nicky, I didn't know that it was Rufus they were going to punish. One of our members called and said that they were going to whip a Negro. I don't even know what he had done to receive a whipping from the Klan. The shooting came as surprise to our entire group. I was powerless to stop it."

Nick responded with sarcasm. "Stan, I saw the *terrible crime* Rufus was guilty of. I was there when he committed that *unpardonable sin*—a Negro touching a little white girl," said Nick. "All he did was pull the little girl away from the traffic in order to save her from getting killed by a car. Because she was so scared, she continued to cling to him. Unfortunately for Rufus, a member of the Klan witnessed it." When he heard Nick's explanation, Stan looked away in shame.

Nick decided to warn him, "Stan, do you realize what could happen if you confess your story to higher authorities? You could spend years in prison for being an accessory to murder! Are you prepared for that?"

"I realize that Nick. But I'm going to confess anyway. I can't bear anymore of this guilt." He wiped away his tears.

"But who would you report it to? The local police? By the way, since the sheriff is now dead, who replaced him as sheriff? I hope to God it wasn't Cowboy Galyon! That bastard arrested me for nothing when I was still living in Cedar Valley!"

Stan gradually became less emotional. "No, the sheriff wasn't replaced by Cowboy Galyon, Nicky. Before the sheriff was murdered, the County Police Department had become dysfunctional. Just before the sheriff's death, he fired all the deputies. Three of them, 'Light Horse Harry' Daniels, 'Bird Dog' Johnson, and 'Cowboy' Galyon were fired for stealing police money. After the jailhouse snitch, Little Billy Sneed ratted on them to the sheriff, Galyon beat the hell out of him. Since Dad was the county mayor, he called a meeting of the county commissioners. They quickly appointed an interim sheriff, George Kirkland, and two new deputies. After that, my uncle resigned as sheriff, and Dad resigned as our mayor."

"Well, what about this interim sheriff that the commission appointed. Is he an honest man?" asked Nick.

"Are you kidding? George Kirkland is as honest as a Sunday school teacher, Nicky! Also, he even got rid of 'Little Billy' Sneed? Remember him?"

"Yeah, I remember meeting that damned jailhouse snitch when I was arrested for nothing and placed in jail," said Nick. "The sheriff was paying him to rat on different people."

Stan laughed. "Yeah, that guy was really contemptible."

Nick changed the subject. "By the way, when do we go into town for the sheriff's funeral?"

"The funeral home receives friends at 2:00 p.m. tomorrow and the funeral is at 4:00. The graveside service will be held immediately after the funeral. And don't worry about being harassed by the Klan. The new sheriff knows that I'm in danger because I told him I witnessed the double-murder. I also informed him that if he wouldn't arrest me for being an ex-Klan member I would eventually reveal to him the identity of the killer. I wanted to wait until you arrived here so you could corroborate the story with me. We'll have plenty of police protection during both of the services."

"Except for the new sheriff, does anyone else know that Rufus and the preacher were murdered?" Nick asked.

"Nobody else knows for sure, but a few people are suspicious about what happened to them."

"By the way, Stan," said Nick, "Since you're going to confess your involvement with the Klan, I'll also report that I witnessed the murder of Rufus and the Preacher. After it happened, the only reason I didn't report it was to protect you and Lauren's dad from going to prison. But since you're going to reveal the name of the killer and Sheriff Mullins is no longer with us, I have no reason to keep quiet about it anymore. Anyway, I never have felt very comfortable with my decision to allow the Klan members to get off scot-free."

"Well, the grand jury is scheduled to convene in a few days," said Stan. "You can appear and testify with me about the Klan murders. Although they're not sure he's guilty of murdering Preacher Temple and Rufus, the T.B.I. is still looking for former deputy, Mike Bronson because he's listed as a missing person. They finally found his car beside a little road in the valley behind Rufus' house. He must have abandoned his police vehicle and high-tailed it out of town for parts unknown. Nobody knows his whereabouts. Immediately after the murder, no one knew about it because nobody missed the victims; after all, neither of them were well-known by most people. There have been a few vague rumors about the reason that Rufus and the preacher just suddenly disappeared. Two law enforcement agencies are trying to locate Bronson for opposite reasons: The T.B.I. wants to question him about the murders, while the former county deputies want to locate him to kill him in order to shut him up. Most of them were Klan members, so they were accessories to the brutal murder. Nobody knows where Bronson is."

Nick only smiled. "I know where he is, Stan. He's probably in the western part of the state floating somewhere in the Tennessee River—At least his body is."

"What do you mean?" Stan was surprised.

"He's dead. It happened during a terrible storm. Lauren and I were standing in the meadow behind Rufus' house in the driving rain after Bronson stopped us, He meant to kill us to keep me from testifying about the Klan murders. Rufus' twelve-year old grandson, Caleb saved our lives when he stepped from behind a tree and killed him with a shotgun. He also avenged the killing of his grandfather, Rufus."

"Are you kidding me?" Stan asked. "Where was Bronson buried? The police looked everywhere for his body, or a grave, but never found it. They figured he just abandoned his police car and skipped the country."

"No, he's dead, Stan. After Caleb shot him, Bronson fell into the creek. Then he floated about a half-mile down the creek and disappeared into the Tennessee River." Nick said.

"But that little creek is only a trickling stream," said Stan. "How could he have floated anywhere in that tiny creek?"

"On that stormy day, the creek had swollen into a gushing torrent of water," said Nick. "It didn't take long for his body to be washed downstream and disappear into the river."

"Damn!" said Stan. "The police just figured he left town!"

Nick chuckled. "Let's face it, Stan. The Cedar Valley County Police weren't very intelligent when investigating anything. After all, they weren't exactly mental giants."

Nick was almost sorry he had told Stan of the event, for he still wasn't sure if he could trust him with the shocking news. "Stan, neither of us can ever tell anyone—particularly the grand jury about what happened on that day. If we let that information slip, little Caleb could be charged with murder. Also, his mother, Mary Rose could be tried as an accessory. I never reported it to anyone, because I felt that a certain kind of justice had been achieved. I remembered what you once told me about justice: 'It's sometimes delivered in unusual packages.' Can I trust you to keep this story a secret?"

"Sure, Nicky. By the way, when did you start bending the rules of justice? That's totally unlike you! You've always been strict about conforming to the letter of the law!"

"Sometimes you just have to choose the lesser of two evils, Stan," said Nick. "Justice isn't always so simple."

Stan only smiled. "I never thought I'd hear you say that."

"What else has been going on in your life, Stan? Are you still working for your dad in the house construction business?"

"No, I quit working for him after you and Lauren left town. Since then my father has retired."

Nick looked at the dirty carpet on the floor and the dingy walls of the dilapidated house. "Stan, this place doesn't look as well as some of your usual homes. It isn't exactly a mansion, is it?"

Stan only laughed. "Nick, when I leased this house, I wasn't looking for something stylish, I was looking for something safe… a place where the Klan couldn't find me. We only moved into this shack hurriedly, right after the sheriff was killed. Immediately after his death, I stayed with Lauren's mother at her home in order to comfort and protect her."

"Does the Klan know that you've been staying with Lauren's mother at her house?" asked Nick. "Do you think they'll try to find you there?"

"I don't think the Klan knows that I've been staying there," Stan replied.

"But what if they do?" Nick asked, "Maybe you should get the interim sheriff to keep an eye on the place. The Klan may be so pissed at Sheriff Mullins for his decision to confess his evil deeds while a member of the Klan that they might even do damage to the place."

"I don't believe we have to worry about that, Nick. I just stayed there overnight until we rented this hidden place. There won't be much risk when we return to the sheriff's home to get a few items that are necessary for normal living. After that, we need to stay hidden."

Nick changed the subject. "Have you heard from 'House Cat' Jennings, the guy who worked as your foreman in your construction business before he joined the army? I really enjoyed working for him. He was a good boss."

Stan's expression became sad. "Yeah…It's too bad about House Cat. He lost a leg in Korea. He got a medical discharge several months ago. Hell, after he returned to Cedar Valley, he even got arrested by the sheriff."

"Really?" Nick was surprised. "What was he arrested for?"

"He held an organized protest against the war, right on the main street. The sheriff had to arrest him…He had no choice. The mob was raising hell. It seems that the people were equally divided about whether or not the war was justified."

32

"Damn! I hate to hear that! Does he live in Cedar Valley? If he does, we should pay him a visit. How is he coping with the missing leg?"

"Yeah, he lives in Cedar Valley. The missing leg doesn't seem to bother him. But you can never tell how he's feeling...You know House Cat's weird attitude. Yeah, you and I will have to visit him soon."

Nick again changed the subject. "Do you have a job now?"

"No, I'm not employed at the present time, and Dad recently retired. Kathy and I are just living off the money I've saved. I plan to re-enroll in college for a graduate degree soon; that is, unless the authorities put me in jail. We might even go to New Orleans so I can attend college with you." He smiled at Nick. "I guess Kathy will have to support us for a while."

"Did it piss your father off when you quit working for him?" asked Nick. "I remember he used to try to control you."

"No...In fact he was relieved. Since my life is in danger because I'm going to testify about my involvement with the Klan, he knows I need to stay hidden until this thing is over. Do you remember how Dad didn't have any respect for me? Well, now he's really proud of me for stepping up and taking my punishment like a man. Dad was never involved with the Klan; as a matter of fact he hated the organization. He and I are now on the best of terms." The untimely death of the sheriff had introduced a family closeness between Stan and his father—a bond that hadn't previously existed.

"Well, as I recall, your father wasn't the best influence on you. Did he ever stop dealing with bootleggers?" Nick asked.

Stan grinned. "Nicky, when the sheriff mended his ways and I decided to come clean, my father also turned over a new leaf. He had a spiritual conversion! It was lucky for Dad that he stopped his illegal activities before he was exposed. Nobody could really prove that he was in the bootlegging business. Some of the jailbirds suspected it, but they had no proof. The sheriff was the only person who really had proof of Dad's involvement in illegal activities. For the first time in my life, Dad and I are innocent of any wrongdoing and we're best friends."

"Well, that's great, Stan! At least you have *something good* that's happening in your life!"

"Well, there's also something bad that happened a few months ago," said Stan. "After you left Cedar Valley, I vacated the apartment that you and I had rented and moved back into our home to live with Mom and Dad. But Mom left Dad when she found out about his former involvement in his bootlegging activities. She moved to Memphis to live with her sister. Dad's alone now. He's retired and living in a large house by himself. After Mom moved away, both Dad and I moved out of our big house, and Dad sold it. I've been living by myself in a small apartment until I moved to this hidden place where the Klan members can't find me. I guess Kathy and I will continue to stay with Lauren's mother and hide until this entire police investigation is resolved."

"I hate to hear about your mother leaving," Nick said.

Stan again hung his head. "Yeah, it's really sad. I regained my father, but I lost my mother."

A voice from the kitchen interrupted their conversation when Kathy called out, "Dinner is served!"

When Stan slowly rose from the couch, Nick also stood. He immediately hugged Stan and said, "Pal, I'm proud of you for stepping up and being a real man. As far as I'm concerned you and I have just renewed our friendship. And I trust you again." Nick noticed that Stan had tears in his eyes.

When the group shared dinner in the kitchen, conversation was limited, for there was an awkwardness among them. No one wanted to discuss the obvious; as a result, most of the talk was limited to trivial and courteous conversation. The sudden death of Lauren's father and the beginning phases of dementia of her mother were too tragic for any of them to discuss.

Shortly before preparing for bed, Stan called Nick aside and smiled. "Nicky, before we retire for the night, you should move your car behind the house so it can't be seen from the road. Just park beside my vehicle in the back yard, okay?"

"Sure, Stan," He walked outside to the driveway and drove Lauren's car to the weedy backyard and parked beside Stan's old station wagon When viewing the shabby condition of the vehicle, Nick noticed that it was far inferior to the former classy cars to which Stan had become accustomed when he was still working for his father.

When Nick stepped out of the car, he hesitated before returning to the house. For a while he took a seat on the back porch steps, enjoying the beauty of East Tennessee. Unlike Stan, who was outgoing and talkative, Nick was a quiet, private person. He could always think more clearly when alone. He was grateful for this moment of solitude, for it gave him a brief respite from enduring the despair that was so evident inside the house. He pondered the recent tragic events and the unknown circumstances that he and Lauren were destined to face in the future.

A full moon illuminated the misty panorama of the forest as he peered at the distant array of sprinkled lights in the faraway lowlands of Cedar Valley. This beautiful Tennessee evening brought cherished images back to him. It evoked memories of his close association with Stan and his former romance with Lauren many months ago. For a while he remained in the moonlit backyard, pondering the capricious nature of life.

When he retired to his bed beside Lauren for the evening, he was very tired. The recent stress that he and Lauren had endured plus the long drive from Louisiana to Tennessee had left both of them exhausted, both physically and emotionally. But in spite of his weariness, he experienced difficulty when attempting to sleep; for his mind flowed with mixed feelings: Although he was saddened by the trauma facing Lauren, he was happy about his mended relationship with Stan.

Chapter 4

After a brief breakfast, Stan, Nick, and the other family members encountered a stormy morning when they collected their umbrellas and left to attend the funeral of Sheriff Mullins. While the others in the group slowly followed, Stan held an umbrella over the wheelchair as he pushed Lauren's mother to the parked vehicle. He lifted her into the back seat, carefully folded the wheelchair, and placed it inside the rear compartment of the station wagon. Since the entire family was in a somber mood, their conversation was limited as they closed their umbrellas and entered the vehicle.

Peals of thunder rolled from the distance as the sky grew darker, and the rain began to fall more heavily. Puddles of water began to collect on the road and the tires pulled a trail of foggy mist behind the car. To Nick, who was a war veteran, thunder had previously brought back memories of exploding artillery. He recalled his terrible fear of storms shortly after his discharge from The Korean War. He was thankful that most of his former fears were now behind him.

Stan slowly drove the old station wagon down Kingston Hill toward the funeral home. Smith Mortuary was located in the suburbs of the small town only about three miles from

Stan's rented house. The group remained silent throughout the short journey. Stan finally pulled the station wagon into the long row of vehicles that had been reserved for the family of the deceased. To identify the cars that would lead the procession of vehicles as they left for the cemetery, a funeral home attendant wearing a raincoat quickly fastened a flag to the radio aerial of each car. Nick noticed two police cars parked near the mortuary.

The stone building was old, but well-preserved. Several maple trees and large beds of flowers covered the neatly-mowed lawn. Because Sheriff Mullins had been a prominent figure, throngs of people were in attendance. Stan's father, Lester joined Stan and his group as they prepared to enter the building. His appearance was much like Nick remembered: He was a muscular man, and more than six-feet-four in height. Like most of the other men, he was dressed in a dark suit. While shielding her with the umbrella, Stan pushed Lauren's mother through the door in her wheelchair as the family folded their umbrellas and blended among the large group of mourners inside.

Once inside the hallway, Stan's father immediately smiled and vigorously embraced his son. "Just continue to be brave, Stan," he said, reassuringly, "I know how you feel. This sad event is equally tough for me." After leaning over the wheelchair to hug Lauren's mother, he embraced both Lauren and Stan's wife, Kathy. He then turned to face Nick. He smiled warmly at him and enthusiastically shook his hand. "It's really great to see you again, son," he said, "It's too bad that we meet again under such dismal circumstances. And congratulations in regard to your marriage to Lauren!" Nick had previously considered Stan's father an insensitive man. He was now surprised by his compassionate demeanor.

Following the directions of one of the attendants, the sheriff's immediate family members assembled in a line in front of the open casket. The large assemblage of people stood in the aisle on the right side of the crowded room. One by one they stepped forward and offered condolences to the grieving family members of Sheriff Mullins. When this procedure finally ended, the family took their proper seats in an adjoining room only a few feet to the left of the casket. The open front wall of the room offered the immediate family a full view of the crowded main room of the mortuary. The women sat in seats to the right of the men, with Lauren's mother resting in her wheelchair in the aisle. Stan was seated between his father and Nick. Close friends and relatives took seats in the front pews of the mortuary directly in front of the open casket. The lighting was dim, and the subtle aroma of roses permeated the room. The soft, peaceful organ music was an ironic contradiction to the final moment of life for the sheriff and the terrible manner in which he had died.

When Nick turned and peered across the sanctuary at the large crowd of people, he experienced a moment of anxiety when he noticed two of the sheriff's former deputies, Cowboy Galyon and Bird Dog Johnson among the group of mourners. He wondered about the significance of their presence: Did they know that Stan had moved to a safer location? *Had they attended the event for the purpose of discovering Stan's hidden house by following his vehicle after the funeral was over?* He hoped that the deputies were unaware that Stan had moved, but was still living in his rented apartment. When Nick nudged him and nodded toward the ex-deputies, Stan glanced over his shoulder and also saw them.

The lights in the mortuary dimmed with a sharp flash of lightning, and the immediate crack of thunder intruded on the soft organ music. The music continued as Nick noticed Lauren dabbing at her eyes with her handkerchief. *What a terrible time for a storm,* thought Nick.

Stan's father had tears in his eyes when he affectionately draped his arm around his son. At last the music stopped and the pastor stepped up to the pulpit to deliver his liturgy. Thunder rumbled in the distance as Reverend James Williams, the pastor of Sheriff Mullins' First Baptist Church delivered the sermon. His words were filled with praise as he related the many noble and charitable works of the sheriff: his tithes, his

38

visitation of the sick, and the many donations he had made to worthy causes. As the minister told of the sheriff's good deeds, Nick realized that Laurence Mullins was a very complicated man. While he had no doubt that the sheriff had offered many services to mankind, he also realized that he was guilty of unspeakable wrongs. In his awareness of the complexity of the sheriff's character, Nick began to realize that nearly all people, regardless of their charitable deeds, were guilty of similar sins. When he thought of his own conflicted life, he realized that he was among those people.

During the soft organ music, Nick experienced many contradicting thoughts. He realized that, like all people, the sheriff was a mixture of both good and bad. Nick felt that Sheriff Mullins had divided mankind into opposite categories: the *deserving* and the *undeserving*. Deserving people regularly attended their church and offered service to their fellow man. They were hard workers; therefore, they usually had money and status, and with certain exceptions obeyed the law. To the sheriff, the end justified the means; for whenever profitable, law-breaking, such as accepting bribes from bootleggers was acceptable; besides, regardless of prohibition, some people were going to drink anyway. Also, it gave the deserving people more money to help finance their churches and worthy causes.

But the undeserving people were lazy and ignorant; consequently, they had only a paltry amount of money and absolutely no influence nor status. Many of these people were shiftless and often spent some of their time in jail. Nick wondered how many of his fellow men shared this skewed and judgmental attitude.

The service finally ended and people rose from their seats. Many of them remained, shaking hands, and engaging in small talk, while others slowly made their way to the exit and began to leave the building. Members of Sheriff Mullins' family again assembled in front of the open casket to pay their last respects. Lauren openly wept. She held her father's hand, leaned over the casket and gently straightened his tie. With slumped shoulders, Lauren's mother only sat in her wheelchair and stared at the floor in bewilderment.

Mortuary attendants finally closed the casket and six grim-faced pallbearers carried the casket to the exit and slid it into the rear of the black hearse parked outside. The reappearance of sunshine and the distant rumble of thunder beyond the mountains indicated that the storm had moved eastward. Nick was thankful for the return of sunshine on this miserable day.

While Nick and Stan's father helped the sheriff's family into their vehicle, Stan said to Nick. "Pal, before we proceed to the cemetery for the burial, I need to talk to one of the new deputies parked nearby. I'll be back in a minute, okay?"

"Sure, Stan...Take your time. We'll wait here for you." When the family had entered the old station wagon, Stan strode to the recently-hired deputy, Joe Wilkerson, and extended his hand in greeting. "Hi Joe," Stan said, "I'm glad to see you here. Man, this has been an unhappy occasion!"

The deputy, who was standing beside his car appeared to be about thirty years old. He was a tall, very slim man who was beginning to grow bald at his temples. He returned Stan's handshake. "Hello, Stan. I'm sorry about your uncle. It's good to see you again. I only wish it was under more favorable circumstances. Did you need to see me about something?"

"Yeah, Joe. We're going to attend the graveside service right away. Could you follow us home after the service? I'm still not sure what some of Sheriff Mullins' enemies might do to our family. Sheriff Kirkland guaranteed that we'd be under his protection during and after the funeral service."

The deputy expressed a reluctance. "Stan, I'll protect you during the burial ceremony, but I can't follow you home. The sheriff told me that after the burial, you're on your own. Since the former sheriff is now dead, and some of the deputies have left the force, our entire police department is undermanned."

The deputy suddenly looked away from Stan and abruptly changed the subject. "By the way, Sheriff Kirkland wants to see you immediately. He said that there are several things he needs to discuss with you. Maybe you should see him right away."

"Yeah...You're right. Tell him I'll get with him soon," Stan replied. He then left the deputy and returned to his family relatives in the station wagon. He was followed by his father's car as he drove toward the burial service in the nearby local cemetery.

The drive to the burial ground was completed in silence, before Stan finally parked behind a long line of cars. With the open grave only a few yards to their left, the family left the vehicle. Stan retrieved the wheelchair from the rear of the station wagon and placed Lauren's mother inside it as other family members slowly walked to the graveside. They occupied chairs at the front of the gathering of people beneath the canvas shed. The closing service was brief, and concluded with a lengthy prayer from the church pastor. While the sheriff's closest family members remained seated, many friends and relatives walked in line in front of them, offering hand embraces and condolences.

After a multitude of handshakes and idle conversation the large crowd of people slowly dispersed, ultimately leaving only the closest members of the sheriff's immediate family by the graveside. While her mother sat in her wheelchair and expressed no emotion, Lauren continued to cry as the mortuary attendants lowered the casket into the grave.

Before they left the burial site, Stan's father informed the group that he wished to follow their vehicle to their hidden residence in order to have knowledge of their location. Stan breathed a sigh of relief when he realized that, other than his father's car following closely behind, he saw no evidence of any other vehicle following him as he left the cemetery. Because of the recent storm, Stan's old station wagon splashed through the standing water on the road. Except for the occasional sobbing of Lauren, the ride to their hidden hovel was silent. The group of family members was exhausted from stress and sadness when they arrived at their rented shack.

41

While Lauren's mother wordlessly sat in the corner of the room in her wheelchair, Kathy and Lauren entered the small kitchen to begin their preparation for dinner. Kathy noticed the paltry amount of remaining food. "We'll need to buy some groceries soon," she remarked, "Because we moved here so hurriedly, we didn't buy much to eat."

Nick joined Stan and his father when they took a seat on the living room couch. They discreetly avoided any discussion of the recent funeral. Stan's father, Lester Mullins draped his arm around his son and smiled. "Stan, I just wanted to come here to see for myself where you're living, and how you're getting along." When he noticed the condition of the decrepit living quarters, he remarked, "To be honest, I can't be very complimentary about your choice when it comes to a style of living. This place isn't exactly a palace, is it?" He chuckled.

Stan returned his smile. "No Dad—it's certainly not a palace, but it is sort of like a castle, because it offers us some protection from people who might want to kill us. When I chose this place, I wasn't looking for style, but safety."

"Are you *that afraid* that someone might be gunning for you?" Stan's father asked. "If you need that kind of protection, you could have come and lived with me and I'd have hired protection for you. I have several rooms in my house."

"Dad, I didn't have time to consider that. After my uncle was killed, I had to move fast. Also, I had to help Aunt Bonnie, Lauren's mother."

Stan's father skeptically eyed him. "Do you still believe that my brother was killed by someone and didn't commit suicide?"

"Yes Dad. We've discussed this before! I'm sure of it!"

For the first time, Nick spoke. "Stan, you may be jumping to conclusions! You don't have any proof that somebody murdered him! As hard as it might be to accept, we all may have to live with the fact that he killed himself!"

"You'll never convince me of that!" Stan replied.

Nick only smiled. "Don't get paranoid, Stan. Committing murder is a strong accusation to make against someone."

Stan's father turned to face Nick and smiled. "Son, I guess Stan told you about the way that both he and I changed our ways after you and Lauren left Cedar Valley."

"Yeah, he told me. And I'll have to admit that I was really surprised." Nick replied. "What brought about this drastic turnaround?"

"Well, it all began with my brother—the sheriff. When Lauren condemned him, he was crushed. I guess you might say that both the sheriff and I had become arrogant, and felt justified in our actions. Serving as mayor, or sheriff in a small town isn't an easy job. Trying to maintain order and peace without compromising to sin is very difficult. But as the Holy Bible says, 'Your sins will find you out.' I have paid dearly for my past sins. They cost me the love of my wife, and I almost lost the respect and love of Stan because of my dishonest ways. But I wasn't guilty of some of the things that the jailbirds accused me of." He placed his arm around his son. Nick looked into his eyes and noticed a suggestion of tears that reflected a deep sincerity.

Nick smiled at him. "Well, I'm sorry about what happened with your wife, but I'm happy about your drastic change, sir!"

"Thank you Nick," he replied. "I had a spiritual conversion when I began to realize that I was on a path to destruction. As the Good Book says—'you might gain the whole world, but still lose your own soul!'" He then smiled and patted Nick on the shoulder.

"You sound a lot like my old friend, Preacher Temple," Nick said. "He was really a devoted man, but like all men, he wasn't perfect."

Lester Mullins looked at his son. "I've been trying to get Stan to dedicate his life to God, but he isn't interested. I'm still praying for him to attend church with me."

Stan answered, "Dad, I'm proud of you for the commitment you made, but I don't believe in any kind of religion—at least not for me."

There was an awkwardness between the men until Nick abruptly changed the subject. "Stan, when we were at the funeral home and you approached the deputy to ask him questions, what did he have to say?"

Stan replied, "Well, he expressed his sympathy about Uncle Laurence, and then he told me that the interim sheriff, George Kirkland wanted to see me in his office right away. I plan to go to his office in the next couple of days. Maybe you can go there with me."

"Sure, Stan. I'd be glad to join you," Nick replied.

Kathy called from the kitchen, "Dinner is served!" Nick followed Stan and his father into the small kitchen. While Stan's father and Nick gathered around the table, Stan carried a tray of food to Lauren's mother, who was only staring into space from her wheelchair. When everyone was seated at the kitchen table, Lester Mullins winked at Stan's wife, Kathy and said, "You're going to make Stan a good wife, Kathy." He then offered a brief blessing prior to everyone beginning their meal.

In her attempt to avoid talk of the funeral, Stan's wife, Kathy commented, "Well, Stan, we're gonna have to buy some groceries tomorrow. All we have to eat for dinner are hamburgers and these fried potatoes."

"Yeah, we'll go to the store tomorrow. Also, I need to go talk to the new sheriff about a few things," Stan answered.

While the group finished their evening meal, the silence was only broken by trivial conversation. Finally, everyone vacated the table while the women cleared away the dishes and began kitchen work. The men walked into the tiny living room where Lester Mullins placed his arms around both Nick and Stan. He smiled. "Well, I have to be going. Stan, if you need anything, you know you can call on me. Tell the womenfolk 'goodbye' for me". He then walked to vehicle and drove away.

Nick turned to face his friend. "Stan, your father is indeed a changed man!"

Chapter 5

At 10:00 a.m. on the following morning, Nick and Stan walked up the concrete steps into the office where Sheriff Kirkland was seated behind his desk poring over some kind of paperwork. He was a short, heavy-set man who appeared to be about sixty years old. His bifocals magnified the size of his eyes when he looked up at them.

The sheriff's office was directly below the jail. When Nick recognized the unchanged interior of the office and heard the upstairs clamor of prisoners, unpleasant memories again haunted him. They emotionally returned him to the times when, many months ago he was unjustly arrested and locked in this jail, and the filthy and noisy environment that he had repeatedly attempted to forget.

The sheriff left his chair and extended his hand. "Hello, Stan. I'm glad you stopped by. I was beginning to think that you had forgotten our little appointment." Peering over his glasses, he looked intently at Nick.

Stan shook hands with him and replied, "Sheriff, I've been a busy man. I made it here as quick as I could. I wanted to wait until Nick got into town so he can verify my story." He turned toward Nick. "By the way, sheriff, meet Nick Parilli.

He's the other witness I was telling you about. And Nick, this is Sheriff Kirkland." The men exchanged handshakes as the sheriff carefully inspected Nick's demeanor. "Are you guys related, or are you just friends?" asked the sheriff.

Stan said, "Well, we're definitely friends, but we're kinda related too—by marriage. Nick married the daughter of Sheriff Mullins. Her name is 'Lauren.'"

"Well, have a seat, fellows," said Sheriff Kirkland. After the others were seated, the sheriff quickly reoccupied his seat and got to the point. "Okay, Stan—you said that you had more to tell me about the Klan murders. Let's have it."

"Well, sheriff, both Nick and I are eye-witnesses to a double-murder. I was a member of the Ku Klux Klan when I witnessed it, and Nick sneaked into the meeting with a preacher friend for the purpose of preventing the punishment of an innocent Negro man. The Negro's name was Rufus Headrick, and the preacher's name was Luke Temple. Nick and I witnessed both of them being shot by a Klan member. The murderer was Mike Bronson, a former deputy of the county police. He was also the Grand Dragon of the Klan."

Sheriff Kirkland eyed Stan with skepticism. "Well, where is this guy, Mike Bronson? I know that he was once a deputy sheriff, but what ever happened to him? Does anyone know where he is? How can the police question him?"

"Nobody knows where he is. He just disappeared. He's listed as missing by the T.B.I. as a possible fugitive."

The sheriff asked, "Stan, can you name all of these Klan members? I'll need a complete list of their names—including this Bronson deputy, so they can all be indicted for murder. If this Bronson guy can never be found, he'll have to be tried for the murder in absentia."

"Sheriff, I'm kinda dumb about trial terminology," said Stan, "What do you mean by 'absentia'? Does that mean that he can be convicted of murder without being at the trial?"

"It means *exactly* that, Stan. Even if we can't find him, he can be convicted of the crime and someday pay for it."

Stan smiled. "Well, that's a good policy, sheriff."

46

The sheriff appeared to be puzzled. "But you two guys were on opposite sides. You said that you were a member of the Klan, so you bear a measure of responsibility for the murders. On the other hand, you said that Nick sneaked into the Klan meeting with the intention of preventing any mistreatment of the Negro. How did you two guys ever join forces?"

"Well, actually we were close friends at the time. Nick didn't know that I was a member of the Klan. Because I regretted my bad judgment and misdeeds so much, I decided to come clean about the tragedy."

The sheriff curiously eyed Stan and said, "Son, you come from a good family. In Fact, I've known you since you were just a snotty-nosed kid. How in hell could you ever get involved with an outlaw gang like the Ku Klux Klan?"

Stan hung his head. "I guess you could say I was stupid in those days. I came to my senses when I witnessed the leader murder two men who were my close friends. I've been living with the guilt for a long time. That's the reason I'm confessing my involvement to you now."

The sheriff peered over his bifocals at Stan. "Young man, I admire your intentions, and the way you're standing up to the sins of your past like a man. But do you realize what could happen to you if you testify that you witnessed those killings? You could spend years in prison as an accessory to murder!"

"I realize that," Stan answered, "but I just couldn't stand to bear the guilt any longer. The judge and jury members will just have to punish me any way they choose."

The sheriff stared at him in amazement. "Son, you are an unusual man. I admire your loyalty and honesty."

Stan changed the subject. "Sheriff, I also came here to see you for another reason: the recent death of our former sheriff, Laurence Mullins. Did the coroner perform an autopsy to determine the cause of his death? Most people have accepted the theory that he simply committed suicide."

Sheriff Kirkland carefully studied Stan before answering him. "Yes, in spite of our disarray in the police department, I managed to cover all the details of his death. The autopsy didn't reveal anything except that he was killed by a single gunshot wound to the left portion of his forehead from a .32 caliber pistol. We did a ballistics test on the weapon, but the serial number had been removed. Obviously, it was a stolen gun. Since the weapon was found only a few inches from his extended right hand, most everyone assumed that he probably killed himself. This discovery may shock you, but evidence proved that he was murdered."

Stan seemed unperturbed; however, Nick slowly rose from his chair. "Murdered?" he asked, "How did the investigators determine that?"

"Actually, it was easily determined. First of all, the weapon was found near his right hand, but the gunshot wound was on the left portion of his head. It is highly unlikely that a man would shoot himself in that manner. It would be too awkward. But the real proof was the lack of any fingerprints on the gun. If the sheriff had killed himself, his prints would be on the weapon—but there were no prints. Whoever killed him wiped away the prints and placed the gun near his right hand to make it appear that he had shot himself."

"That isn't surprising to me, sheriff!" Stan declared. "It only confirms my claim that he was murdered!"

Nick slowly returned to his chair and turned to face Stan. "Damn! You were right, Stan! Somebody killed him!"

The sheriff was puzzled. "But why would anyone hate him enough to *kill him?* I realize that any law enforcement officer is going to make some enemies…Maybe some people who might want to criticize him, or aggravate him, or seek some kind of vengeance against him…But who would hate him enough to *kill him*?

"That's another thing I want to talk to you about, sheriff," Stan replied. "I know some people who might have been determined to kill him."

"Who…and why?" asked the sheriff.

"I can give you some names later. But first I want to give you the *motive*. How well did you know Sheriff Mullins?"

"Well, I knew him only casually. I believe that he was an honest man, and most everybody liked him. Did someone you know have a personal grudge against him?" asked the sheriff.

Stan leaned forward in his chair. "Whoever killed him had *more than a personal grudge* against him, Sheriff. Let me give you my own assessment of Sheriff Mullins' character: He was a mixture of good and bad. In many ways he was a good man. He did charity work and tithed to the church; also, he performed many good deeds."

Stan paused, and then continued. "But he was a member of the Klan; and although he wasn't at the Klan meeting on the night of the killings, just by being a member he is partly responsible for the murders of Rufus and Preacher Temple. Also, a couple of his deputies were Klan members, so they were also partly responsible for the Klan murders. Not only that, but as sheriff, he was involved in illegal activities: bootlegging, payoffs, and favoritism to his friends. His deputies were also crooked. This gave them a double-motive to kill him. Because he began to feel guilty, Sheriff Mullins decided to repent of his former sins. Actually, he said that he had been converted and became a Christian. I talked with him about it. He told me that he was going to confess his illegal activities to the T.B.I., which meant that he would also incriminate his deputies. I believe that one of the deputies discovered the sheriff's intentions, and to avoid going to prison, killed him before he confessed his crimes to the authorities. Also, Sheriff Mullins was too lenient on some of the privileged. He never adhered to the letter of the law. He bent the rules of justice."

Sheriff Kirkland asked him, "Stan, can you give me some names of some of the deputies who might have had a motive to kill him?"

"Sure," answered Stan. "Ernie Galyon was one of them—he was also known as 'Cowboy' Galyon. Also, one of the deputies was known as 'Bird Dog,'...I think his last name is *Johnson.* Then there were a couple of other guys who worked as part-time deputies. And, of course, there was a 'volunteer' prisoner the sheriff always protected—Little Billy Sneed, the 'jailhouse snitch.' He'd do anything for money, even if it involved killing the sheriff."

While the sheriff scribbled down the names mentioned by Stan, he asked, "Well what about the deputy and Klan leader that you saw shoot the two men—Mike Bronson? Is there any way I can locate him so I can question him?"

"I don't know, sheriff," Stan answered, "As I told you before, the general public doesn't have a clue where he is, or what happened to him. I doubt if we'll ever see him again."

Sheriff Kirkland looked at Nick. "Son, you are married to the sheriff's daughter, so you must know some details about his family. In order to investigate his death, I need to discover more about his life. I understand that he had an invalid wife. Didn't he have a maid working for him—someone to help him take care of his wife? Whatever happened to her?"

Although Nick was aware of Sheriff Mullins' adulterous love affair with his maid, he was reluctant to discuss the details; however, because of the necessity of a thorough police investigation, he felt that a full disclosure would be helpful to the sheriff. "Sheriff Kirkland, I'm going to give you all the information that might help in the investigation. But I need your assurance that some of the lurid details will go no further than this discussion between you and me."

"You have my assurance, Nick," the sheriff answered.

"Thank you," Nick replied. "It was like this: The maid was an attractive Negro woman named 'Willie Mae.' I never learned her last name; after all, a lot of Southern people never bother to learn a Negro's last name. Anyway, to Sheriff Mullins she was more than *his maid*...She also served his sexual needs, if you know what I mean."

"Yes, you have explained their relationship quite clearly, son." the sheriff answered. "I suppose when their wife is an invalid, many men seem to share the need to satisfy their sexual urges with someone else on certain occasions."

"Well, that was the relationship that existed between Sheriff Mullins and his maid." Nick said.

The sheriff slowly rose from his seat. "Well, unless you have more to tell me, I guess that about does it, gentlemen." Stan and Nick left their chairs, shook the sheriff's hand, and walked toward the door.

The sheriff opened the door for them "Stan, a while ago you told me that Sheriff Mullins often ignored police protocol, favored his friends, and refused to adhere to the letter of the law." He smiled at Stan. "Well, I'm guilty of the same things, because I'm ignoring the letter of the law and bending the rules of justice for *you*. After all, you just confessed to being an accomplice to a double-murder. I should have locked you up in our jail as soon as you confessed. When we consider many of the merciful decisions of Sheriff Mullins, maybe he was only guilty of being human."

Chapter 6

With Stan seated beside him, Nick drove Lauren's car away from Sheriff Kirkland's office. "Where to, Stan?" Nick asked.

"Turn left here and drive to the Mullins home," Stan answered. "We need to pick up a few things for Lauren and her mother and some household items. We moved out of there too fast to take enough stuff with us. Besides, you and I need to check on the place and make sure that everything's okay there. Also, we need to buy a few groceries before we go back to that shack we moved into."

"Do you think it's risky to go back to the Mullins' house?" asked Nick.

Stan answered, "Hell, risky or not, we'll need to check on Lauren's former home occasionally. Besides, we'll only be there for a few minutes. We can't stay away from the place twenty-four hours a day, Nicky."

"What did you think of Sheriff Kirkland, Stan?" asked Nick. "Do you think he believed your story?"

"Yeah, I'm sure he believed me. Why else would I confess to witnessing two murders that might incriminate me? Except for one statement I made to him, I tried to be totally honest."

"What did you say that wasn't honest, Stan?" asked Nick.

"I withheld evidence. Both you and I know that Mike Bronson is dead. After all, Bronson is the man who murdered both men at the Klan meeting. Naturally, he's the person that the T.B.I. will most want to interrogate. But they can never do that, because he's dead. This might complicate the case."

"Man, I'm sure glad you didn't tell him the truth about that, Stan," said Nick. "If you had revealed the truth about Rufus' young grandson killing Bronson, both he and his mother could be indicted for his murder."

"Yeah. I guess I kinda told the sheriff a *white lie*—a lie by omission, you might say. I just said that he disappeared from sight, and that nobody could find him. And I guess, *technically*, that's a true statement." His rationale brought a smile from Nick.

As the car approached the Mullins home, Nick noticed a vehicle parked in the driveway. He wondered who the visitor could be. He considered that it could be someone who might wish to express condolences in regard to the untimely death of the sheriff.

When Nick parked behind the car, he again remembered the magnificence of the Mullins Estate when he noticed the splendor surrounding the home. Although the uncut grass confirmed the emptiness of the place, the overall condition of the stately home seemed as well-manicured as ever. The shrubbery and the randomly-arranged maple trees that stood in the front yard were in full bloom.

When Nick parked the vehicle, he peered at the large front porch. Standing in front of the door stood a Negro man, apparently ringing the doorbell. When both Nick and Stan got out of the car and strode across the expansive lawn toward the man, he turned toward them and stared.

Stan was the first to speak. "Hello there! Can we help you?" Both men quickly stepped up onto the porch and approached the stranger. Having never seen the man before, they were curious about his motivation for stopping at the recently-deserted home.

Nick closely examined the man: He was a tall, handsome muscular man who had the appearance of a mulatto, for his features mirrored those of a man of mixed breed. When he spoke, his diction was more like that of a white man, for his words and expressions were lacking in the traditional Negro dialect. He appeared to be a middle-aged man. None of the men offered a handshake.

The Negro smiled. "My name is Arthur Bowman. Are either one of you related to Sheriff Mullins, the county sheriff who used to live here?"

Without formally introducing either himself or Nick, Stan replied, "Yeah, I'm his nephew, and this man married the sheriff's daughter. How can we help you, Mr. Bowman?"

The man replied, "You people have been hard to locate. This is the third time I've been here."

Stan studied the stranger. "Well, you must have something important to discuss. What is it?"

"Could we possibly go inside?" the man asked, "I have several important questions I'd like to ask you."

Stan glanced at Nick and shrugged. He then looked at the visitor. "Sure, come on inside," he answered, "Just sit down anywhere you like."

Nick's first glance at the luxurious living room brought memories back to him. The fact that Sheriff Mullins had been a wealthy man was obvious. The interior of the house reflected a modern theme of casual affluence: colorful, modern furniture, with an abundance of modern lamps and throw-cushions; also, several abstract paintings were displayed on the walls. Nick felt that the interior design had been influenced by Lauren.

Arthur Bowman adjusted a throw-cushion and took a seat on the couch, while Nick and Stan occupied seats facing him in the two recliners. An awkwardness existed between them until the stranger finally spoke. "Well, gentlemen, I really don't know how to begin this discussion. I realize that you are both under a lot of stress after only recently burying Sheriff Mullins. First I want to tell you who I am, and why I'm here. I am Willie Mae Bowman's brother. She was my younger sister, and I have always felt protective toward her. If you'll remember, she was the sheriff's maid. She served him faithfully for several years before his death."

Nick responded. "Yeah, I met her several times. She was totally loyal to the sheriff."

Arthur Bowman hesitated before continuing. "Well, I'll tell you why I'm here. After all of those years of being loyal to the sheriff and serving him as if she were his slave she was suddenly fired from her job with no warning. I don't want to anger you, but he used her for years and then put her out onto the street without her even having a job! That wasn't fair! She always served him well!"

Nick was beginning to become angry. "Yeah, she served him…But she also *serviced* him, because she slept with him for years! You say that Sheriff Mullins wasn't fair to her! Hell, Lauren's mother was totally unaware that anything improper was going on! Do you think that was fair?"

The man sat upright on the couch. "Well, the fact that she also had a sexual relationship with him and served as his wife is even more reason for Sheriff Mullins to treat her as a human being! I believe she was in love with the man!"

Stan interrupted. What's the bottom line here? What do you expect out of us—Nick and me?"

"I don't want a damned thing out of either of you! But I think that the sheriff should have made some kind of provisions for Willie Mae! But instead of doing that, he committed suicide!" Neither Stan nor Nick thought it relevant to reveal that he had been murdered.

The Negro sat for a while before he continued his accusations. He finally said, "Let me tell you something! I had some very long talks with Willie Mae about her romantic relationship with the sheriff! It was only after the sheriff was dead that I learned from Willie Mae that during their relationship, he made many promises to her. He vowed that he would always provide for her. He even promised to buy her a piece of property! As a matter of fact, Willie Mae is going to sue the Mullins estate for restitution! It's a good thing the sheriff took his own life! If he hadn't, I'd kill him myself!"

Nick quickly rose from his seat. "Listen, Mr. Bowman! We're all still suffering from Sheriff Mullins' death and you come in here with more depressing stories about how evil he was! I think it's time for you to leave!"

Arthur Bowman left the couch and faced Nick. "You haven't heard the last of this! You're going to rue the day that Willie Mae ever met that heartless man! Willie Mae and I will see you in court!" He then walked out the door to his vehicle and backed out of the driveway.

Nick and Stan stood beside the door and watched the man drive away. Stan slowly left his seat in the easy chair and smiled. "Nicky, don't you think you might have been a little hard on that poor guy?"

"Why do you say that, Stan?" asked Nick.

"Well, maybe you should look at it this way, Nicky... Lauren's mother wasn't capable of having sex with her husband, but he always expressed his love and did his best for her. But, hell, Man, who expects a man to go all of his life without having sex? Maybe that's just another illustration of what Sheriff Kirkland said about my uncle. Maybe that just shows he's human!"

Nick angrily glared at him. "It also shows that he's an inconsiderate human who had no respect for the feelings of either Lauren or her mother! If he needed sex that bad, he should have gone to a prostitute!"

Chapter 7

Stan and Nick were seated at the breakfast table with Lauren while Kathy poured cups of coffee and dished out the small serving of scrambled eggs and toast. In obvious dismay, Stan gazed at his skimpy breakfast in his plate. "Damn, Kathy...Is this all we have to eat?"

"Yep, that's it," Kathy answered. "We're completely out of groceries. Since you and Nick slept so late, we saved the remaining food for you. The rest of us got up early, so Lauren and her mother only had coffee, and I finished the orange juice. You forgot to buy groceries yesterday. Sometime today you'll need to go to some market and buy us some food."

Kathy refreshed their coffee. As Lauren leisurely sipped on it, she asked, "Well, how did yesterday's discussion go with Sheriff Kirkland? Did you give him a complete account of the Klan murders?"

Stan answered, "The session went well. Nick and I told him everything."

"Did he believe you?" asked Lauren.

Nick finally spoke. "Yes, I think he believed us. Stan told him *almost* everything. But he left out the fact that the killer, Mike Bronson is dead, and that you and I saw him get killed."

Lauren pondered the answer. "But will that have any bearing on the murder case?" she asked.

"Who knows?" Stan asked. "We won't know until the case comes to trial. What difference does it make as long as a jury decides he's the guilty party?" He hesitated before continuing. "Brace yourself, Lauren!" he said, "My conclusion that your father was murdered was correct! Sheriff Kirkland has proof that somebody shot him!"

Lauren was shocked. She buried her head in her hands and stammered, "Oh God No!"

Stan only smiled. He patted her on the shoulder and said, "Lauren, don't you think that's much better than to always believe that he committed suicide?"

Nick changed the subject. "I want to tell you what we did for the rest of the day, Lauren. Stan and I went by the sheriff's home to check it out and pick up a few items of clothing. A guy named Arthur Bowman, the brother of your daddy's former maid was waiting on the front porch. He was as mad as hell about Willie Mae being abruptly fired with no provisions for earning a living. He knows about your dad sleeping with her, and said that he's going to sue your family for damages."

Lauren appeared to be sad as Kathy hugged her. "I have such mixed feelings about the relationship between Willie Mae and my father," she said. "I feel betrayed by them, but I still feel sorry for her. She was almost like a second mother to me. If Daddy hadn't been suddenly killed, I believe he would have made some kind of provisions for her."

"I agree, Lauren." Stan replied. "In most ways your father was a good man"

Nick interrupted. "Stan, if we're gonna buy groceries we'd better be going."

They all walked into the living room where Lauren's mother, Bonnie Rose was seated in her wheelchair. Both Nick and Stan smiled and hugged her. "Is there anything special we can buy for your mother while we're gone?" Nick asked Lauren. "Maybe I should bring her a little present. She may be getting bored with nothing to do but sit around all day."

"You might bring her a candy bar," she answered. She stepped forward and hugged Nick. "You guys be careful," she warned. "Do your grocery shopping somewhere in the outskirts of city...Don't go to a big market in town where you'll be exposed to the public."

Nick smiled at her. "Don't worry so much, Lauren...We'll be careful." The men stepped outside and Nick drove away in Lauren's car. He steered the vehicle down the winding road of Kingston Hill and finally turned onto Broadway. "Where do you suggest we buy these groceries, Stan?"

"Let's stay clear of Cedar Valley and drive into Loudon," suggested Stan. "We can safely buy our food there. Besides, we can stop in Loudon and have a couple of beers before we return home. I haven't enjoyed a beer in several days. Hell, it'll be like old times! Remember those 'good ol' days', Nick?"

"Yeah...I remember. But I also remember that some of those days weren't so good, Stan."

Stan glared at him. "Damn, Nick! Why are your memories always so sad? Try to remember the good times!"

"I'm trying, Stan...I guess the sheriff's recent funeral has depressed me."

When Nick continued his drive toward Loudon, he looked to his left and saw the road that led to *Bucktown*, the section of the local area that had been consigned to the Negroes and poor white residents of the small city. He remembered the former home of Preacher Temple before he had been brutally murdered by the Klan. Also, Rufus, his daughter, Mary Rose and her handicapped son, Caleb had once been residents of this shabby community, and his former friends.

He suddenly steered the vehicle into the road toward Bucktown. "Stan, if you don't mind, I'd like to take a look at this old community. I have many old memories about it."

"Nick, you're too sentimental! Why do you want to visit this hellhole again? This place was one of the worst experiences of your life! You know, that's where you and I are completely different! You hang onto old memories even when they're bad. Hell, this place is forever gone from your life! It's dead and buried! Put the past behind you and move on!"

Nick only smiled at him. "Stan, my memories of this place are not *all* so terrible. Some of them are precious to me. This community is like everything else in life. It's not all good or all bad. It's a mixed bag!"

"Damn, Nick! What's good about it? Just look at the run-down condition of these dilapidated houses! Every one of them even has an outdoor toilet!"

Nick only chuckled. "Let's face it, Stan. You were raised in a damned mansion. Join the *real world,* man."

The drive into the small settlement bore proof of Stan's appraisal; however, as Nick drove further into the shabby downtown area, sentimental memories came flowing back to him. The community looked the same as Nick remembered it. The narrow street was situated in a low-lying area and was surrounded by steep hills that were scattered with several dilapidated houses. Beyond the hills, the Tennessee River was only a quarter of a mile away. This business section consisted of only two blocks of ramshackle buildings that offered only the bare essentials for survival to local residents: a grocery store, a drugstore, a hardware business, a barber shop, a shabby tavern, a pool room, and a small Baptist church. As he drove through the area Nick noticed that many of the business names and window ads were only cheap imitations of those of the more affluent businesses in Cedar Valley, for they had been crudely hand-lettered by the merchants themselves.

Nick remembered that the small community of Bucktown was a mixture of poor people that consisted of about 90% Negroes and 10% poor whites; however, the shabby community was mainly for the Negro—it was *his town,* a habitat that had been assigned to him by his white neighbors—and a place where he was expected to spend his time at the end of each day, for Negroes were not allowed in the city of Cedar Valley after sundown.

When he drove up the hill into the residential area, Nick again viewed the run-down shacks beside the gravel street.

Some were sagging and unpainted. He again noticed the trash that littered the area: old, abandoned cars, worn-out tires, and discarded appliances. He viewed the outdoor toilets that were scattered among the weed-infested back yards of most of the houses. As he remembered the luxurious upbringing of Stan, he understood his friend's loathing of the area.

When he approached the former home of Rufus, Mary Rose, and little Caleb, he was almost overcome with sadness. When he pulled into the driveway of the dilapidated dwelling, he noticed the eerie silence, the sagging porch, and the weeds that had invaded the yard. "Stan, I want to stop here for a minute. I've got a lot of memories associated with this place."

Stan only rolled his eyes. "Suit yourself, Nicky," he said. Nick studied the decrepit porch, where he had engaged in many conversations with the Negro woman, Mary Rose shortly after Deputy Mike Bronson had murdered Rufus, her father. Nick also remembered Caleb, Mary Rose's young son.

Stan asked, "Nicky, why did you want to stop here? This will just make you miserable!"

"Stan, I wanted to remember Mary Rose and little Caleb. After all, Caleb is the little boy who killed Bronson, the murderer of his grandfather with his shotgun. And my memory of that doesn't make me miserable."

"As I recall, little Caleb was unable to speak," said Stan. "How did he comprehend enough to go after Mike Bronson, and that it was Bronson who killed his grandfather?"

"Stan, Caleb couldn't speak but he wasn't stupid. As a matter of fact, he was a very smart little boy." Nick answered.

Nick pulled out of the driveway and drove up the hill to the former home of Preacher Temple, where the condition of the property was even worse. The whitewashed exterior had faded to a dull gray, and the tin roof was covered with rust. Weeds covered the entire yard. Fond memories of the preacher came back to him, as he realized the many ways that Preacher Temple had influenced his life before he was murdered.

"This house is familiar to me," said Stan, "I met you here once...Remember? I took Lauren home for you."

"Yeah, I remember," said Nick. "Lauren was mad at me because I revealed to her some of the sins of her father. I wasn't able to take her home because I didn't want to be seen in public. I was afraid that the Klan was gunning for me. After all, I saw their leader, Mike Bronson murder two men."

Nick slowly pulled the car away from the preacher's house and drove toward Loudon. For a long while he remained silent. Because of his renewed memories of the distant past, he became even more aware of the ordeal facing him.

Stan smiled and patted Nick on the shoulder. "Nicky, I was just studying you when you stopped at those two houses. Man, you live in the past! Hell, Nicky, put that shit behind you! Think of the future! After visiting this terrible place you're gonna be depressed! It sure as hell depressed me!"

"Yeah, I can see how it might depress you, Stan," said Nick, "You were born with a silver spoon in your mouth! You know, you're the guy who's not living in the *real world*. For many people, living in places like Bucktown is the world of reality!"

Stan only laughed. "You know, Nicky…You and I are totally different in the way we view life! It's a wonder that we ever became friends!"

Nick smiled at him. "Well, maybe the differences in our attitudes make a good blend! But in spite of our differences, we agree on many things."

"I agree with you again, Nicky," Stan chuckled.

The men remained silent while Nick drove the car down Highway 11 until he crossed The Tennessee River Bridge into Loudon. Nick said, "You know, Stan, in superficial things, like the way we were raised, we're very different. For instance, you were raised in a wealthy family, while my family barely scraped by in order to exist. But in the more important issues, you and I are mostly in agreement. We both recognize the unfairness in the world and fight like hell to resist it! In fact, that's what we're doing now!"

"Yeah, but you're *obsessed* with being fair," Stan said.

"In what way am I obsessed, Stan? Give me an example."

"Okay, pal...I'll give you a perfect example! Do you remember my comment about Lauren's dad sleeping with his maid? I said that it proved that he was *just being human!* Then you made some self-righteous comment about what a bastard he was for betraying his wife and Lauren! I was just recommending a practical solution to the problem! Hell, his wife was no longer able to perform! It's not practical for a healthy man to spend his life without sex! I hope you're not the same old 'goody-two-shoes' Nicky of the past!"

Nick was slightly irritated. "Stan, I recognize that it's only a natural urge in all men to crave sex. But if Lauren's dad had visited a brothel it would have made the act less personal. It's better than betraying his family with a misplaced affection for his maid. Betrayal of our wives or friends is probably the worst offense we can ever commit!" Stan quickly remembered the manner in which he had betrayed Nick during his time in the Klan. Nick's remark created an awkwardness between them. Both men remained silent as Nick parked in front of a small grocery market in the suburbs of Loudon.

"Does this little store look okay to you, Stan?" Nick asked.

"Well, it's pretty small. They may not have a very large variety of food, but at least it looks like a safe place where nobody will be looking for us," Stan answered.

To both Stan and Nick, grocery shopping was a feminine job. Typically of men when spending time in a store, their shopping venture was brief. After buying the bare essentials, they quickly left the small market and placed the groceries in Lauren's car. Stan said, "Nicky, let's go to a tavern and drink a couple of beers."

Nick drove Lauren's vehicle a few blocks further into the outskirts of town. As directed by Stan, he parked in front of *The Red Top Tavern,* a sleazy bar sporting a red canopy over the front windows with a bright red neon sign in the window. The interior of the tavern smelled like vomit, and a generous amount of sawdust covered much of the floor.

Nick cast a disdainful look at the dirty, dark interior and sarcastically said to Stan, "My, what an elegant place, Stan! I can tell you're accustomed to luxurious living! You couldn't have chosen a nicer place! Hell, this tavern is state-of-the-art!"

Stan only laughed as both men entered the tavern. Nick quickly noticed the sweltering heat of the interior and the burly bartender who was busy serving beer to customers. Sweat and body odor saturated the backs of some of the overweight drinkers who were seated at barstools. One of them wore his pants so low on his hips that it revealed the upper portion of his butt crack. An obese man was seated on a barstool at the end of the counter. Apparently, he had consumed too many beers, for he was slobbering on the bar as he snored in his sleep. Nick noticed a spittoon amid the sawdust on the floor. Splotches of tobacco spit surrounded the filthy receptacle. Obviously, many tobacco chewers were inaccurate with their aim. A stray cat darted through the sawdust on the floor.

Stan and Nick walked to the rear of the tavern and took seats in the corner booth. Nick was facing the bar, so he signaled the beefy bartender, who slowly trudged to the booth. Nick ordered their beers while Stan lit a cigarette. The overweight bartender brought their order, and while Nick was sipping on his beer, Stan commented, "Nick, I know this isn't a very classy place, but hell, man, we're safe here! What sane man would ever frequent this low-brow dump?"

"You're right, Stan," Nick answered. "Obviously, you and I are insane. I'd almost rather take the risk of being discovered by one of the Klansmen than drinking beer in this joint! Let's just drink this one beer and get the hell out of this lousy dump!"

Loud conversation and the blaring jukebox eliminated any possibility of engaging in conversation. From the ceiling hung a strip of fly paper that had captured dozens of flies, and the noisy overhead fan labored uselessly in an effort to reduce the swelter of the hot and humid day.

With a bored expression, Stan turned his head and peered toward the front of the tavern and idly watched two men as they vacated their barstools and left the tavern; however, his interest was quickly restored when he observed the two men who replaced them. He leaned across the booth, nudged Nick and pointed toward the men. "Nick! Look who just came into the bar!"

Nick sat upright in the booth as he gradually remembered the pair of ex-deputies. "Are those two guys the people I think they are? Do you think they might have seen us come into this damned sleazy place? Could they be following us?"

"Nicky, those two guys are Cowboy Galyon and Bird Dog Johnson! I don't think they're following us. They're acting too casual to indicate that they're looking for anybody. I think it's just a coincidence they came into this tavern."

In order to keep his eyes on the barstools in the front of the tavern, Stan slowly stood and moved to sit beside Nick on the opposite side of the booth. He and Nick continued to eye the two ex-deputies as they sipped on their drinks at the bar.

Nick cautioned his friend, "Listen, Stan...I know how much you hate those guys, but don't do anything foolish! Let's just play it cool! Maybe we can sneak out of here and get back to our house before they even see us, or even know we've been here! It's obvious that they're not looking for us!"

"Damn, Nicky! Don't expect me to cringe from those bastards! I'd just as soon settle our differences here and now!"

"I'm not scared of either of them, Stan! But we need to avoid these guys until we can see that they're convicted by the court! We don't want them to see us and follow us home!"

While casually holding a can of beer in his hand, Cowboy Galyon slowly turned on his barstool and faced the rear of the tavern. His new position enabled him to get a full view of both Stan and Nick, who kept staring at him. Bird Dog also turned to face the rear of the bar. A scowl of hatred was reflected in the eyes of Stan as he and Nick scrutinized the ex-deputies.

After recognizing Stan and Nick, Galyon slowly stood and cautiously eyed them. In order to be clearly heard above the chaotic noise inside the tavern Cowboy yelled, "Well, I see that Parilli is back in town! What the hell are you doin' here, Parilli? And what are you starin' at, Mullins?"

Nick reached out to restrain Stan as he began an advance toward Galyon. In a deafening voice, Stan answered, "What am I *staring at?* Well, Galyon...I guess you could say that I'm staring at *a piece of shit!"*

The tavern suddenly became eerily quiet, as the customers all turned toward the shouting quarrel. Only the repetitious humming of the overhead fan could be heard inside the bar. The burly bartender stared at the disruptive squabble as Bird Dog Johnson abandoned his barstool and scurried out the front door where he immediately entered his car.

Galyon slowly reached into his pocket and removed a pair of brass knuckles. He openly displayed them, making sure they were seen by his adversaries. Then, with an angry sneer, he attached them to his fists. Before Stan had time to react he suddenly hurried toward the corner booth and struck Stan in the side of his head. The blow was quick and vicious. Stan was completely unconscious when he immediately fell to the floor. Galyon then swung his fist at Nick, who easily avoided the clumsy attempt. Nick hammered Galyon's face with several ruthless punches that sent him sprawling onto the sawdust that covered the floor.

The customers stared in awe and the room was enveloped in silence. The overweight bartender reached behind the bar, grasped a baseball bat, and immediately advanced toward the melee. "Get the hell out of my tavern!" he screamed. "I'll bash your heads in if you ever enter this place again!"

Cowboy Galyon slowly rose from the floor. While the bartender held the bat in a threatening position, Galyon staggered toward the front door. He suddenly turned and said, "Listen Parilli! You guys ain't seen the last of me! You'd better keep your eyes wide open, because your days are numbered!" He then left the tavern and entered the vehicle driven by Bird Dog and the car quickly sped away.

Stan gradually awakened. Nick helped him to his feet and led him toward the front door. In an even more threatening gesture the bartender raised his bat higher. "Don't you guys ever again come back to this tavern!

When they climbed into Lauren's car, Nick inspected the laceration that the brass knuckles had left on Stan's temple. He applied his handkerchief it to the bleeding gash, and swabbed the wound before finally handing the cloth to Stan. "Here, Stan. Press this against the wound until the bleeding stops."

"Thanks, Nick," said Stan.

Nick suddenly asked, "Stan, I wonder why Galyon didn't follow us to try to find our hide-away?"

"Hell, I don't know, Nicky. He *still* may be planning to follow us. What happened inside that joint, anyway? I don't remember anything after Bird Dog fled the scene." Stan said.

"You were knocked cold by Galyon. He was wearing brass knuckles on his fists." Nick answered.

"Well, what happened to Galyon?" Stan asked.

Nick grinned. "I beat the hell out of him!"

Stan appeared to be sad. "Nicky, I sure wasn't much help to you in that little altercation, but I'm glad you beat the hell out of Galyon! No wonder he didn't follow us to find out where we're living! I guess he'd had enough stress for today!"

When Nick drove away, he noticed that Stan seemed despondent. "Stan, don't feel bad about that little brawl. I'm sure you could have whipped Galyon if he hadn't used those brass knuckles! You shouldn't feel depressed!"

Stan looked up at Nick. "I'm not worried about getting the hell beat out of me, Nicky."

"Then what's bugging you?"

"I'm depressed about the terrible way that we messed up that elegant, state-of-the-art tavern." Both men laughed.

Chapter 8

Shortly after having breakfast at their hidden shack, Nick and Stan climbed into Lauren's car and Nick drove down the curvy mountain road to Highway 11. They had decided to visit Gilbert Jennings, or 'House Cat' as he was commonly called by local residents. Nick hadn't seen him since House Cat had abruptly joined the U'S. Army and was immediately sent to fight in the Korean War where he was severely wounded.

Stan was anxious. "Nicky, I'd sure like to see House Cat, but I don't really know if I should even mention his missing leg. You're a war veteran, so you've obviously had to deal with that kind of trauma. Do you think he'll be suffering from combat fatigue?"

"We have no way of knowing how he feels, Stan. Combat injuries affect most people differently. But I can assure you of one thing…He'll never again be the same." Nick said.

"Well, you'll probably feel comfortable talking to him, but I feel pretty awkward even thinking about it. I believe I'll let you do most of the talking, if you don't mind." Stan nervously lit a cigarette.

"Well, if House Cat is like most veterans, he'll probably heal fairly quickly from his physical wounds. He'll experience more pain in his psyche. But you'll need to consider House Cat's personality. His weirdness will probably mask any of his true emotions. We may never know how he *really* feels. Do you remember how he seemed to never give a damn about anything?"

Stan smiled. "Yeah, I remember. But I still don't know how to act toward him."

"Just be yourself, Stan," answered Nick.

Several months earlier, Nick had worked as a carpenter for House Cat Jennings, who had been the foreman of a house construction crew. The business was owned by Stan's father, Lester Mullins, while Stan, as building superintendent, was House Cat's boss. Although House Cat had supervised several men, he only developed a special bond with Stan and Nick.

The day was warm and sunny as Nick drove eastward down the main road. In order to shield his eyes from the rising sun, he adjusted the sun visor and turned toward Stan. "Tell me when to turn, Stan. When you called House Cat did he tell you exactly where he lives?"

"Turn right onto Martel Road and go about three miles. He lives out in the country. You know how he always hated city living." They continued their journey on Martel Road until Stan pointed and said, "Turn here. I think he lives in that little shack up in that field. He said that it's the only house within a half-mile of civilization."

Nick smiled. "Same old house Cat. And I'll bet he's still calling me, 'Ace' instead of 'Nick'."

Nick wheeled the car into a rutted road and parked beside a dented pickup truck and a deteriorating two-room shack. The shabby hovel was even worse than the shanty where Stan and his family members currently lived. Weeds and saw briars covered the surrounding area, and trash littered the yard.

Stan and Nick got out of the car, walked to the front door and softly knocked. After a rather lengthy wait, the front door opened and House Cat appeared in his wheelchair. Nick was shocked by the change in his appearance. His missing right leg quickly captured Stan's attention. He had lost several pounds, and instead of his customary sun-tanned complexion, his skin bore an unhealthy pallor; however, he had maintained his crew-cut hair style. He shielded his eyes from the bright sun as his bewildered expression gradually changed to a smile. "Well, I'll be damned!" he shouted, "If it ain't my ol' boss Stan! And I'm glad to see that you brought my ol' buddy 'Ace' with you! Welcome to my mansion, fellers!"

The men exchanged handshakes. Nick only laughed and sarcastically said, "Damn, House Cat. I see that you still have good taste in your choice of living style. I can also see that you're still calling me, 'Ace.'"

House Cat laughed. "Hell, 'Ace' sounds a lot better than 'Nicky.' That sounds like a girl's name. How did you ever get labelled with that?"

Nick smiled and said, "I explained that to you a long time ago when I was one of your employees. 'Nicky' is just a disgusting tag that Stan hung on me. My real name is 'Nick.' But it's okay with me if you keep calling me 'Ace.' I'm kinda getting used to it. You've been calling me that since we worked together, many months ago." Except for his initial greeting, Stan still hadn't spoken a word. He seemed to be ignoring his former friend.

House Cat switched his gaze to him. "Stan, when are you gonna say something, pal? Has a cat got your tongue? All you've done since you got here is act as dumb as hell and stare at my missin' leg! Ain't you ever seen a one-legged man before?"

Stan became embarrassed. "I'm sorry, House Cat. I'm just not used to seeing you like this." His attempt to embrace House Cat was quickly rebuffed when his old friend pulled away from him. "Don't start goin' sentimental on me, Stan," he said. His cutting remark caused even more embarrassment to Stan.

Nick ended the awkwardness when he quickly changed the subject. "House Cat, how are you doing financially? Do you have enough money to get by?"

"I'll make it okay, Ace. I had some money saved before I joined th' army. I'm mostly livin' off th' government."

"Well, what about the future? Do you think you'll be able to hold down some kind of regular job?" Nick asked.

"Hell, I don't have th' slightest idea, Ace. I'm just livin' my life one day at a time. When you think about it, ain't that what most ever'body else is doin'?"

Stan entered the discussion. "Maybe you could hold down some kind of job where you don't have to use your legs."

"God, I hope so. I sure won't be any good in a job that requires climbin' ladders. And I could never play golf, or take part in sports. Hell, I wouldn't be worth a damn in an ass kickin' contest." His friends laughed.

Stan asked, "Are you able to drive a vehicle?"

"Yeah, as long as I use that damned gadget." He pointed to that prosthetic leg in the corner of the room.

"Let's go into the living room and sit down where we can relax and talk," Nick suggested. In preparation of pushing his friend in the wheelchair, Nick grasped the handles; however, he was quickly censured by House Cat. "Let me manage this by myself, Ace! Hell, if I start dependin' on everybody to do simple things for me, it won't be long before some complete stranger will be wipin' my ass for me!"

Nick and Stan followed him into the shabby living room. The small, rumpled cot in the corner was cluttered with items of discarded clothing, and the room had a musty odor. Not a single picture adorned the walls, and the dirty rug on the floor was stained by leaks from the ceiling. House Cat remained in his wheelchair, while Nick and Stan took seats facing him in straight-backed kitchen chairs.

When they were seated, Nick said, "Well, House Cat, other than your missing leg, you seem to have survived the war with little emotional damage. Stan was telling me about the war protest you staged on the main street in Cedar Valley, and the rioting that resulted from it. I guess you feel the same way about the Korean War as I do. It was a needless war!"

71

House Cat's expression became grim and he spoke in an angry voice. "You know, Ace, I should have listened to you when you tried to talk to me about the war before I joined the army. What did we gain in that senseless slaughter? Hell, a peace treaty was never even signed! Ever'body just grew tired of th' war and quit fightin'! And I lost my damned leg for nothin'! That friggin' war was just a bunch of crap that was devised by idiots!" He toned down his loud rhetoric. "Hell, I got carried away. It won't do any good to whine about it!"

Having personally experienced the horrors of war, Nick was less reluctant than Stan in discussing House Cat's war wounds and anxieties. "Tell me how you lost your leg, pal. That must have been a terrible experience! Did you suffer any other wounds?"

House Cat's vision became a vacant stare, almost as if he were reliving the memory of the horrible event. His voice was like a rehearsed monotone, indicating that he had told the story many times. "The North Koreans were blastin' us with mortar fire. I crawled down inside this bunker and one of th' mortar shells landed in th' bunker. I don't remember anything else except waking up in th' hospital. Th' Medics found me before I bled to death. I didn't receive any other wounds—unless you consider th' wounds to my emotions. Ordinarily, I don't like to talk about th' war, but I don't mind discussin' it with another guy who's been there…"

"I understand," said Nick." Do you sometimes experience panic attacks?"

House Cat's eyes became misty. "Well, Ace, it's more like a feeling of worthlessness. But mostly I experience guilt. I was in th' infantry, so I killed a lot of enemy soldiers. Some of 'em were too young to even serve in th' military. Although I'm takin' sleeping pills ever' night, I still can't sleep. I keep havin' these morbid thoughts. Hell, sometimes I wish that mortar shell had killed me."

Nick sadly recalled the time he had killed the young North Korean teenager in the war. He reached over and patted House Cat on the shoulder.

Stan quickly changed the subject. "I told Nicky about the protest against the war and about how you got arrested by my uncle, Sheriff Mullins. I'm sure that must have pissed you off. I guess he put you in jail for your own protection. What was the final result of that arrest anyway?"

House Cat's face displayed anger. "Th' final result was Sheriff Mullins tellin' me that I should leave this county! He said that Cedar Valley don't need *rabble-rousers* like me! I realize that you just buried him, and probably don't appreciate criticism about him! But Cedar Valley is my home! I don't ever intend to leave this county! I know he was your uncle, but I'm kinda glad he committed suicide! That man was so dishonest, it's lucky somebody didn't kill him!"

"Somebody *did* kill him, House Cat!" Stan said. "The investigation proved that somebody shot him in the head and placed the gun beside his hand to make it appear to be suicide. They realized the truth when no fingerprints were found on the weapon. Obviously, the killer wiped away the prints. The fact that the sheriff was murdered will be common knowledge as soon as the newspaper prints the story. By the way, how do you know he was dishonest?"

House Cat said, "Do you happen to know a guy named 'Little Billy' Sneed? He knew the sheriff well, and told me about his dishonesty. Little Billy even sometimes visits me."

Nick answered, "Yeah, I know him! He was the jailhouse snitch! I met him in jail when one of the deputies arrested me for nothing! You'd better keep an eye on that guy, pal."

"Well, I 'pologize for being so critical of th' sheriff. I know it's tough for you guys. Hell, you just buried him."

Stan only chuckled, for he was well aware of House Cat's bluntness. "Hell, don't worry about it, man. The sheriff was like all of us…He was both good and bad."

House Cat changed the subject. "Well, what's been happening with you guys? I kinda lost track of you whenever I joined th' army. Ace, I got word from somebody that you ended up marryin' th' sheriff's daughter…Is that a fact?"

"Yes, that's true," Nick said. "We have a good marriage. Stan is also married now. Did you ever marry, House Cat?"

"Hell no. I'll probably never get married, now. What woman in her right mind would ever want to marry a one-legged man?"

Stan grinned and commented, "House Cat, when a man marries a woman, his leg is not his most important appendage. Just be thankful you didn't lose that portion of your anatomy!"

House Cat failed to see the humor. "Well I knew a couple of soldiers who did lose their peckers. Too bad. They'll never again be th' same. That's just another example of th' terrible price paid by suckers like me!"

Stan apologized to him. "I'm sorry, House Cat. I was just trying to interject a little humor into our conversation. I didn't mean to trivialize your loss."

"Hell, forget it Stan. I guess I'm a little sensitive since I returned from th' war."

Stan made an effort to explain his insensitive remark. "I never had to endure the terrible trauma that you and Nicky suffered. I'm beginning to realize the misery you endured."

House cat returned to the original subject. "Well, you guys were going to bring me up to date about what's been happenin' in your lives. Ace, you were just tellin' me that you married the sheriff's daughter. What else has been goin' on in your lives?"

Nick said, "House Cat, after you joined the army, many unbelievable things happened to me." He continued the story by telling about his unjust arrests, and the way that Sheriff Mullins had reacted by ordering him to forever stay away from his daughter, Lauren as well as the town of Cedar Valley. He related the tragedy at the Klan meeting, when Rufus and Preacher Temple were murdered. He told of the poetic justice obtained when Rufus' grandson, young Caleb had evened the score when he killed the Klan member who had murdered his grandfather. He then mentioned his escape to Louisiana with Lauren, and how they had returned to Cedar Valley for Sheriff Mullins' funeral. He completed the story by explaining that he and Stan planned to 'finish the job' that he had left unfinished; for they intended to exact revenge on the remaining Klan members. He also told of a more recent burden: to discover and help convict the murderer of Sheriff Mullins.

"Wow! You've been a busy man, Ace. I heard through th' grapevine about the possibility of th' Klan murders, but nobody knew for sure if th' story was true. I began to believe th' story when I didn't see Rufus around town anymore. But I didn't know about little Caleb killing th' murderer of his grandfather. You say that you came back to Cedar Valley to *finish th' job*. What do you mean?"

"Well, Stan and I intend to see the Klan members pay for their part in the murders. Stan is going to confess his Klan membership to the authorities. Also, since I witnessed the Klan murders, I've decided to testify about the killing to the grand jury. Because the Klan members are aware of this, Stan and I are in constant danger!"

House Cat was shocked. "Damn, Ace!" You'd better stay hidden!" He turned to Stan. "How about you, Stan? What's happened in your life since I left Cedar Valley?

"Well, I guess you could say that I really veered off-course with my life. I foolishly became a member of the Klan. In the beginning, I thought they did a lot of good in our community. But now, I'd love to kill any of those bastards!"

House Cat agreed. "Hell, I'd like to kill *every damned one of 'em!* It became public knowledge when I held my protest against th' war. When the Klan heard about it, they staged a protest against *me!* Those cowards are *for th' war!* But like most ignorant hicks, they're too yellow to fight in it! They should be wiped from th' face of th' earth!"

Stan said, "I quit the Klan when I saw them murder the preacher and Rufus. You know, Rufus was like a father to me. You remember Rufus, don't you, House Cat?"

"Sure I remember him," House Cat answered. "He used to work for me occasionally. I remember that he was the handy man around your dad's home. He was a hell of a nice guy for a nigger. So when Sheriff Mullins was killed, I guess you called

Ace and Lauren so they could return to Cedar Valley and attend his funeral…Right?"

"Yeah, that's right," Stan replied, "And I suppose that kinda brings you up to date on Nicky and me. And by the way…Rufus wasn't a *nigger*, House Cat."

"Then just what in th' hell was he?"

Stan replied, "He was a *Negro.*"

"Damn it Stan, don't start gettin' technical with me! Hell, 'nigger' is just a word!" With a sarcastic emphasis on the pronunciation of the last word, he said, "I ain't got nuthin' against **Negroes**. By the way—speakin' of niggers, I met a guy recently that you guys might know. His name is Arthur Bowman, but he was only a *half-nigger*…So I guess that means he's only *half bad*." To irritate Stan, he sneered before continuing. "Do you remember th' maid that worked for Sheriff Mullins? I think her name is 'Willie Mae.' Well this guy claims that she's his sister." With the mention of the man's name, both Nick and Stan became interested.

Nick was first to speak. "Where did you meet this guy?"

"He came here to my house, Ace."

"What did he want?" Nick asked.

"He asked a lot of questions. He asked if I knew th' sheriff, or either of you guys. He was as mad as hell! He talked about th' way the sheriff had taken unfair advantage of his sister, and in his opinion, Sheriff Mullins was obligated to provide for her. I believe he came here before th' sheriff was killed. He even said that he would like to get his hands on him! If the sheriff was murdered, maybe this guy is th' guilty guy."

Stan interrupted the discussion. "I realize that the sheriff was bad in many ways. But Willie Mae was more than just his maid. She was more like a wife to him. Hell, he was sleeping with her! In personal matters like this, my uncle was a good man! I know that if he had lived, he would have provided for her, and if Willie Mae's brother had met him before his death, the sheriff would have assured him of that. In fact, Arthur Bowman even told us that when the sheriff dismissed her,

Willie Mae had received the sheriff's assurance that he would provide for her. "

"Do you think that Arthur Bowman knew this before Sheriff Mullins was killed?" Nick asked. "If Willie Mae only told him this after the sheriff was dead, maybe Bowman *did kill him!*"

"Hell, I have no way of knowin' the answer to that," House Cat answered. "Why does that matter?"

"It matters because if Bowman knew this, and believed that the sheriff was true to his word, he would have no reason to kill the sheriff. In fact, he would have hoped that the sheriff lived a long life, so he could continue to provide for his sister. When did he come to visit with you?" Nick asked.

"It was a few days ago...Hell, I can't remember th' date."

"Well, was it before, or after the sheriff was murdered? If it was *before,* then this guy would only have a motive if the sheriff refused to provide for her. But if it was *after* the sheriff's murder when he came to see you, he would never have talked to others about how much he hated Sheriff Mullins. After all, suspicion would have fallen directly on him. After the sheriff was murdered, Bowman would be a fool to go around telling people how much he would like to kill the sheriff! Hell, the police would already have him in jail as a suspect in the sheriff's murder!"

Stan entered the conversation. "There's another aspect that should be considered. I realize the fact that he was murdered will soon be public knowledge. But when the sheriff died, the general public believed that he committed suicide. Except for the authorities and a few of our family members there's only one person who knew that he was murdered: *the killer.* If a person thought that suicide was the proven cause of death, he would have felt free to express his hatred of the sheriff, so he is obviously innocent of the crime."

House Cat only chuckled. "Well, I guess that eliminates me as a suspect, because I still thought he committed suicide, and I didn't like him worth a damn!" His crude remark brought laughter from both Stan and Nick.

Nick remarked, "It also eliminates Arthur Bowman as a suspect, House Cat. Why would he kill the sheriff and then brag about how much he hated him? He would immediately become a suspect! It doesn't make sense!"

House Cat agreed. "Yeah, I guess you can eliminate him as a suspect. If you want my opinion, I'd say that one of th' Klan members killed him. That shitty deputy, Cowboy Galyon hated him; in fact, I've heard rumors that he once threatened to kill th' sheriff. As a matter of fact, th' sheriff wasn't that well-liked by his other deputies."

Nick said, "I didn't know he was that unpopular with the officers who worked for him. Where did you get all this information, House Cat?"

"Do you remember when I asked you if you knew Little Billy Sneed? Well, he told me."

"House Cat, you must be seeing of lot of Billy Sneed to obtain so much information from him. Maybe you should steer clear of him. After all, he's not very trustworthy."

"You're right, Ace. He talks to me a lot whenever I buy drugs from him."

"You buy drugs from Billy Sneed?" Stan asked.

"Hell yes. Since I was wounded in Korea I've suffered almost constant pain. I can't even get around without some kind of pain-killing drug. I've even still got a piece of shrapnel lodged in my spine! Hell, Billy Sneed is beginnin' to cost me about half of my government check!"

"Where does Billy get these drugs? Stan asked.

House cat shrugged. "Hell, I don't know. He can get a gun for you, or even dynamite if you want to blow up a building. Hell, he can get about anything a man wants if he's willin' to pay for it."

"House Cat. I'm sorry to hear about your addiction."

House Cat changed the subject. "Ace, how long do you intend to stay in Cedar Valley?"

Nick replied, "I don't know. I guess I'll just stay as long as it takes to tie up all the loose ends."

"Where are you stayin'?"

"Lauren and I are staying with Stan and his wife, Kathy. Also, Lauren's mother is staying with us for now."

"I'll bet you're stayin' in one of those fancy Mullins mansions." House Cat laughed.

Stan laughed and answered, "Not quite, House Cat. The place where we're staying is about like this place, *in all its glory!*" To sarcastically illustrate the illustrious character of the shabby hovel, he looked upward and swept his arms in a glorious gesture.

House Cat asked, "Stan, what's your dad doin' these days? I heard that you and him closed your construction business. Are you goin' to start buildin' houses again?"

"*I'm* not," said Stan. "And my father has retired. He recently got religion. I think he would like to work in the church in some way." Stan didn't mention that his mother had recently left his father.

House Cat stretched and suddenly yawned. "I ain't tryin' to be rude, but if you guys will excuse me, it's time for my afternoon nap. As usual, I didn't get much sleep last night. Doctor's orders, of course."

For a while Nick and Stan continued to reminisce with House Cat about the past. After saying their goodbyes and promising to revisit, they finally drove away. They journeyed homeward in silence and with sadness, for they wondered what the future held for their old friend.

Chapter 9

Lester Mullins was a lonely man. His wife, Mary Jane had recently left him, and during his son's teenage years and early adulthood, Stan had grown to dislike him. In addition, he had recently abandoned his beloved mansion and moved into a large house that was unfamiliar to him. He was further saddened by the headlines in the morning newspaper stating that Sheriff Mullins' death was not suicide, but murder.

As he drove toward Stan's residence, he reminisced about his many regrets of the past. His selfish misdeeds during the years when he served as mayor of Cedar Valley and his former inconsiderate ways had driven Mary Jane away. Since his recent conversion to Christianity and regular church attendance he had partially recaptured Stan's respect for him; however, he wasn't able to escape the feelings of guilt and regret that tortured him.

He drove the vehicle up Kingston Hill and turned right into the property that his son had recently rented. Since he knew that Stan wanted to keep all vehicles hidden from the road in front, he steered the car into the weedy back yard and parked behind Lauren's car and Stan's old station wagon. When he peeked at his wristwatch, he noted that the time was

5:30 p.m. *Perfect timing*, he thought. Sharing dinner with kin would assuage his loneliness.

Soon after he knocked at the front door, Stan immediately responded. He was somewhat surprised to see his father standing in front of him. From the small kitchen the pleasant aroma of frying chicken filled the living room. Stan smiled and said, "Why hello, Dad! Come in! You're just in time for supper…or *dinner*, as Nicky refers to the evening meal".

Stan's father immediately stepped into the living room and hugged his son. "Hello, Stan! I hope you'll excuse my rudeness. I realize you didn't know I'd be coming here, but I was hoping you'd allow me to share supper with you. I'm not hungry, so I won't eat very much. I mostly just got lonely for company."

Lauren's mother, Bonnie Rose, was seated in the small living room while the others were preparing dinner in the kitchen. Stan turned and called out to them, "Hey, you guys! Dad's here! Come in and say 'hello' to him!"

Kathy immediately appeared and briskly walked to Stan's father and hugged him. Nick and Lauren quickly followed her. Nick shook his hand and Lauren warmly greeted him. After exchanging pleasantries with them, Stan's father immediately walked to Lauren's mother, Bonnie Rose and knelt in front of her. He reached out and warmly embraced her. "Well, how have you been doing, young lady?"

At first, Bonnie Rose only stared at the floor. She finally raised her head and looked straight ahead without really seeing him. "Where's my husband?" Her voice resembled an angry whisper. "He's been gone for several days! When's he coming back home?"

Stan's father looked into her eyes. "Bonnie Rose, he may be gone for a while, but maybe he is just waiting for you to go to him. It may not be too long until you can be with him all of the time."

She looked away from him. Suddenly, in a loud voice she angrily shouted, "When in hell are we going to eat?" Her incongruous question brought surprise to everyone in the

81

room. Their emotions became a contradicting composite of humor and sadness. Lauren began to openly cry and hurried back into the kitchen.

To offer comfort, Kathy followed her. Nick joined Stan and his father when they took seats in the living room. Soon, sounds from the kitchen could be heard as Lauren and Kathy finished preparing the meal. When Kathy called out, "Come and get it!" Nick went into the kitchen and brought a tray of food out to Lauren's mother in the living room and placed it on a table in front of her wheelchair

The table had been neatly set when Nick followed Stan and his father into the kitchen where they all sat in chairs around the table. The women dished out the food and sat down. Soon after, Lester Mullins said a brief blessing.

Although their accumulation of groceries had been limited, the cuisine was good: fried chicken, mashed potatoes, green peas and biscuits. The meal was complemented by iced tea and store-bought cookies for dessert. Because of the sadness that resulted from the confused mind of Bonnie Rose, Stan's father only nibbled at his food and the meal was consumed mostly in silence.

While the women cleaned the kitchen and put away the dishes, Bonnie Rose was still munching on her food when Nick followed Stan and his father into the living room where they chose seats facing each other. Stan's father watched her as she ate. "Poor woman," he remarked, "Her mind seems to have gotten worse since the last time I saw her. Do you think she can comprehend what we're saying?"

Stan looked sadly at her. "No, Dad…She is completely in a different world. She can hardly make sense of anything we say or do." Nick was amazed when he noticed the drastic change that had occurred in the attitude of Lester Mullins since his religious conversion. In Nick's past memories of him, he was an insensitive man who cared little about the problems of others; however, his past misfortunes had altered his thinking. Apparently, he had changed to a man of gentleness and compassion. Nick admired him.

Stan's father asked, "When are you going to start attending church with me, Stan? I get lonesome, and I worry about you."

Stan smiled. "Maybe I will one of these Sundays, Dad."

The women entered the living room to join the men in their conversation. To afford them a place to sit they were carrying chairs from the kitchen. While Kathy took a seat, Lauren set aside her chair and immediately walked to her mother and knelt beside her wheelchair. She became misty-eyed as she brushed her mother's hair and soothed her with affectionate words. She then stood and carried her mother's empty food tray into the kitchen. Upon her return she sat in her chair beside Kathy. In the South during the Fifties it was an unwritten rule that when a conversation took place between members of the opposite sex, men had the floor. As a result, both Kathy and Lauren remained quiet.

Lester Mullins asked, "Stan, what are you and Nick going to be doing tomorrow? Could I help you in any way?"

Stan answered, "I got a phone call from a guy named Billy Sneed. He wants to meet with Nicky and me. He said he had some valuable information for us about your brother's murder. You're welcome to go with us to meet him, Dad."

Stan's father was surprised. "Do you mean, *Little Billy Sneed?* Wasn't he the guy that was known as the 'jailhouse snitch'? What kind of information could he have that would interest you?"

"I don't know, Dad. He just wants us to meet with him. After all, he had pretty intimate knowledge of the sheriff's activities. Maybe he can give us some information that will help find your brother's killer."

Stan's father seemed puzzled. "Do you know where he lives? Does he have a home now? He used to make his home at the jail. He was just a volunteer prisoner. My brother provided him a place to live, and occasionally slipped him a little bit of money in exchange for some information he uncovered about potential criminals. He is a very contemptible man, and nobody respects him—not even his fellow prisoners. Since he's not staying at the jail, I wonder where he is living."

"Dad, I think he's homeless. He simply called and asked if Nicky and I could pick him up at Humpy Keener's pool room. Would you like to go with us?" Stan asked.

Stan's father frowned. "No thanks, Stan. I try to be open-minded, but I don't believe I could tolerate that man!"

"Well, Nicky and I are going to meet with him. Maybe he can give us some information about several things," said Stan.

Lester Mullins slowly stood and walked toward the front window that overlooked the lengthy front yard. He shaded his eyes and looked downhill toward the distant road. "Hey, come here, you guys! Take a look at the road at the bottom of the hill! There's a car parked there with a man standing beside it!" With the exception of Lauren's mother, everyone in the room left their seats and gathered in front of the window. Stan's father became more curious. "Look!" he said, "I believe he's looking at this house through a pair of binoculars!"

Stan strained his eyes to capture a better look. He then remarked, "Do you think that he's part of the Klan trying to find out where we live?"

Nick was less suspicious. "Stan, don't get so upset! That guy might be simply conducting some kind of survey. I'm afraid you're getting paranoid!"

"But what if it is a Klan member? That might mean that our hideout has been discovered!"

Nick was still skeptical. "Don't worry, Stan...We're all inside. That guy can't see any of us. All he can see is an old empty house." The intruder slowly re-entered his vehicle and drove away.

Lester Mullins was still worried. "Stan, I'm afraid that your little hiding place has been discovered! My offer still stands! All of you should abandon this place and move into my house with me. I've got plenty of room! And it's sure better than living in this little shack. I'll even hire some protection for all of you!"

"Dad, you've given me something to think about!" Stan said. "But maybe we're still safe here!" However, after Stan's father followed his family away from the window, he continued to worry.

Twilight was descending when Stan's father said his goodbyes to the group. They invited him to sleep on the couch and stay for the night, but he politely declined. He again hugged Lauren's mother and thanked the others for their companionship and for dinner. Finally he playfully kissed both women on their cheeks and hugged Stan and Nick before leaving the house. Both men peered through the front window and watched him drive away.

It was a rainy, gloomy morning when Nick and Stan entered the old station wagon and Stan drove toward Cedar Valley and their meeting with Billy Sneed. Nick was filled with curiosity about the visit. "What time are we supposed to meet him, Stan?" he asked.

"I told Little Billy that we'd meet him at 10:00 a.m." Stan answered. "Hell, that bum is so unreliable I doubt that he even shows up."

"Well, if he doesn't show up, we can probably locate him at some tavern or either one of the two poolrooms. Where did he tell you to meet him?"

"At Humpy Keener's poolroom," Stan answered.

"I believe he'll be there, Stan," Nick said, "He's trying to make a little easy money for whatever information he might give us. But it may be worthless."

"Well, any idle gossip we get might be helpful. How much money do you think he expects us to give him?" Stan asked.

"I think that's up to us. We'll pay him according to how much the information is worth. Damn, Stan! Can you imagine a guy so worthless that ratting on people is his major source of income?"

"He's just out for whatever he can squeeze out of us, Nick. I even brought a pint of booze with us to loosen him up."

Nick became depressed as he peered out the window at the accumulating puddles of water, for he was reminded of some of the dismal rains of Louisiana in the springtime. He became even more depressed when he thought of the scheduled meeting with Little Billy Sneed. "Stan, this meeting might be totally worthless, you know. We may be wasting our time."

"Nicky, that may be so, but we have to start somewhere. Think positive. We may actually learn something."

They became silent as Nick's mind wandered. He began to think of the recent visit by Stan's father. Nick began to have second thoughts about the unexpected appearance of the stranger they had seen spying on their property with binoculars. "Stan, what do you think about that guy who was parked beside the road looking at our house yesterday? Do you really think the Klan suspects we are hiding there?"

"Damn, Nicky! I don't know! I sure hope not!"

"Well, what do you think about your father inviting us to move into his apartment with him?"

"You know, Nicky…I really believe Dad is worried about us, and he's really trying to help us. But mostly, I just think that he is lonely. Since my mother left him, he's nearly become a recluse. Maybe we should consider his proposal. Dad has really changed for the better—but I still hate to think of again living under his domination!"

"Don't worry, Stan. I'm still not sure we need to change locations. But if we decided to move in with him I don't really think your father would ever try to control your life again."

Stan entered the downtown area and drove the old station wagon through the puddles of water in the street. He finally angle-parked in front of a shabby brick building on the corner of First Avenue. The sign on the faded surface above the windows read, *'Keener's Billiard Parlor'*.

They left the vehicle and in an effort to avoid the drizzling rain, dashed into the pool room. The smell of stale beer and cigarette smoke permeated the room. Noisy conversation and the repetitious clicking of billiard balls were constant. Several were playing pool, while many onlookers sat in a row of seats that bordered the pool tables. Nick followed Stan as he walked past the billiard tables toward the rear. Sitting in the last seat among the onlookers was Little Billy Sneed.

When Nick again saw him, old memories returned. His features were exactly as he remembered them. He was a tiny, elfish, middle-aged man, short in stature and was so frail that he appeared to weigh less than a hundred pounds. The top of his head displayed a few wispy strands of jet-black hair that thickened to a fluff on the back of his head and extended to his shoulders. A thin patch of silky hair sprouted like tiny wires from his upper lip. He had a large, beak-like nose, oversized ears, and yellowing teeth with protruding incisors hanging over his lower lip like fangs. When viewing his features, Nick decided that he bore a striking resemblance to a rat. This assessment reminded Nick of the occasion when he had first met Billy Sneed: the time that he had been thrown into jail when he hadn't broken any law. He also remembered that Billy Sneed had a pet rat named, 'Oscar.'

When Nick and Stan approached him, Billy Sneed immediately recognized Stan; however, he had no memory of Nick. Stan offered a handshake and introduced him to his friend. "Hello, Billy. In case you don't remember me, I'm Stan Mullins and this guy is Nicky Parilli."

"Howdy, fellers," he responded. "I wanted to see you guys because I read in th' paper that th' sheriff was murdered and didn't commit suicide. I'm glad ya could make it. I was afraid this rain might keep ya away. Man, it's rainin' outside like pourin' piss out of a boot! By th' way, Stan…I can't seem to place this-here buddy of yours. Have me an' him met somewhere in th' past?"

Nick said, "Yeah, Billy. I met you once when one of the deputies threw me in jail for nothing. You obviously don't remember me. I recall that you had a pet rat named, 'Oscar.' Do you still have him?"

Billy's face reflected anger. "Hell no! I lost ol' Oscar a long time ago. That shitty deputy, Cowboy Galyon came into the cellblock one day and killed him!" He then mumbled, "That son of a bitch!"

"Damn, Billy! Why would anyone want to kill a rat? That was terribly cruel of him!" Nick sarcastically replied.

The poolroom noise became louder, making it difficult to hear normal speech. Billy Sneed cupped his hand behind his ear and asked, "Whut did ya say? I didn't hear ya!"

Stan spoke loudly when he suggested, "Let's all go outside and talk in my vehicle. It's too noisy in this poolroom!"

"Good!" said Billy."Ya can't here ya'self fart in here!"

Little Billy followed Nick and Stan toward the entrance of the noisy and smoke-filled poolroom. As they moved down the row of seats that were occupied by poolroom loafers, a large, beefy man suddenly stopped Billy Sneed. He was obviously very angry. "You damned rat-fink!" he shouted, "I've been hoping to run into you somewhere! Because of your snoopin' around and rattin' on me, I spent a month in jail!" He viciously shoved Little Billy into one of the pool tables. "If you wasn't so pint-sized, I'd beat th' damn shit outta you, you little bastard!"

Although Nick sympathized with the angry man, he quickly restrained him. While Little Billy regained his balance, Nick pushed the huge attacker backward and held him firmly. "Back off, mister! Leave him alone! I understand your complaint, but you're too big to beat the crap out of a little guy like him. We're taking him out of here, so give us room to get through! Okay?" Nick smiled at the large man.

The man remained angry; however, he stepped aside and allowed the three men to walk past him. As they made their exit from the poolroom, he shouted, "I'll run into you again sometime, you asshole!" he shouted.

The rain had subsided when Nick and Stan led Billy Sneed from the poolroom onto the sidewalk. Stan noticed a stranger standing beside his station wagon. Upon closer inspection, Stan recognized him: The man was 'Bird Dog' Johnson, the ex-deputy and former employee of Sheriff Mullins. When Bird Dog quickly trotted away, Stan shouted, "Hey, mister…Wait a minute! What were you doing hanging around my car?" But his question remained unanswered as Bird Dog continued to hurry down the sidewalk.

While Billy Sneed stared in curiosity, both Stan and Nick stood by the old station wagon and watched Bird Dog until he disappeared around the corner.

Nick was puzzled. "Stan, I wonder why that guy was standing beside your car?"

"I'll be damned if I know! Obviously he was looking for something! Or maybe it was just a coincidence!"

When they entered the vehicle, Stan and Nick sat in the front seat while Billy Sneed climbed into the back. When they were comfortably seated, Stan looked around at Little Billy. "Okay, Sneed. You said you had some information about Sheriff Mullins' murder. Let's have it!"

"Hell, fellers, let's not git in a big hurry. We need to git down to bizness first! How much do ya intend to pay?"

"That depends," Stan said.

"Depends on whut?" asked Billy.

"It depends on how reliable the information is."

"Damn! I can't tell you if it's reliable or not! Shit, that's yore problem to figger out. All I can do is to give you some names! You guys will have to fit the pieces together!! How much are ya willin' to pay?"

Nick turned and addressed Billy. "Listen, Sneed. We don't have time to fool around with you. You give us whatever information you have, and we'll evaluate it. Then we'll decide whether or not if it's worth anything! Now stop badgering us for money and start talking!"

"Can't we go somewhere and eat first? Hell, I'm as hungry as a damned bear!" It seemed that Billy Sneed wanted to pilfer anything he could get from either Nick or Stan.

Stan became angry "Forget about eating, Billy. Nick and I don't have time for that! Now let's get down to business!"

"Damn! You guys shore ain't very sociable! Ain't ya at least got a little somethin' to drink? Hell, ya just jerk me outta a poolroom and expect me to start solving a murder fer ya!"

Stan reached under the front seat and withdrew the pint of whiskey. "Does this help any, Billy?" he asked. Billy's eyes immediately ogled the bourbon. He reached over the seat, secured the bottle, and immediately took an enormous drink.

Nick began to reflect on the time when, many months ago he had first met Little Billy Sneed. Nick had been unjustly arrested and thrown into the Cedar Valley county jail. He remembered that Billy Sneed was one of the men behind bars; however, he was languishing in jail by choice, for he had always been homeless and loved the atmosphere of the jail. He managed to survive by favors granted to him for informing on other people. He provided information to the sheriff regarding suspicious activity among the inmates, and his fellow citizens of Cedar Valley. He also performed some of the janitorial work around the jail. In return, the sheriff rewarded him with free room and board in the jail, and sometimes with a rather generous tip. When Nick thought of Billy's dismal lifestyle, he began to feel sorry for him; however, his sorrow was a feeling of pity that was born of revulsion, for Nick disliked the man and had absolutely no respect for him.

After another drink from the bottle, Billy placed it between his knees and loudly belched. "Aaah! Now that's more like it!" he exclaimed "Okay, fellers, how can I help you?"

"You can start by telling us who you believe might have killed the sheriff...and why." Stan said.

Billy lifted the bottle and fondly examined it. He then took another small drink, lowered the bottle, and smiled. "Well, I've got a few suspects for ya," he said. "First of all, it might have been Cowboy Galyon."

"Why do you suspect him?" Nick asked.

"Because I personally overheard 'im threaten to kill th' sheriff. A few days after th' sheriff decided to come clean about th' crookedness of th' county police force, Galyon got as mad as hell. He was in th' office with Sheriff Mullins, and I was in th' next room helpin' clean up th' place. Galyon and th' sheriff started quarrelin' and Galyon finally said, 'Mullins, your days are numbered! If you go through with this betrayal of all your deputies, you're th' same as a dead man! Because I'll kill you!'"

Nick answered, "That's an interesting story, Billy. Are you sure you don't simply have a grudge against Galyon? Stan told me that Galyon once beat the hell out of you. And wasn't it Galyon who killed your pet rat?"

Billy only shrugged. "Well, I'm just tellin' ya th' facts. I can't make you believe my story."

Stan asked, "Billy, who are the other suspects?"

Billy lifted the bottle and took another long drink. "You may not suspect him, but Bird Dog Johnson once told me that Galyon had offered him a bunch of money to kill th' sheriff for him. Of course, I still kinda believe that Galyon did th' job hisself."

Both Nick and Stan shared the same suspicion. However, Nick remembered their visit with House Cat Jennings in which House Cat had mentioned the mulatto, Arthur Bowman, the brother of Sheriff Mullins' maid. "What about a guy named Arthur Bowman, Billy?" Nick asked.

"Hell, I don't know very much about him." Billy took another hefty drink.

Both Nick and Stan felt that the interview was over. Stan reached into his wallet and withdrew a couple of bills and handed them to Billy, who momentarily stared at the money before stuffing it into his front pocket.

Billy Sneed temporarily remained in the car as Nick asked him some personal questions. He became curious about Billy's means of survival. "Billy, now that you can no longer live at the jail, where is your home now?"

"Anywhere I can lay my head, fellers. I guess most people would say I'm homeless. But I've sorta got a home now."

"Where?" asked Nick.

"For th' last month or so, 'Marble Head' Matthews has been lettin' me sleep in his barn loft. I do a few chores around his farm in order to pay him back." He opened the door and stepped out of the car.

"Well, how can you afford to eat?" Stan asked.

Little Billy reached into his front pocket and withdrew the money that Stan had given him. He simply displayed the two ten dollar bills and smiled before walking away.

The rain had stopped when Stan drove the old station wagon away. Suddenly, the valves began to slightly miss. Nick quickly noticed the hesitation of the engine rhythm. "Stan, what's wrong with this old trap? Have you had it serviced recently?" However, the men became less concerned when the engine gradually began to function more smoothly. As a result, Stan began to ignore the irregularity of the engine and began to focus his concern on their visit with Billy Sneed. He continued to drive the old station wagon away from the downtown area into the suburbs.

Stan asked, "Nick, just how much credibility should we give the suspicions of Billy Sneed? Do you think any of the people he named might have killed Sheriff Mullins?"

"Well. Cowboy Galyon is a likely suspect...and Author Bowman might have killed him. Bird Dog Johnson is mean enough, but he's probably too stupid to devise a complicated scheme involving murder."

Stan shook his head in doubt." Damn it Nick, I don't believe we made much headway with Little Billy. We're right back where we started!"

"We'll just have to give every shred of this information plenty of thought. By the way, how much did you pay him for the information, Stan?" Nick asked.

"I gave him twenty dollars. I only wanted to give him a ten and a five, but except for a couple of ones, all I had were the two tens. Hell, I should have only given him the ten, because I don't feel that the information he gave us is worth a damn!"

Stan had now driven the old station wagon out of the downtown area into open country. Unexpectedly, the vehicle became slower as the engine began to sputter. Stan pulled out the choke and continued to press the accelerator, but the engine finally died. He engaged the clutch and steered the coasting vehicle into a wide space beside the road. His repeated attempts to restart the vehicle were unsuccessful. Stan's expression displayed a look of hopelessness. He stared straight ahead and sighed, "Damn, Nick! What do we do now? Here we are stranded in the country several miles from nowhere! I can't figure out how this ever happened!"

Nick pondered the situation. "Stan, here's a possibility. We caught that bastard, Bird Dog Johnson snooping around your car. Do you think he did something to it?"

Stan was immediately suspicious. "That son of a bitch! I'll bet he disconnected a spark plug or did something else to our car. Hell, there's no telling what he might have done!"

When Nick peered across the wet meadow to an adjoining thoroughfare about a half-mile away, he noticed that the road displayed a few random businesses. He punched Stan on the shoulder. "Stan, look over across that meadow. There is some kind of civilization on that road over there. See those buildings? Maybe we can locate a garage that can get this old trap of yours running again. It's worth a try."

Both men left the vehicle and entered the field toward the other highway. Because of the recent downpour of rain, the ground was a sea of standing water and mud. As a result, their feet began to squish in the slime and their shoes became covered with mud. Nevertheless, they wordlessly trudged toward the scattering of small buildings located on the nearby highway. When they arrived at the other road they discovered *Earl's Garage* among the small businesses. They stomped mud from their feet and entered the door.

The interior was semi-dark and reeked with the smell of oil. Two employees were on duty. One worker was installing tires to an old pickup truck. A second mechanic, while holding a flashlight in his hand, had his head buried beneath the raised hood of an old convertible. The man withdrew his head and wiped the grime from his hands with a rag as Stan approached him. His denim pants were spotted with grime and the tee-shirt he wore over his muscular body bore numerous stains of oil and grease.

The mechanic continued to clean his hands as he stared at the mud that Nick and Stan had tracked onto the garage floor. Stan also took note of it and offered a lame apology. "Mister, I'm sorry we got your floor so dirty. We had to walk across that swampy field to get here."

The mechanic continued to sourly look at the muddy floor. In an unfriendly voice he asked, "How can I help you, sir?"

Stan began to explain. "Our car is parked just across that field over on Highway 11. The motor started missing and then the car just quit on us. Can you either tow it into your garage, or drive us back over there and get our car running again? It may be the plugs, or maybe it's the battery. You may want to bring some parts with you. I know you may be busy, but I can make it worth your while if you could stop what you're working on and help us."

The mechanic appeared to be reluctant. He finally replied, "Just give me a few minutes to get some parts together, and I'll be with you." He pointed to a nearby vehicle. "I'll drive that wrecker over there, so you can wait for me inside it. And clean the rest of the mud off your feet before you get into the vehicle!"

"Okay, mister," Stan answered. As the man walked away, Stan whispered to Nick, "That guy must have a bug up his ass about something!"

Nick only laughed. "Hell, Stan…He's probably just having a bad day. Besides, we sure muddied up his floor."

Almost an hour passed before the mechanic returned. He was carrying a kit into which he had packed away some tools and parts. After placing them into the back of the wrecker, he drove away in the vehicle. The man remained silent as Stan gave him directions to the location of their car. He hesitated as he slowly pulled the wrecker into the open space beside Stan's station wagon. Before parking, he pointed to the muddy tire tracks beside Stan's vehicle. "Somebody's been parked here beside your car, buddy," he said. "Did you see those tracks when you parked here?"

94

Both Nick and Stan were suspicious. "No, I sure don't remember seeing them," said Stan.

"Well, I might as well get started. Let me have your car keys," he said to Stan. "I'll try to start it before I look at the engine. It may just be flooded."

Stan handed him the keys. "I'm sure it's not flooded, mister. It appears to be just the opposite. It doesn't seem to be getting *enough* gasoline."

The mechanic said, "Don't give me instructions! I know what I'm doing!" He left the wrecker and walked to the side of the station wagon and opened the door of the driver's side. Apparently, he changed his mind about attempting to start the car, for he hesitated for a moment before moving to the front of the car and opening the hood, exposing the motor. He only briefly examined the engine before quickly jumping back. He called to Stan and Nick, "Come here you guys! What kinda trick are you tryin' to pull on me? Hell, there's several sticks of dynamite under the hood beside your battery!"

Nick followed Stan to the open hood. They both stared in shock at the bundle of explosives that had been wired together beside the battery. All of them took several steps back from the vehicle when the mechanic angrily said, "Damn! If I had turned that key to start this trap, I'd be a dead man! That dynamite is wired to the battery! I sensed that you guys were trouble when you first walked into my garage! Who are you guys, anyway? Are you part of a damned gang?"

Nick angrily glared at him. "Look, Mister! Don't get so riled up! We're just as surprised as you are!"

When he realized that he had narrowly escaped death, the mechanic sighed with relief. "Well, what do we do now? I can't get your car started! And I'm sure as hell not gonna try to dismantle that bomb!"

Stan was apologetic. "Look, pal. I'm sorry about the way this little repair job turned out. We're not bad people...We're just trying to live the best we can. We need to get the police to come and investigate this. I want to ask a favor of you. When you get back to your garage, will you call the county police for us? If you can remember, ask to speak to Sheriff Kirkland. Tell him what happened and that Stan Mullins needs him right away! He'll know to bring somebody with him who's qualified to dismantle these explosives."

In order to partially compensate the mechanic for his harrowing experience, Nick reached into his wallet, withdrew a ten-dollar bill and handed it to him. The man nodded his head. "Okay, buddy. I'll call 'em for you." He slowly climbed into the wrecker and drove away.

Nick and Stan watched the wrecker speed down the street. In order to distance themselves from the dynamite, they walked across the road and sat down among the weeds in a hilly section of dry ground.

Stan was depressed. His mind was overwhelmed with the contradicting emotions of relief and anger. "What do you think happened here, Nicky? How in the hell did that dynamite end up in our car?"

Nick pondered the event. "Stan, I think it all began with Bird Dog Johnson—when we saw him hanging around your vehicle. Apparently, he disconnected a spark plug, or maybe he did something else to your car. As a result, we had to stop and abandon your car in order to find a mechanic. Realizing this, either Bird Dog or one of his accomplices followed us. The muddy tire tracks beside your vehicle indicate that somebody parked there within the last hour. When the auto mechanic took so long in bringing us here, it gave them time to place the dynamite in your car."

With his handkerchief, Stan wiped the sweat from his forehead and sighed with relief. "Whew! Do you realize that if that mechanic had turned the key to start my car, we'd have all been blown to hell? Nicky, I'm impressed by the way you analyzed this attempt on our lives. Maybe you should have been a detective!"

Nick smiled. "Maybe I should have, at that, Stan. I guess you could say that my past experiences have taught me to be suspicious and cynical!"

The sheriff responded in less than fifteen minutes. With flickering lights, a county police car pulled in and parked at least twenty yards behind Stan's vehicle in the broad expanse of mud beside the road. Both Sheriff Kirkland and an overweight man left the police car and quickly strode across the road to meet Nick and Stan. The sheriff shook hands with both men and quickly addressed Stan. "What's going on here, Mullins? I received a call from a guy who told me about finding a bunch of dynamite stashed away in your car! The caller didn't identify himself, so at first I suspected a hoax! But when he identified you guys, I knew that his report was true! You guys are turning out to be bad news!"

Stan was embarrassed. "I guess you're right, sheriff. 'Bad News' is starting to become my middle name. I've sure had my share of it for the past several months!"

The heavy-set man who had arrived with the sheriff walked to the open hood of Stan's station wagon. He cautiously peered inside. Nick and Stan followed the sheriff back across the road toward the vehicle; however, they stopped short, keeping their distance.

The man examining the dynamite turned and stepped back to join the sheriff. He then shook hands with both Stan and Nick while the sheriff introduced him. A tall, affable man, he was almost completely bald, and bordering on obesity. He smiled as he said, "Don't worry, guys. I'll have that dynamite out of there in a heartbeat."

When he slowly reached into the engine and removed the explosives, both Nick and Stan kept their distance. The man laughed. "Whoever planted this in your car was a complete amateur. Hell, it wasn't even hooked up correctly to the battery." When Nick and Stan continued to retreat, he said, "You don't need to be afraid of this stuff anymore, fellows. Without an electric charge to ignite it, it's harmless." He smiled at the sheriff. "Sheriff Kirkland here says I'm nuts, and claims that I've got a death wish. But every time he wants to do something dangerous, he asks me to do it for him! Maybe he'd like to see me dead!" He then laughed and carried the dynamite and placed it in the rear seat of the police car. "I'm ready to go, sheriff!" He took a seat in the front of the cruiser.

The sheriff walked toward the police cruiser. He suddenly turned and spoke to Stan. "Listen, Mullins! After this little episode, I can see that your entire family is in terrible danger! I don't have the manpower, or I'd offer protection for you and your family. You need to consider taking all of your kin and leaving this town until this case is solved! And by the way, the grand jury is going to meet next week. So if you do leave town, both you and your friend, Nick need to come back and appear so you can testify!"

"You can count on both of us to appear, sheriff," Stan replied. The sheriff entered the police car and drove away.

The remainder of the day was almost a hopeless nightmare for Nick and Stan. Since Stan's old station wagon was now inoperable, it again became necessary to walk across the muddy field to the nearest telephone at a small pharmacy. Stan called a wrecker service to tow his vehicle to a garage for repairs. He then called his father, Lester Mullins, who picked up Nick and him at the pharmacy.

Lester Mullins was shocked when Stan told him about the Klan's recent attempt to bomb his car. "Stan, you're going to have to be more cautious! All of your lives are in danger!"

"I realize that, Dad!" Stan said, "We have two separate murder cases we're dealing with: the murder of Rufus and Preacher Temple, and Sheriff Mullins' murder!"

Stan's father quickly took a renewed interest in the murder of Sheriff Mullins. "Speaking of my brother's murder…Did you find out anything worthwhile about who might have killed him? What did Billy Sneed have to say about who his killer might be? Did he name any suspects?"

"I don't know, Dad," Stan answered, "Little Billy Sneed is too sneaky to trust. All he's interested in is how much money he can steal from suckers like Nicky and me. He'll offer any kind of information, even if it's nothing but lies if he thinks a person will pay him for it."

"Well, did he provide you with the names of any suspects? Surely he must have given you some clues." Stan's father said. He eyed his son with curiosity.

"Yeah, he named a few people, but Nicky and I didn't put much credence in what he said." Stan said.

Stan's father grew even more curious. "Well what were the names he provided? Did he name any actual suspects?"

"Yeah, he finally mentioned the usual scumbags: Cowboy Galyon, and Bird Dog Johnson; also, when we mentioned a half-black guy named Arthur Bowman, Billy said that he doubted his involvement, but you can't believe anything Billy Sneed says."

Lester Mullins dropped the subject. "Stan, you need to accept my offer to move all of your kin to my apartment! I can hire someone to protect you! I don't know if I told you, but I'm going to hire a private detective to investigate the murder of my brother. Maybe he can also offer some protection." He paused, and in a pleading voice said, "Just look at what's happened to you recently! Some creep came snooping around, checking out your hideaway, and now you have to deal with this recent attempt on your lives! Please do as I ask, Stan! Assure me that you'll move in with me!"

"I'll consider your offer, Dad." he looked at Nick. "What do you think, Nicky?"

"That's your decision, Stan. I'm only along for the ride." Nick wondered how many more threats awaited them.

.

Chapter 10

It was late in the evening when Lester Mullins parked his car behind the shack that his son had recently rented. The women had retired for the night, and since he was so exhausted from the trauma of the day, he decided to spend the night with his son, which meant sleeping on the couch. After a near sleepless night, everyone awakened and prepared to share breakfast.

Lauren's mother ate breakfast while sitting in her wheelchair in the small living room. Stan's father was seated in the tiny kitchen sharing breakfast with the others. After Stan and Nick had explained yesterday's traumatic experience about the bomb that had been placed in their vehicle. Lauren and Kathy were stunned. When Lauren had finally regained her composure, she exclaimed, "Oh my God, Nicky! Our lives are in danger!"

After a long silence, Stan's father finally said, "I want every one of you to listen to what I have to say! After yesterday's episode of that stranger spying on this place, and Stan and Nick's terrifying ordeal of finding dynamite in their car, it's obvious to me that the Klan members know where you are all hiding! They are also able to identify Stan's old station wagon, because they placed explosives inside it!"

In obvious dismay, Stan shook his head, and looked at his father. "Yeah, Dad…And I know exactly what you are about to suggest. You're going to tell us that we need to move into your house and live with you, so you can hire somebody to protect us. Well, that's not a bad idea, but we'll have to move all of our belongings to your place, and that's a big job! Are you sure you have room for all of us?"

"I've got plenty of room, Stan, and you'll find that the place is safer and much more comfortable." Lester answered.

"What am I gonna do about my station wagon?" Stan asked. "I suppose I'll have to get rid of it."

"You'll have to trade it, Stan. And you need to do that immediately. If you're short on finances, I can help you."

"No, Dad…I've got enough money. And speaking of my vehicle, I'll need to call Gibson's Garage and find out when they'll have it running again so I can pick it up."

When breakfast was over, Lauren left the table. She walked into the living room, and soon returned with her mother's empty tray. While Lester temporarily remained seated at the breakfast table, Stan followed Nick into the living room where they both smiled at Lauren's mother and greeted her. Then, Nick quietly called Stan aside and whispered, "Stan, don't tell your father that Lauren and I witnessed Mike Bronson being killed by little Caleb that day by the creek."

"But why shouldn't I tell him, Nicky? If he's going to help us find justice for these two murders, he has a right to know all the facts!" Stan answered.

"Because telling him the truth would only put him on the spot!" Nick explained. "Your father has only recently become a Christian! He wouldn't want to lie, by withholding facts in a criminal case! But if he told about Caleb killing Bronson, Caleb would be indicted for murder, and his mother would be accused of withholding evidence!'

"Damn it Nicky! How long do we have to keep up this facade? You're also withholding evidence! It's totally unlike you to bend the rules of justice! We'd be better off if you'd just told the truth from the very beginning!"

Nick reacted angrily. "Stan, several months ago I withheld evidence to help both you and Sheriff Mullins! I didn't reveal to anyone that you were a member of the Klan, and I didn't tell anybody about the sheriff's illegal activities! I bent the rules of justice to protect both of you from going to prison! Don't try to tell me how I should conduct myself! You once swore to me that you'd never tell about this. I expect you to keep your promise!" Stan seemed angry as they both sat down in living room chairs.

While the wives cleaned the kitchen, Lester Mullins walked into the living room. He immediately approached Lauren's mother and knelt in front of her wheelchair. He smiled and asked, "And how's my favorite lady doing today?" He ruffled her hair and stood. He then sat in a chair facing Nick and his son. "What do you think about everyone moving into my place?" he asked.

"We haven't made up our mind, yet, Dad," Stan answered.

"Well, why don't we decide on it the democratic way?" asked Stan's father, "Let's take a vote on it!"

"Okay, Dad," Stan said. He turned his head toward the kitchen. "Lauren! Kathy! Come in here! We're gonna take a vote on something!" His commanding words brought an immediate response from the wives. They obediently entered the living room and sat in the kitchen chairs they had brought with them.

When they were comfortably seated, Stan's father smiled and announced, "Ladies, the menfolk have decided that we need to take a vote on whether or not we all move into my house. All in favor of the move, raise your hand!" Except for Nick and Lauren's mother, everyone in the room responded.

Stan stared at Nick. "Well, how about it, Nicky? Are you for the move or against it?"

Nick only smiled. "Stan, I'm not *against* it! But it's not my place to make a decision about where you people want to stay. I guess it's completely up to the Mullins family. I'm willing to stay here or move to wherever all of you decide. I just don't want to inconvenience your father."

"Then, I guess this issue has been resolved!" Stan's father said. Except for Lauren's mother and Nick, everyone else in the room clapped their hands.

Stan suddenly stood. "I've gotta make a call," he said. He walked to the telephone and called Gibson's Garage. He was told that his vehicle had been repaired was ready to be picked up. He hung up the phone and returned to his chair. He told his father of the conversation.

Lester Mullins said, "Stan, after you get your station wagon back from the repair shop, we need to trade it right away." Stan agreed with him.

Nick changed the subject and asked, "Stan, what's on the agenda for today?"

"I suppose we should go to Sheriff Kirkland's office and have a little chat with him," said Stan, "He said that the grand jury is supposed to meet next week, so I guess we need to get all the details."

Stan's father quickly sat upright in his chair. He seemed excited. "Do you guys mind if I go with you? Maybe I could be of some help. I may have something that I can contribute to this investigation...especially regarding the murder of my brother."

"Are you sure you want to get involved in all this mess, Dad?" Stan asked. "What do you think, Nick?"

"I guess it's okay if your father wants to go with us. Maybe he can give us some moral support. We're sure going to need it!" Nick answered.

Stan's father suddenly stood. "Well, let's get moving!"

When Lauren's mother fell asleep in her wheelchair, Lauren stood. "Since it's all settled where we're going to live, Kathy and I will start packing some things away," she said. They both hugged the men and told them to be careful.

When they left the house, Nick immediately climbed into the back seat of Lester Mullins' car while Stan sat in the front seat beside his dad. Stan's father then drove from behind the house and down the steep hill toward Cedar Valley. At the bottom of the hill, the vehicle entered Highway 11.

103

Stan and his father engaged in idle conversation as the car passed through the countryside toward the sheriff's office, Nick became lost in thought as he gazed out the window at the beautiful summer morning. Precious memories returned as he recalled the beauty of Cedar Valley, and the wonderful days of summer when he was beginning to overcome his combat fatigue. It was in this small Southern town that he had first met Lauren, the love of his life. He remembered the evening by the lakeside when he first realized that he had fallen in love with her, and how his hopes and dreams had seemed so bright; and although it had happened only months before, it seemed so long ago… And now he was confronted with dire circumstances that were almost as fearful and malignant as his wartime experience. He wondered how he and Lauren had ever fallen into such a predicament.

It was 11:30 a.m. when Lester Mullins parked beside the sheriff's office, which was located on the first floor of the upstairs county jail. He left his car and followed Stan and Nick up the concrete steps into the office of Sheriff Kirkland, who had not yet arrived. The layout of the office was well-remembered by Nick. To the right was the sheriff's desk, and behind it rested an oversized, comfortable chair. The powerful odor of disinfectant permeated the room. From the upstairs jail they could hear the muffled conversation and clamor of prisoners as they engaged in their jailhouse activities. The men took seats in the three chairs that were aligned against the left wall. When he recalled his past experiences in this horrid place, Nick was again haunted by unpleasant memories of the times when he had been unjustly arrested and condemned by Sheriff Mullins.

After a half-hour's wait, Sheriff Kirkland entered the room from the side door. The men quickly stood and the sheriff shook their hands. Although he fully expected the appearance of Nick and Stan, he seemed surprised to see Lester Mullins standing beside them. "Well, hello, gentlemen!" he greeted, "And I see that you brought the former mayor with you! Are you fellas here to discuss the meeting of the grand jury?"

104

Stan was the first to speak. "Yeah, sheriff. Also we would like to discuss a couple of other things with you. Actually, we're talking about two separate cases: the double-murder committed by the Klan members, and the murder of Sheriff Mullins. As I mentioned to you when we were here before, Nicky and I want to testify before the grand jury against the Klan, and I brought my father along because he's interested in finding out if there's been any progress made in solving his brother's murder."

"Well, let's sit down and talk about it, fellas," said the sheriff. He walked around his desk and sat in his chair while the men took seats in the three chairs that bordered the wall. As soon as he was seated, the sheriff leaned forward on his elbows and and studied them with intense interest. "The grand jury meets a week from next Monday at 10:00 a.m. Make sure you.re there on time! And Stan—as I told you before, I'd be within my legal rights if I locked you in jail right now! After all, you were part of a group that committed murder! I'm only letting you walk free because of your courageous decision to come clean about witnessing those two murders!"

Stan's father intervened. "Sheriff, you did the right thing by letting Stan remain free. By testifying against his former Klan members, he is displaying great courage! I'm extremely proud of him!"

"You should be proud of him, Mr. Mullins—or should I call you 'Mayor Mullins'?" Sheriff Kirkland asked.

Lester Mullins only smiled. "No, sheriff...I gave that position up after my brother was killed."

The sheriff nodded. "That reminds me. This town needs to elect a new mayor to replace you." He changed the subject. "Well, what can I do for you today, Mr. Mullins?"

"My main concern is the murder of my brother. I realize that the murder is recent, so it is still unsolved. I don't like to meddle into police business, or pry into private matters that don't concern me, but this case is a bit different! After all, we're talking about *my brother!*"

"I understand that, sir," answered the sheriff.

Lester Mullins pressed him further. "Sheriff, do you have any suspects? Do you know of anyone who would like to see my brother dead?"

"Yes, Mr. Mullins. Your son gave me the names of a couple of people who had a grudge against Sheriff Mullins. Since you are the ex-sheriff's brother, I suppose you have a rather intimate knowledge of Sheriff Mullins' responsibilities, as well as how the county police department operated. And I'm sure you are aware of the names of the couple of suspects that your son, Stan gave to me."

Lester Mullins carefully studied Sheriff Kirkland. "Well, I believe Stan mentioned a couple of people who might have had a reason to kill him. He mentioned Ernie 'Cowboy' Galyon, and 'Bird Dog' Johnson. They were former deputies, and also members of the Klan. I suppose you'll want to investigate them."

"Yes, we'll certainly do that, Mr. Mullins. You know, maybe you should simply sit back and relax. Let the police solve this crime."

While listening to the discussion, Stan and Nick continued to remain seated; however, Stan's father rose from his seat and stood over the sheriff's desk. He was beginning to lose his patience. *"What police,* Sheriff Kirkland? The only deputies you have working for you are a couple of incompetent yokels who couldn't even arrest a person who ran a red light!"

Sheriff Kirkland carefully remained calm. "Mr. Mullins, when your brother resigned, he left the police department in complete disarray. Since it has recently been reorganized, we've only hired two deputies to replace the officers that were fired by your brother when he resigned. Their names are Joe Wilkerson and Elmer 'Bull Dog' Simpson. We are in the process of trying to hire a couple more deputies if we can afford it. Most small cities in the South aren't prepared to solve complex murder cases. Why do you need this information, Mr. Mullins? Am I supposed to inform you every time we bring a suspect in for questioning? You need to learn to show a little more patience about solving this case."

Stan's father answered, "I'll tell you the reason I need the information! I've decided to hire a private detective to investigate the murder of my brother. Actually. He'll be *working with* your department to stay on top of the case. Let's face it, Sheriff Kirkland! Your department doesn't have either the brains or the manpower to solve this case!"

Sheriff Kirkland smiled. "You're right, Mr. Mullins. At this moment we're not prepared to solve even a *simple* murder case. But beginning tomorrow, we'll have both the brains and the manpower! The T.B.I. has decided to enter the case! And I'm certainly glad that you're hiring a private investigator to give this case his full attention. Maybe this private eye can join forces with the T.B.I."

Lester Mullins became less irritated as he returned to his chair beside his son and Nick. He again addressed the sheriff. "By the way, sheriff...how did you learn that the people I mentioned are suspects?"

"Your son, Stan told me," the sheriff replied. "Also, I had a little talk with a guy named Billy Sneed. 'Little Billy,' most people call him. He seems to know a lot about several people. As a matter of fact, he even named another suspect that might have had a hand in killing Sheriff Mullins."

Stan's father became curious. "What's his name, sheriff?"

"His name is Arthur Bowman. He's a man that's half-black. According to Billy Sneed, he's the brother of Sheriff Mullins' former maid, Willie Mae. So, at this point in the investigation, we have three suspects."

"Are you certain that you don't have any other suspect, sheriff?" Stan's father asked.

"Not at this point. But I'm gonna keep questioning Billy Sneed. I realize that he's untrustworthy, but he's also well-informed. Maybe he can come up with another person who had a motive to kill your brother"

Lester Mullins shook his head. "Sheriff Kirkland, I believe that your interrogation of Billy Sneed would be a complete waste of time. That guy is full of lies. If I were you, I'd steer clear of him. I don't believe he can help your investigation."

"What kind of relationship did Billy Sneed have with Sheriff Mullins?" asked the sheriff. "Maybe he had some kind of quarrel with the former sheriff and held a grudge against him. It's possible that he killed Sheriff Mullins."

"I don't know what their exact relationship involved. I think he was just a handyman for my brother—doing odd jobs around the jail, and running errands. I believed they liked each other. I can't see where he had a motive to kill his boss."

"Well, Mr. Mullins, I sure hope you can hire a competent private investigator," said the sheriff. "When we started this conversation, I suggested that perhaps you should stay out of the investigation and let the police handle it. I didn't know that you were going to to hire a private eye. Now that I realize that, I'd just like to say, 'welcome aboard! 'I want you to know that you can count on me to supply either you or him with all the information that we obtain from our investigation!"

Stan's father smiled. "Thank you, sheriff!"

Throughout the conversation between Sheriff Kirkland and Stan's father, Nick and Stan had remained quiet. They had carefully listened to the discussion with profound interest; for all information regarding the murder of Sheriff Mullins was of utmost importance and essential to solving the case.

The sheriff turned his attention to Stan. "Okay, Stan. Let's discuss the grand jury meeting. As I told you before, the grand jury will meet next Monday at 10:00 a.m. And this information is for both you and your friend, Nick. First of all, after you testify against your former Klan members, if the grand jury believes your story, they will issue a true bill against the accused—which means they will be indicted for murder. The indictment may be for either first degree murder, or possibly second degree. After they are all located, they'll be arrested, of course. Then each of them will hire a lawyer—or maybe just a single lawyer will be appointed to handle the entire case. After a lawyer is hired or appointed, all of the defendants will post bond in order to stay out of jail. Stan, if you want to stay out of jail, you'll also have to post bond. This doesn't apply to Nick because he's not guilty of anything."

Stan sighed. "Man, I'll sure be glad when this whole mess is behind us! All of my kinfolks and I are forced to live like cowering animals! We've been hiding from all of the Klan members for several days. And when they planted that bundle of dynamite in my car—that was the last straw! Now that they recognize my vehicle, I have to get rid of it! Sheriff, you advised us to leave town until this trial is over! But we have a better solution! We're going to move into my father's house, and he's going to provide protection for us!"

"Good for you, Stan!" the sheriff replied, "that's a great solution! It's perfect—as long as you have the money to pay someone to provide protection!"

The sheriff stood, while Lester Mullins, Nick, and Stan left their chairs and shook hands with him. When Sheriff Kirkland held the front door open for their departure, Stan's father stopped and apologized to the sheriff. "Sheriff Kirkland, I'm sorry if I offended you in any way. We've just been under a terrible strain recently."

The sheriff only smiled. "Don't worry about it. By the way, if you think you've been under a strain, just put yourself in my position for the next few weeks! I'm still trying to figure out why I ever took this job!"

It was mid-afternoon when Stan retrieved his station wagon from Gibson's Garage. When he picked up the vehicle his suspicion was confirmed; for he was told by the mechanic that someone had tampered with the engine by disconnecting some of the wiring. When they arrived at their home that afternoon, the men were all relieved that this meeting with Sheriff Kirkland was now behind them.

Chapter 11

The initial relocation to the Lester Mullins home was simpler than expected, for when Stan, Kathy, and Lauren's mother had moved from Sheriff Mullins' house to the isolated shack, they had only brought with them the bare necessities for living. The removal of all clothing and household items was accomplished by delivering only one large load of miscellany in their three vehicles. While Lauren and Kathy attended to the needs of Lauren's mother and generally supervised the placement of their sparse inventory in the new location, Nick and Stan helped Lester Mullins carry items into the house. Although the initial movement of the articles was accomplished in only three hours, their final arrangement required more time, for it was almost twilight before the energetic crew completed the relocation.

The home of Lester Mullins was familiar territory to Stan and Kathy, for they had visited him on numerous occasions in the past; however, this was the first time that Nick and Lauren had seen the place. When he first saw the enormity of it, Nick was amazed. Although it lacked the warmth and splendor of his former home, the house was indeed impressive, especially for a unit of rental property. Although the dwelling was rather sterile and nondescript in character, the roomy interior was large enough to accommodate a dozen people. The huge living room contained a large arrangement of expensive furniture.

When Nick and Lauren strolled through the remaining rooms of the two-story house they were even more impressed; for as well as a large kitchen, the house contained a spacious dining room, five large bedrooms and three bathrooms. The interior was immaculately clean, and the fresh smell of paint introduced the aroma of cleanliness and newness.

The house was located atop a sloping hill behind a large front yard. Four small recently-planted trees were evenly-spaced in front of the house and a few shrubs hugged the small front porch. The house was lacking in uniqueness; however, it was large and accommodating. It was quite obvious that Lester Mullins had retained a fondness for luxurious living.

Because the house already contained adequate furnishings acquired from Lester's previous home it became necessary to store many of the less expensive items in the garage. When the chore was finished, the entire group was exhausted.

The leisurely dinner was brief, and consumed mostly in silence, for everyone was tired and ready for bed. It was 10:00 p.m. when Nick and Stan lifted Lauren's mother from her wheelchair and placed her in bed. Lauren talked softly to her for a long while before finally kissing her goodnight. With the exception of Lester Mullins, everyone went to their separate bedrooms and crawled into their beds. Lester sat in the spacious living room in his easy chair. For a long time he reminisced, before finally kneeling in prayer. He then went to his bedroom and retired for the evening.

The women slept late as Stan's father joined his son and Nick in the dining room for a brief breakfast of oatmeal and coffee. Before beginning his meal, Stan's father bowed his head and said a brief prayer of grace. To display proper respect, Stan and Nick echoed the gesture by saying, 'amen'. Lester then raised his head and began to sip his coffee. "Well, what do you guys have on the agenda for today?" he asked.

Stan said, "Nick and I are going to trade my old car."

111

"That's good news. You need to get rid of that old trap as soon as possible. I'd go with you, but I have some things I have to accomplish in town," he said. "If you need some help paying for it, I'll be glad to do my part."

When the men had finished their breakfast. Stan stood and said to his dad, "I don't need any financial help, but thanks, anyway." He was followed by his father and Nick as they walked into the expansive living room and sat in facing chairs. Lester Mullins studied both his son and Nick. He lowered his voice when he said, "I'm glad the women are all sleeping late this morning. I need to discuss a situation with you that we may have to soon deal with, and I'd rather they'd not hear it. But we'll all have to face it later."

The secretive tone of his voice caused both Stan and Nick to lean forward in their seats, as both men quickly expressed an intense interest. Stan asked, "What's on your mind, Dad?"

"It's Bonnie Rose—Lauren's mother. Her dementia seems to be rapidly getting worse. It won't be very long until she'll be suffering from a severe case of Alzheimer's disease." He looked at Nick. "Have you and Lauren explored any long-range plans about how you're going to deal with this problem, Nick? We can temporarily handle this situation, but what will any of us do when the illness gets worse? She'll finally reach the point where she can no longer function! With all of this legal mess going on, we've already got our hands full!"

Nick answered, "Mr. Mullins, I don't honestly know what to do. I guess we'll do the best we can for now. But when all of these problems are resolved here in Cedar Valley, Lauren and I will be going back to Louisiana. I'm sure that she will want to take her mother back with us."

"But Nick—Lauren's mother is going to continue to get worse. What will you do when she becomes completely helpless?" Lester asked.

Nick shrugged. "When she becomes unmanageable, I suppose we'll have to place her in a nursing home. I don't know what else we could do. Until then, we'll just have to deal with it the best we can."

"When you get back to Louisiana...do you have the time to deal with this problem, Nick? Remember, you're trying to go to college, and Lauren's time is tied up with a full-time job. And how could you pay for it? Also, it may be months before you and Lauren can return to Louisiana. Bonnie Rose is rapidly getting worse. She may not be able to function at all by the time you leave here."

Nick asked, "What do you suggest we do?"

Stan's father looked sadly at Nick. "I'll tell you what I'm prepared to do, Nick. If she gets totally helpless immediately, we can place her in a local nursing home and I'll pay for it."

"But she's not that bad, yet. How can we take care of her right now—before she gets worse?" Nick asked.

Listen, Nick," Stan's father said, "I feel terribly sorry for the poor lady. I'm retired now, so I'm not very busy. .If necessary, I'll stay at home and take care of her. I'll help in any way I can, because we're all in this crazy mess together!"

Stan suddenly stood and said, "Well, Dad, both Nick and I really do appreciate your compassion. We'll have to give this situation some serious thought, but we can't solve this problem right now. Nick and I need to go car-shopping for the rest of the day." He moved toward the front door and added, "This problem concerning Lauren's mother is just another enormous obstacle that we'll have to overcome before we can again start living normal lives."

Lester Mullins said, "Just put your trust in God, Stan." He followed his son and Nick to the front door. "Choose a late model car, Stan. And remember, I'll help you pay for it!"

"Thanks, Dad," Stan said. He and Nick walked to Stan's station wagon and drove away.

Stan drove the vehicle down the long driveway and turned onto Fifth Avenue. He remained silent for a couple of miles before he said to Nick, "You know, Nicky, I don't know how either of us could survive without Dad. He even wants to help me pay for the car we're trading for. But I'm not gonna let him do it. Hell, I don't want to start depending on him again. I'm just now getting to the point where he respects me again."

113

Nick only chuckled. "Stan, I just noticed that when we're in the company of your father, you never utter a small cussword! In your last statement to me, that's the first time I've heard you say the word, 'hell' in a long time."

"I'm still not accustomed to the fact that he only recently became a Christian. I'm still trying to adjust to him!"

"Just be yourself, Stan. I don't think your father would disown you for using a little cussword occasionally! But he is certainly different from the way I remembered him when I lived in Cedar Valley a few months ago! By the way, where are you planning to trade your car?"

"I thought we'd steer clear of Cedar Valley and drive on down to Loudon to trade vehicles. That way, we don't have to expose ourselves to Klan members. I hear that Loudon has some car dealerships with excellent bargains."

"Loudon?" Nick asked. "Isn't that where *The Red Top Tavern* is located?—That joint where we got into that ruckus with Cowboy Galyon and Bird Dog Johnson? Maybe you and I can do a little *social climbing!* Would you like to stop there for a couple of beers?"

"Are you kidding me, Nicky? I just hope I never see that damned sleazy bar again!"

He turned the vehicle onto Highway 11 and drove toward Loudon. Since the old station wagon was operating smoothly, Stan increased the speed. They were now passing through a hilly section of the countryside that had numerous curves. Stan took his eyes off the road long enough to find some country music on the radio. Suddenly from behind him, a large dump truck turned left into the passing lane and sped up as if to pass him; instead, the driver steered the large truck to the right and smashed into the side of Stan's station wagon. The vehicle was forced off the road into a deep ravine, where it rolled several times before finally coming to rest on its top in the deep gully. The large dump truck continued its journey toward Loudon. Miraculously, except for Stan's bloody nose and a large knot on Nick's forehead, neither of them were badly hurt. Both men finally escaped through the broken windows.

Both Nick and Stan brushed the broken glass from their clothing and briefly sat at the bottom of the muddy ravine. Fearing that the automobile would catch fire, they hurriedly retreated down the gully to a safer location and pondered about the incident. Since the driver of the truck had been sitting so high in his seat and on the opposite side of their vehicle, neither of them had been able to see nor identify him; as a result, it would be impossible to make accusations or file charges. However, it was obvious that one of the Klan members had again recognized Stan's station wagon. It was unfortunate that this event happened just minutes before Stan would forever be rid of the jinxed vehicle.

When they inspected the automobile, they could see that it was a total loss. The top had been completely flattened and every window was shattered. Also, the body was damaged beyond repair. Steam that rose from the mangled heap threatened an ultimate fire and possibly an explosion; consequently, both Nick and Stan kept a safe distance from it.

They walked up the steep, muddy bank to the highway and looked back at the mangled wreckage. Their feelings were ambiguous: Although angered by the tragedy, they were also thankful that they had been spared from death. As they stood by the road, Nick draped his arms around Stan. "Well, old buddy, it appears that we were about thirty minutes too late in trading that old heap. Do you have insurance on it?"

"Hell no!" Stan said, "It wasn't worth enough money to carry an insurance policy on it! It looks like my old station wagon is a total loss!"

"Do you still plan to buy another car?" asked Nick.

"Sure I do, Nicky! Hell, I have to own a car. How else can you and I get around? You're lucky, because you can drive Lauren's car. But I'm up shit creek without transportation! And now I don't even have a vehicle to trade! Hell, I can't really afford a car without something to trade!"

"What do we do now, Stan?" Nick asked. "Hitch a ride? Hitch a ride to where? I'm almost afraid to start thumbing a ride. Hell, we might be picked up by a member of the Klan!"

Stan looked across the field and spotted a house in the distance. 'We can walk to that house and make a phone call."

"Who would we call, Stan? And where are we going, anyway? We can't trade your car, because we've got nothing to trade. Our original mission has been sabotaged! Do you want to go back to your father's house?"

"Damn it Nick! Why would I want for us to go back there? So we can both sit on our asses? I'm going to walk to that house over across the hill and call Dad!"

"And then what?" Nick asked.

"And then we can discuss what we're going to do! Damn it, Nicky! Why are you asking all these questions? You're about to drive me nuts!"

They struck out walking toward the distant house. When they arrived at the door and knocked, an elderly woman answered. After they explained their predicament, she allowed Stan to call his father.

Lester Mullins was almost in shock when he hung up the telephone. Stan had acted irrational when he called about the tragic attempted murder and his demolished vehicle that had occurred on Highway 11. Lauren and Kathy were in the kitchen preparing lunch, while Bonnie Rose was sitting in her wheelchair in the living room. Without any communication with the women in the house, Stan's father hurried out the front door and drove away in his car. He drove down Fifth Avenue, and then increased his speed as he entered Highway 11. He wasn't surprised that the Klan members had recognized Stan's old station wagon; however he was puzzled in regard to the method used by the assailant, for on that dangerous stretch of road, he had risked his own life.

He drove even faster as he made a thorough assessment of the situation. Since Stan had pinpointed the exact location of the incident, he knew that Stan and Nick would probably be standing by the highway near the demolished vehicle. He became depressed when he thought of the incident, for he realized that he had now become burdened with responsibility.

He began to count the obstacles that lay ahead of him. First, *he would have to pick up Stan and Nick, and engage them in further discussion about the murder attempt.* Second, there was the obvious question: *What should be done about the demolished station wagon?* And third, *where should he take Stan? Back home? Or did he still intend to buy another car?* If so, since he had no trade-in auto, it would mean that his father would have to buy it for him—or at least, in the unlikely event that Stan had the money for a down payment, Lester Mullins would have to stand good for future payments. However, the wonderful fact that neither Stan nor Nick had been seriously injured in the murder attempt made the other obstacles seem insignificant. He silently thanked God.

Lester Mullins stopped his Cadillac at the roadside near the site of the demolished vehicle. When he picked up his son and Nick, Stan angrily related to him the harrowing details of their near-fatal crash. Nick remained silent as Lester listened attentively when Stan elaborated on the frightful details. Both Nick and Stan were angry and fraught with anxiety. When Stan's father patiently listened to the full account of the traumatic incident, he only smiled and said, "Stan, get out of that bad mood! You just suffered a simple setback! You should be thankful to God that your life was spared!"

Stan replied, "Yeah, I suppose you're right, Dad. I guess Nick and I are lucky we weren't both killed!"

The men remained silent as Stan's father drove his car into Loudon to *Carl's Wrecker Service* where he gave the manager a full report on the location of the wrecked station wagon. He then drove to a local car dealership, *Jim Watson Motors.* Stan and his father spent more than an hour inspecting cars in the showroom until they finally agreed to purchase a new 1955 gold and white Ford station wagon. Since Stan was unable to offer a trade-in vehicle, Lester Mullins simply paid with a check the full list-price of more than three-thousand dollars.

Stan was ecstatic. He repeatedly thanked his father, who only smiled and pitched the car keys to his son.

When Nick entered the passenger seat of the new car in preparation of his friend driving it home, Stan was in the best of spirits. However, as he was driving the new vehicle home he reflected on his father's generosity. Although he was appreciative of the gesture, he began to have mixed feelings. Instead of gratitude he slowly experienced a feeling of resentment. Since his father had born the entire expense of the transaction, he feared that Lester Mullins would have less respect for him and again try to control him. He was torn between the opposing feelings of thankfulness and regret.

Nick noticed Stan's expression of displeasure. "You're awfully quiet, pal. Is something bugging you again?"

Stan answered, "Nicky, I've just been thinking...I shouldn't have let Dad buy this car for me! I was just beginning to gain his respect! Now, he'll start owning me again! I'm back where I started—I'm right back under his thumb!"

Nick appeared to be irritated. "Damn it Stan! Your father did the only thing that he could do for you! What would you do without a car? Just look at how generous he's been to all of us! He's a changed man, Stan! Hell, show a little gratitude!"

Since Stan had begun to pout, they finished the drive to the Lester Mullins home in silence. When they arrived, Stan received a phone call from *Carl's Wrecker Service.* They informed him that he owed their company fifty dollars for towing the wreck to their garage; however, they agreed to do away with the amount owed and give him twenty-five dollars for the mangled vehicle. Stan became even more irritated.

After a leisurely dinner, the women had again prepared for an early retirement to their bedrooms; however, shortly before bedtime, Lauren's mother fell to the hardwood floor when Lauren attempted to lift her from her wheelchair. The fall resulted in a long period of agonizing pain for her. When they heard her scream, Stan and Nick rushed to help her. They were quickly followed by Stan's father, who applied a heating pad to her back. His expression was sad when he tried to console her with comforting words. "Good night, Bonnie Rose," he said, "That nasty old pain will be gone before you know it. Try to get some sleep." He then gently hugged her and kissed her cheek. When the pain subsided, Lauren placed her in bed and kissed her goodnight. She finally joined Kathy and the women all retired for the evening.

Lester Mullins was a man of habit. During his many years of marriage, even when Stan was a small boy, Lester had always experienced difficulty when attempting to sleep; as a result, he usually stayed in his study or living room until midnight before retiring to his bed. When the women were finally asleep, he joined Nick and Stan into the living room where they all sat in comfortable chairs facing each other.

Stan's father was still upset about the recent fall that Lauren's mother had experienced. He expressed his concern to Nick. "I remember mentioning to you that Bonnie Rose was rapidly getting more helpless. Well, her recent fall is a good example. You told me that Lauren would want to take her back with you when you return to Louisiana. If you do, what will you and Lauren do when the poor old lady gets too helpless to function? She's going to continue to fall, you know! What if she falls out of her wheelchair when nobody else is at home, Nick? Can you afford to hire someone to look after her when you're away?"

"I honestly don't know," Nick answered, "I really hadn't thought about that possibility."

Lester replied, "Well, you'd better start giving it some serious thought. If you'll remember, Lauren's mother hasn't really ever experienced a very happy life. She's been in a wheelchair for years."

"Yeah, I realize that," Nick said. "I've always hoped that she would someday have a happier life."

"I know what you mean, Nick," Stan's father said. "And someday she will! We are most fortunate to have a merciful God! Sometime in the near future she will join her husband in a glorious world of peace and eternal happiness!"

Stan reacted with skepticism. "Oh, come off it, Dad!"

Lester Mullins only smiled and looked at Nick. "I'm sorry Nick, but I'm afraid that Stan has developed the attitude of an agnostic!"

Stan retaliated. "Dad, you are beginning to talk like an old-time Baptist! I didn't realize that you are a fundamentalist!"

"Well, what is your belief, Stan?" Lester asked.

Stan only laughed. "I happen to be a realist, Dad. I don't believe in an afterlife! When we die, it's all over! And that's the end of the story!"

"I'm sorry you feel that way, son. You're not dealing with reality at all!"

Nick entered the conversation. "Mr. Mullins, maybe it's like an old preacher friend once said to me. When I told him I only believed in reality, he asked, 'What is reality, Nick'?' Then he continued by saying, 'Our perception of life is the only reality we have. If we perceive that life is a certain way, then that's reality for us.' Maybe *Stan's perception of life* is reality for him!"

"Nick, I don't enjoy destroying your basic beliefs, but your preacher friend was wrong! There is only *one* reality—and it has already been created and established by God. He alone is the master of our fate!"

Stan carefully studied his father. "Dad, if you're right, and an eternal life of peace awaits us after we die, then Lauren's mother would be better off if she suddenly died!"

Lester Mullins asked Nick. "Do you know if Lauren's mother has ever been saved?"

"What do you mean, Mr. Mullins?"

"I mean, has she ever had a spiritual conversion?"

Nick answered, "Yes, she's been baptized. Also she's been a devout Baptist since she was just a small child."

Stan's father said to his son, "I'm rather hesitant to say this, Stan, but you're exactly right! If Bonnie Rose suddenly died and God brought her into His Kingdom, she'd be better off, because she'd find happiness for the first time in her life!"

Stan hung his head. "Dad, I've just endured one of my worst days...And now I have to hear a religious lecture!"

120

"I'm deeply concerned that you have such a cynical attitude! I love you, Stan! And because of that love, I'm afraid for you! I'm going to pray for you, and maybe God will save your soul!"

With curiosity, Nick sat upright in his chair and looked at Stan's father. "Mr. Mullins, you said that Lauren's mother would be better off dead...Maybe you're right. Maybe we'd *all* be better off if she died. Well, what about your brother— Sheriff Mullins? I remember how much you grieved after his death. If you believe that we are all happier after we die, then why were you so sad? Isn't he *also* better off? Maybe you should be happy for him, too; after all, he's surely in heaven now, for just like Lauren's mother, he also confessed his sins and experienced a spiritual conversion before he died."

Lester Mullins' eyes became misty and he spoke with sadness. "I grieved over my brother for days, and I still miss him terribly. But now, when I think of him, I feel a happiness in my soul, for I know that he is much happier than before, for he is with God."

Nick slowly stood. "Well, it's getting past my bedtime. Today has been tough day for all of us. Maybe you and Stan can talk it over and solve some of these problems that keep bugging all of us. Good night to both of you."

Stan also got up from his chair. "I'm going to bed too, Dad. I'll see you in the morning." He started to follow Nick, but suddenly stopped and turned to face his father. "Dad, I'm sorry I acted so skeptical tonight. And I want you to know that I am proud of you for becoming a Christian. Also, I want to thank you for buying the car for me." He smiled at his father. "Good night, Dad."

Both Stan and Nick slowly walked to their bedrooms while Lester Mullins remained in the living room. After he was sure they were gone, he kneeled in front of his chair and bowed his head in prayer.

Chapter 12

Since the spiritual conversions of Stan's father and Sheriff Mullins had occurred, the safety of Lester Mullins 'adopted family' had been in peril, for it initiated the constant threats and harassment by members of the Klan. As a result, the lifestyles of Stan's father and his kinfolks had undergone a drastic change. While his family members remained mostly hidden and usually idle, only Lester Mullins enjoyed the freedom to mingle with the public, for he was the only one in the group who didn't pose a threat to the Klan. As a result of their inactivity, Stan, Nick, and their wives began to suffer from 'cabin fever.' Lauren's mother was mentally incapable of realizing her emotions.

Lester Mullins became overwhelmed with responsibility to his family members; for it had automatically become his duty to financially provide for the others, as well as run most of the necessary errands for the group; however, he seemed to harbor no resentment about his inherited role, for he envisioned himself as being their protector and father-figure.

In the early afternoon, because of their sheer boredom, Lauren and Kathy were sunbathing on the back deck while Bonnie Rose sat beside them beneath a large umbrella.

Lester Mullins was preparing to leave the home to pay bills and buy groceries, while Nick and Stan were in the living room watching television. They were bored with their inactivity; however, they were also nervous. Their boredom would be brief, for their lives would soon be filled with anxiety and frantic activity whenever the grand jury met.

The ringing doorbell quickly sent Stan's father to the front door. When he opened it, he saw a large, scowling man standing on the front porch. He was a muscular man, about fifty years old. He wore a tan hat, and his black mustache was a contradiction to his graying temples. Although neatly dressed in his sport coat and tie, the mismatch in the contrasting colors between his blue sport coat and brown trousers reflected a terrible choice in his mode of dress. He introduced himself. "Good afternoon, sir," he said "My name is Peter Wilson. Is this the Lester Mullins residence?"

Lester was somewhat taken by surprise, for he wasn't expecting company. "Yes it is." he replied. "How may I help you, sir?"

The man extended his hand. "I've come here to discuss your recent request to hire a private detective, Mr. Mullins. I'm your man." He spoke in a Northern accent.

Stan's father curiously studied the visitor and shook hands with him. "Come on in, Mr. Wilson." When the man entered, Lester Mullins introduced him to Nick and Stan. He then pointed to a lounging chair. "You can sit there, sir." He then continued, "I wasn't really expecting you today, Mr. Wilson. I understood that you were scheduled to see me on Tuesday, but today is Monday...You're a day early."

Peter Wilson took a seat in the chair and offered an apology. "Well, sir, I finished with my case a day early, so I thought I'd get a start on your problems immediately...If that's okay with you, Mr. Mullins."

"You can call me 'Lester,'" said Stan's father.

Peter Wilson grinned and replied, "The same goes for me, Lester. You can just call me 'Pete.' By the way, how did you hear about me, Lester? Why did you ask for my services?" He removed a pad and pen from his jacket pocket.

Stan interrupted. "Mr. Wilson, Dad hasn't asked for your services yet. Before he decides that, He'll need to discuss some things with you, and find out a little more about you." Both Stan and Nick studied the detective before leaving their chairs and moving to the couch. Their move gave Stan's father access to the chair that faced the detective. Since the unexpected appearance of the private investigator had aroused their interest, they intently listened to the ongoing discussion. Something about his demeanor made Stan suspicious of him.

The detective said, "What do you need to know about me, Lester? I guess you'd like to know how I got your name. A local lawyer by the name of Carl Parker said that you had contacted him. He said that you were looking for a private eye for several reasons. He said that you needed protection for your family, and a solution to the mystery of your brother's murder. I can surely help you do those things."

Lester said, "You're right, Pete I contacted a lawyer so I could locate a private investigator. He later called and said that you'd be here on Tuesday, but you're a day early I'm not familiar with standard protocol. Tell me about yourself, Pete"

"What do you need to know about me?" he asked.

"Well, you're obviously not a local man, or I'd be familiar with your name. I know most of our law enforcement people, because I'm the former mayor of this town. Where are you originally from? What kind of cases have you solved?"

"I'm originally from Chicago, where I served as a police detective," he answered. "I moved to the South to be near my aging mother. I've solved many cases. Some have involved murder, others are about detecting thieves, and a few of them involve the investigation of husbands cheating on their wives."

"Can you give me an example of how you operate, and cases you have helped solve?" asked Lester.

"Most of the cases I've solved took place in Chicago. I've only been in the South for about three months."

"If you've been in the South for three months, you must have worked on some cases here. Can you name one? And can you tell me the results of the case, and whether or not the perpetrator was convicted?"

With an expression of annoyance, he answered, "Sir, that information is confidential. Surely you can understand that!"

Stan's father appeared to be slightly irritated; however, he continued his interrogation. "Pete, if I decide to employ you, I need to explain what your responsibilities will be. I'll give you the names of some suspects that you'll need to investigate. You'll need to give me regular reports on them. After I explain the story, you'll need to help decide who had a motive to kill my brother. Also you'll need to report to me any unusual activity of any of the suspects—any deviation from their normal behavior. You'll be working with the T.B.I. during this investigation."

"I can handle that, Lester," said Pete, "Is there anything else you'll require of me?"

"Yes. You said that you could provide protection for my family. I have some relatives in this house who are in constant danger. This involves a different murder case. My son and his friend are going to testify before the grand jury against the Ku Klux Klan—a group that committed two murders. To keep them from testifying, these Klan members have made several attempts on their lives. During times when you're not involved in your routine investigation, I want you to serve as their bodyguard when they leave this house to go anywhere. I want you to protect them from harm!"

"I see no problem doing that," the detective replied, "but your relatives will have to keep me informed about the times they'll be leaving the home and need my protection."

Stan complained. "Mr. Wilson, does this mean that every time I leave this house, I'll have to either ride in your car or ask your permission? That's like living in a prison!"

The detective retaliated. "Look, I don't give a damn when you leave this house! I can't always protect you, so sometimes you'll have to take a chance and drive your own car."

Nick said, "You worry too much, Stan. After the Klan members are convicted of murder, we'll no longer be a threat to them. We'll be free to go wherever we please!"

"But that could take weeks, Nicky!" Stan said. "Indicting them will be easy, but convicting them will be much more difficult! We might need protection for months!"

The detective ignored him. "We need to start somewhere. Can you give me some names of some of the suspects in Sheriff Mullins' murder?" He held the pad in his hand while he removed the pen from his pocket.

"Sure, Pete," replied Stan's father. As the detective began to scribble names, Lester Mullins proceeded to mention all of the people who might have a motive for killing his brother: 'Cowboy' Galyon, 'Bird Dog' Johnson—and the mulatto brother of the sheriff's former maid, Arthur Bowman.

The detective momentarily stopped writing names. He asked "Is there anyone else I could contact who knows more about these people?"

Nick said, "You need to get in touch with Billy Sneed. Most everybody calls him, 'Little Billy.' He used to be the jailhouse snitch who knew something about everybody. You may have a hard time locating him, because he doesn't have an address. He's a street person."

Stan's father shook his head in disagreement. "I don't know about that, Nick. I think it might be a waste of time. You can't believe a word that comes from that liar's mouth. I think our detective should begin his investigation by concentrating his efforts on that guy, Author Bowman. After all, he had a stronger motive than anybody!"

The private detective replaced the pen and pad into his jacket pocket. From his wallet he removed a business card and handed it to Stan's father. "Lester, here's my card with my phone number. We can discuss my pay after I've worked for you for a few days…after I discover the full scope of my responsibilities. If you decide to hire me you'll need to tell me the exact date when I need to start." He stood and tucked away his wallet.

Lester also stood. "Pete, if I decide to hire you, I'll let you know immediately. I need to discuss this with Nick and Stan."

The detective asked, "When do some of your people appear before the grand jury? Is your family going to need my protection for that? By the way, my car is very large. It's a custom-built station wagon, and the glass is bullet-proof."

"The grand jury meets next Monday—A week from today. I'll let you know something before then." Lester said.

Nick and Stan stood and shook hands with Peter Wilson before Stan's father ushered him to the front door. The men watched through the front window as he drove away.

They again sat down in the living room facing each other as they discussed the recent visit of the detective. Stan's father spoke first. "Okay, guys...What do you think? Do you think I should hire this guy?"

Nick responded, "I don't like the guy. I can't put my finger on it, but I don't believe he can be trusted. He has an arrogant way about him!"

"I don't like him either!" Stan said.

"Why not?" asked Stan's father.

Stan punched Nick on the shoulder and grinned. "I don't like him because he talks like a damned Yankee!"

Chapter 13

On the following Monday morning, both Nick and Stan had finished their breakfast with family members and were fully dressed in their preparation to appear before the grand jury. The women were still cleaning up the kitchen while Lauren's mother watched from her wheelchair.

When he walked into the living room with Nick and Stan, Lester Mullins peered at his watch and noted the time: *8:45 a.m.* He realized that Stan and Nick had adequate time to meet with the grand jury at 10:00 a.m. He had recently hired the private detective, Peter Wilson, who was scheduled to meet with him at 9:00 a.m. to offer protection for Stan and Nick during the legal proceeding. However, it was 9:15 before he arrived at the Lester Mullins home. He was sloppily dressed and strongly smelled of alcohol. Lester cast a disapproving look at him and again checked the time. "Pete, we were supposed to meet here at my house at 9:00 sharp! I want to make sure that we arrive in plenty of time!"

The investigator smiled. "*We?* Are you going with them?"

"Yes...I'm going. Maybe I can offer some moral support. By the way, why are you so late?"

"Hell, Lester. I got tied up in traffic. It's bad on Monday."

Stan's father was filled with anxiety. "Now we'll have to hurry! And it'll take some time to find a parking space!"

"Damn, Lester! You act like the world is coming to an end! Just relax!" Both Stan and Nick angrily glared at him.

Lauren and Kathy were drying their hands when they came into the living room. "You guys be careful!" Lauren pleaded. She joined Kathy when they hugged their husbands.

Nick cautioned, "Lauren, make sure that you lock all your doors until we get home!"

"Don't worry...We will," she answered.

Stan's father again peered at his watch. "It's after 9:30!" he said, "Let's get moving!" Peter Wilson only shook his head and smiled.

They arrived at the courthouse at 9:50 a.m. and sat in the front row of seats in front of the judge's bench. However, they continued to sit for more than a half-hour before the complete panel of grand jurors arrived and met in an adjoining room. When the jury foreman came out of the room, he approached Stan and informed him that he would be the first to testify. Stan left his seat and disappeared with the foreman into the small grand jury room.

Stan's father grew even more anxious as he sat beside Nick and the private eye, waiting for Stan to complete his testimony. He worried about the final outcome for his son, for he feared that his testimony and his admission to being an accessory to murder would result in years of prison time for him. He bowed his head and prayed for his son.

In less than an hour, Stan came out of the grand jury room and took a seat between Nick and his father. The private detective had fallen asleep in his seat beside them. Nick was burning with curiosity. "Stan, what was it like in that room? Tell me what happened! Do you know most of the jury members? Did they grill you very much?"

"I don't have time to explain it to you right now, Nick," Stan said, "You're supposed to go in there right now! In fact, the jury foreman is standing there waiting for you." he pointed at the door to the room. "Good luck, Nicky!"

129

Nick saw the jury foreman beckon to him. He stood and followed him through the door into the small grand jury room. The sweltering heat inside the room caused Nick to sweat, as he sat beside the jury foreman at the head of the group of men. He pulled his handkerchief from his pocket and swabbed his face. When he scanned the room, he counted only six grand jury members, instead of the customary twelve. They all eyed him with a mixture of boredom and skepticism.

The foreman was an overweight middle-aged man who was sweating profusely. He was the first to speak. "Sir, let me first tell you what to expect during this hearing. Please give us your full name and then tell all of the jury members why you witnessed this event, and the reason you are offering this testimony. Then you can expect some of the jury members to ask you some questions."

Nick began to relive the nightmare. "My name is Nicolo Donato Parilli. I happened to witness this killing because I went to a location where the Ku Klux Klan was burning a cross and was in the process of whipping a Negro. He wasn't guilty of any wrongdoing. Then I..."

The foreman quickly interrupted, "Mister, we don't need your *interpretation* of the things that happened that night. Just give us the bare facts explaining what you actually witnessed."

"Okay." Nick answered. "I had a close friend with me that night. He was a preacher. The Klan members couldn't see us, because we were both hiding in the bushes. The Klan had this Negro tied to a tree beside that burning cross. The Klan leader began to whip the Negro, but after only a couple of lashes from the whip, this preacher friend of mine stepped out into the open. He defended the black man because he knew that the Negro had done nothing wrong. Then the preacher..."

The foreman again warned Nick. "Just stick to the facts, mister! Don't elaborate on your testimony!"

"Yes, sir," Nick replied. "Anyway, the preacher reached out and jerked the hood off of the Klan leader's head, exposing his identity. So he shot the preacher. And then he had to shoot the Negro, who could now identify him."

"Well, that's a pretty gruesome story, Mr. Parilli," said the foreman. He looked at the jury members. "Do any of you have any questions, gentlemen?"

One of the jury members raised his hand. He was an obese man whose face was dripping with sweat. His expression reflected skepticism. He looked directly at Nick. "You keep repeating that this Negro had done no wrong. How do you know this? Nig...I mean Negroes sometimes are guilty of enormous wrongs against white people! You must have known this black man pretty well, to say that he had done no wrong!"

"Yes, I knew him quite well. In fact, he was a very close friend of mine. He was a man of character who wasn't capable of doing something that would warrant a horsewhipping!"

Another juror asked, "If the preacher yanked the hood off of the shooter, then you must have been able to identify him. Who was he? Do you know his name?"

"Yes I know his name. His name is Mike Bronson. He was a county deputy sheriff at the time of the killing."

"Has he been arrested for the murder?" asked the man.

"No, he skipped town right after the double murder. Nobody knows where he is." Nick didn't elaborate.

Another jury member questioned Nick. "I'm wonderin' how you an' that preacher ever got close enough to witness a double murder without bein' seen by a Klan member. Can you explain that?"

"Sir, if you could only see how thick the foliage was that surrounded the entire meadow on the night of the double murder, you'd understand," Nick said.

The skeptical, obese man commented, "Mister, nobody knows for sure that a murder was even committed. I can tell by the way you speak that you come from somewhere up north. How do we know that some Yankee liberal ain't hired you to make this story up?"

Nick became angry. It became difficult for him to restrain himself; however, he realized that if he lost his wits, he could be cited for contempt of court. Fortunately, the questions from the jury members finally ceased. He breathed a sigh of relief.

He finally said, "Gentlemen, unless you have other questions for me, I have nothing else to add to my story".

"The witness is excused," said the foreman.

When Nick had completed his testimony, he returned to the courtroom where he joined Stan and his father. Pete Wilson, the private eye was now awake and welcomed Nick with an elaborate yawn.

The four men left the courtroom and Peter Wilson drove toward home. Nick was seated beside Stan in the rear of the car, while Stan's father shared the front seat with the detective. Although Nick was exhausted from the recent interrogation, he became emotionally charged with curiosity in regard to Stan's experience in the grand jury room. "Stan, did you recognize some of the jurors? Were they pretty tough on you in there? Did the jurors believe your account?"

"Yeah, I recognized some of the guys on the grand jury, but not all of them. Some of them believed my story but most were skeptical. You know, the same old *'good ol' boy'* Southern mentality. They had difficulty believing that a man from the South would defend a black man. But the thing that puzzled them most was the very idea that I, as a former Klan member would incriminate myself!"

"Well, what happens now Stan?"

"It depends on whether or not the Klan members are indicted. If they are, Sheriff Kirkland will issue a warrant for their arrests. All the Klan members will be taken to jail—including me. Then we'll have to post bond. Most everybody will then try to get an attorney. After that, there will be a trial. If I'm convicted along with the others, I'll have to go to prison. And during that time when we'll be testifying against the Klan, they'll be trying even harder to kill us. That's when we'll all need the protection of Pete Wilson the most!"

"Yeah, if we can only keep him awake," Nick said.

Chapter 14

Nick had been lying awake for hours, for he was absorbed in morbid thoughts. He made repeated attempts to return to sleep, but his efforts were in vain. His thoughts became a confusing montage of images. Beginning with his melancholy youthful years, his sequence of memories continued to haunt him: His despondent memories of the Korean War depressed him, and his mind began to dwell among the dreadful memories of more recent times. His thoughts often vacillated, for they sometimes drifted backward in time, conjuring up old images of incidents that he had tried so hard to forget. His mind wandered as he began to relive the double-murder of Rufus, the Negro handyman and Preacher Temple.

He peeked at his watch in the semi-dark room and noted that the time was 3:45 a.m. With the realization that his quest for sleep was futile, he decided to abandon future attempts; consequently; he threw back the covers and slowly stood. To avoid awakening the others in the house he tried to remain quiet.as he slowly dressed himself in the dim-lit bedroom and then tiptoed into the kitchen; however, the hour was too early for either coffee or breakfast. He then stepped through the kitchen door into the darkness of the early morning.

Nick wasn't even aware of his intentions, for he only knew that he desperately needed movement—activity of any kind, anything except lying awake in bed while absorbed in disturbing memories. Even during his brief stroll to the end of the driveway and his leisurely return, his depressing thoughts followed him. He finally stepped into Lauren's car and drove away to an unknown destination.

Nick was a reclusive man: He felt a desperate need to be alone, to sort out his thoughts, to ease his anxiety. Being confined to the home of Lester Mullins, combined with a recommended need of protection made him feel like he had been imprisoned. *To hell with precautionary measures and protection,* he thought, *I'll continue to go wherever and whenever I please!* His mind gradually cleared as he began to experience a renewed sense of freedom.

As if he were obeying an unexpected impulse, he steered the vehicle in the direction of the Tennessee River, toward the site of last year's murder of Preacher Temple and Rufus. Although the horrid event brought back depressing memories, Nick still had some unanswered questions in his mind, for he had developed a morbid curiosity about the cause of such a senseless act of violence.

Nick drove slowly as he steered the vehicle through the center of town, for he was in no hurry. He drove across the railroad tracks, and on toward the river. As he reduced his speed, he noticed the diminishing street lights, and their reflection on the dew that covered the grassy meadow. When he continued to drive down the dark street, memories of the long-ago journey returned, for he vividly recalled traveling this identical route with Preacher Temple in their attempt to thwart the Klan's grisly mission. He turned right and travelled parallel to the river, and into the thick forest. The road narrowed to a weedy lane that was only a path across the flat river-bottom land. His anxiety increased when he recognized that this was the location where he and the preacher had seen the cross burning. Nick began to experience the same spooky feeling that he had felt on that long-ago night.

Although the eastern horizon had begun to display a faint glow, the early morning was mostly dark and eerily quiet. Over the river, the crescent moon that hung low in the eastern sky was a sharp contrast to the full moon that he and the preacher had viewed on the night of the double-murder. The fishy odor of the river and the musty smell of damp leaves melded into the cool, early-morning air, and the incessant chirping of the night insects spoke of a peaceful early-summer morning. The serene setting was a sharp contrast to the horrible event that was to follow later on that fateful evening. Once again, he recalled the sense of foreboding that he had experienced several months earlier on that horrendous night.

Nick continued to drive until he finally stopped at a dead-end at the border of a large meadow. At the edge of the clearing was the previous location of the burning cross that he and Preacher Temple had seen. He vividly recalled the terrifying sight of the flames that leaped skyward, scorching the overhanging branches of the surrounding trees.

When Nick left his car and sat among the fallen leaves, he breathed heavily as he relived those haunting memories. He vividly remembered the way that he and the preacher had witnessed the heinous event from their hidden haven among the dense foliage. The memory of the moment that Rufus was tied to the tree to await his brutal beating haunted him. But the most terrifying memory of that ghastly night was the moment when the Klan leader had shot both Rufus and the preacher. Reliving the terrifying event was difficult for Nick; however, he felt a compelling need to better understand the brutal injustice. Also, reliving the cruel event would strengthen his resolve to seek justice through the court system.

Nick had always been a meticulous examiner of all moral issues; as a result, he pondered the reasoning that initiated such a brutal act as the Klan had perpetrated: *What motivates man's inhumanity to his fellow man?* he asked himself. Upon reflection, he realized a profound truth: All moral conclusions are composed of two elements: *causes and results.* When a cause is noble, the result is usually good; however, if misguided or prejudiced the result can be disastrous. A perfect example was the senseless murders of Rufus and the preacher.

The cause of moral depravity begins with the ignorance and insecurity of some people. *Those well-educated, snooty people think they're better than I am,* complain the emotionally insecure. *But I must be better than somebody! Surely I'm superior to that poor man, that drunk, or that nigger! Hell, he ain't even worthy of associating with decent people like me!* As a *result*, the insecure become prejudiced. They begin to mistreat minorities and commit inhuman acts against the underprivileged. When considering his own worth to humanity, the insecure man becomes immersed in denial, which he disguises. In his unconscious mind, he is aware of his lack of self-esteem; however, this realization remains hidden behind a veneer of pretentiousness, causing him to justify his behavior. When multiplied a million times, this discriminating attitude becomes a movement that affects much of humanity.

Unfortunately, the meanings of the words, 'causes' and 'results' have become synonymous. The *results* often become the *causes*, for when man's insecurity and ignorance become repetitive and continue to endure, they become imbedded in his personality, and grow like a malignant cancer. When the result becomes part of the cause, man's insecurity has created a phenomenon much like perpetual motion. The prejudice feeds on itself; for ignorance begets more ignorance, and insecurity spawns more insecurity. The process ultimately becomes a downward spiral that creates a sustaining pattern in our society, particularly in the South.

However, Nick also concluded that the dismal cloud has a silver lining. Although every species of animal continue to evolve, only man is unique among all of his fellow creatures; for the pace of his mental development and understanding has accelerated. He has gradually but surely developed an insight and compassion at a faster pace than his less adaptive creatures. Man may stumble and sometimes slip backward, but

136

his inevitable path is forward movement. Nick realized that only knowledge and self-examination will ultimately deliver mankind from the primitive attitudes that perpetuate man's inhumanity to his fellow living creatures.

But there is a dark blemish that temporarily obscures the silver lining. Although knowledge, reason, and compassion will be the ultimate and *permanent* victor, the *temporary* solution can only be strong, and sometimes violent resistance against the savagery of evil men. Nick knew that harsh opposition, however justified, can sometimes be as inhuman as the gravest sins of evil men. But he also realized that now was the time for reasonable men to rise up and stand firm in their preparation of stamping out ignorance and prejudice.

On the horizon beyond the river, the morning sun slowly appeared, filtering through the trees and illuminating the meadow where Rufus and the preacher had died. For a long while he remained seated, as he carefully pondered his recent thoughts. He had mixed feelings in regard to passing judgment on the Klan members, for he began to envision them as mere ignorant sheep—blind followers of the Klan leader, a man who had lost all reason; and yet, Nick realized that only through his testimony would justice finally prevail.

Strangely, he felt better after visiting the gruesome meadow where his friends had died; for his examination of the underlying reasons had given him a better understanding, and helped clarify their senseless motive. Nonetheless, he hoped that this would be his final journey to this place. He re-entered Lauren's car and drove toward the home of Lester Mullins.

Chapter 15

On Monday morning at 8:00 a.m., Nick followed Stan when he stepped into his new Ford and they immediately drove away from the Lester Mullins home. Both were nervous, for they were headed toward the Loudon County Courthouse where they were to testify against the Klan members. Nick attempted to avoid a discussion of the nerve-wracking issue with casual conversation. "Damn, Stan! This is a great car! It was nice of your dad to buy this beauty for you"

"Yeah, and I really appreciate it. I just hope he doesn't start trying to control me again."

"Oh, you worry too much, Stan," Nick replied.

Stan redirected the subject, focusing on the trial. "Well the Klan members have been indicted. Are you ready to testify?"

"Yeah, I guess so," said Nick

"Are you nervous?" Stan attempted to hide his anxiety

"Yeah...A little. But I'm gonna try to keep calm. What time do we need to be there, Stan?"

"At 10:00 a.m. But I wanted to get an early start." Stan replied. "The jury has finally been selected, but it was difficult to find anybody who wanted to serve. Hell, some of them were sympathetic toward the Klan. Are you surprised?"

"It doesn't surprise me at all," said Nick. "But it will surprise me if we're even able to get a conviction. How many spectators do you think will be there?"

"I expect the courtroom will be full. A lot of country hicks will be attending because this trial is a big deal for them. They've never witnessed a murder trial before. This is probably the most sensational thing that's happened in this little hick town since that rape and murder trial that happened fifteen years ago. Hell, this is something that they'll always remember, and tell to their grandkids."

Nick peered at his watch. "I guess you know we're gonna be early. It's only 8:15. We'll be there before 8:30. What will we do for an hour and a half?"

"Well, we have to meet my dad, and that lazy private eye he hired will probably be tagging along with him. He stayed all night with us last night. We'll need to talk with them before the trial begins. I wish we'd brought our wives, but they didn't want to attend the first day of the trial."

"Speaking of the private detective—Peter Wilson. Isn't he supposed to be watching over us, and carrying a weapon for our protection? Wasn't he supposed to escort us to the trial?"

Stan grinned. "Yeah, but he's still asleep in one of Dad's beds, and I couldn't get him awake. Anyway, the Klan won't recognize my car anymore, because I'm driving this new Ford. Peter Wilson can ride to the trial with my dad, and protect him...That is, if my dad can wake him up."

But Stan...This trial may last for a long time. The Klan will eventually recognize your car! If they do, they'll trail you, or harass you every time you leave the house!"

"Nicky, don't worry about it. For the remainder of the trial, you and I can ride in Pete Wilson's car. He can protect us then. That is, if we can..."

Nick interrupted. *"If we can keep him awake."* Both men laughed. They continued to ride in silence until Nick suddenly asked, "Stan, speaking of the Klan recognizing your car...I've been driving Lauren's car on a limited basis. I'm afraid they'll finally recognize her vehicle."

"Nicky, I don't believe you'll have to worry about a Klan member recognizing Lauren's car. After all, I was one of their group, so I'm more threatening to them. They try to harass me by doing damage to either me or my car." He mischievously grinned. "Also, you're a Yankee. When you testify against them, they don't feel as threatened. They figure, 'who in his right mind would ever believe a Yankee?'" He then laughed and said, "Speaking more seriously, Nicky, maybe we need to keep that private eye close by our sides until this trial is over. We can ride in his car. He says that it's bullet-proof. He's as lazy as hell, but I believe he's capable of protecting us."

"But your dad hired him to investigate Sheriff Mullins' murder. Maybe Wilson should place his emphasis on that— not hauling us around in his car and protecting our families from harm."

"Nick, Dad is naive. He should have checked Wilson's credentials more closely. That guy doesn't have the brains to ever solve any kind of murder. The T.B.I. can handle that job. I'll bet they'll have the murderer of my uncle in jail in less than a week!"

"I sure hope so," Nick said.

."Nicky, I'm beginning to worry about Dad. Since he 'got religion,' he's too easy on people. He sometimes allows them to play him for a sucker."

"How so, Stan?"

"For instance, he bought that line of bullshit from Peter Wilson about his being a private detective. Hell, he's no more of a private eye than I am!"

"Yeah, I was a little suspicious of him myself. Why do you think he wanted to pose as a detective if it's not true?"

"Hell, I don't know. Maybe that's always been his lifetime dream. I guess having false hopes is true for all of us, Nicky."

"What do you suggest we do about it?" asked Nick

"I Know what I'm gonna do about it! I intend to confront Pete Wilson. First of all, he hasn't done any investigating since my father hired him. Also, he's been drinking too much. I think he's unreliable as an investigator."

140

Nick smiled. "Stan, your father is gonna be surprised that you're stepping in and taking charge of this problem."

"You're right, Nicky. That's always been the biggest problem in the relationship between Dad and me. In the past, I've always let him do my thinking for me."

"So what's going to happen to Wilson?" Nick asked.

Stan said, "Dad hired him, so I don't have the authority to fire him...or the guts either, for that matter. But I think I have a solution that will be acceptable to everybody. Dad should fire him as a private eye, and just use him as our protector. When we leave the house, he could drive us around. Nobody could harm any of us. After all, his car has bullet-proof glass, and he's packing a gun. We'd all be much safer. Of course there would be times when Wilson wouldn't be available, and we'd just have to take a chance and drive our own cars."

"Sounds like a winner to me," said Nick.

For a while Stan drove in silence. Nick turned on the radio which was broadcasting a local news story. The message quickly captured the attention of both men. The report stated that, during the previous night, a residence in the immediate area had burned to the ground. The house appeared to be an inexpensive shack that sat in a forest behind an open field at the top of Kingston Hill. Since they were travelling only a half-mile south of the specified location, both Nick and Stan looked in that direction. From the top of Kingston Hill, a column of black smoke rose high into the sky. Apparently, the fire was still smoldering.

Nick was concerned. "Do you think that the news report was talking about that old shack that we just moved out of, Stan? We've got plenty of time before we have to report to the courthouse. Let's drive up there and check it out!"

Stan suddenly turned right into Kingston Hill. As they rapidly ascended the hill, the smoke became more obvious, and they began to smell the fumes. They finally drove up the long driveway toward the smoking remnants of the small house, cautiously keeping their distance as Stan slowed the vehicle. He finally stopped the car. In total shock, they stared in horror at the smoldering remains of their former home.

Stan was suspicious, "Nicky, do you think the Klan burned the house in an effort to kill all of us? We just barely got moved out of that place! If we'd stayed, we'd all be dead!"

"It's obvious Stan!" Nick said, "Of course that was their intention! We're lucky we moved to your father's house!"

They sat for several minutes and studied the diminishing column of smoke as it lazily rose upward. Nick, who was more sentimental than Stan, looked sorrowfully at the heap of smoking embers. "You know, Stan…It makes me kinda sad to look at that pile of rubble. It might sound crazy, but it brings back some pleasant memories. It's the place where you and I mended our broken relationship. Remember?"

"Yeah, I remember. But it also brings memories of the way we had to hide from the Klan, and how all of us were constantly scared shitless! Nicky, you're too sentimental! You say it brings back pleasant memories! Damn! You'd believe that a funeral is a happy occasion! I hated this lousy dump!" Stan started the car, turned it around, and sped back down the hill toward the Loudon County Courthouse.

When they Stan arrived at the courthouse, Stan found it difficult to find a parking space, for many of the county residents had arrived earlier than necessary. They had already parked their vehicles and were in the process of crowding into the building. By sheer coincidence, Stan was able to park beside Pete Wilson's car. Stan followed Nick when they stepped out of the vehicle.

Stan immediately saw 'Skip' Hickman, a current member of the Klan. He nudged Nick and whispered, "There's one of the guys we'll be testifying against. He was recently arrested along with the other Klansmen. They were all released after they posted a bond. I didn't even have to report to the sheriff. Dad paid my bond for me. Damn, Nicky! I'm gonna owe my father a ton of loot when I start making money again."

"How are you fixed for money, Stan?" Nick asked.

"Actually, not too well. I haven't worked in a pretty good while, you know."

"Well, I'm not loaded with money, either," said Nick. "I sure hate to sponge off your dad, Stan."

"Hell, don't worry about it Nicky. Dad's got plenty of money. If you mention it to him it'll hurt his feelings."

They began to walk toward the courthouse entrance. As they started to walk up the steps, they bumped into Skip Hickman, the Klan member that Stan had earlier seen. Midway up the steps, he stopped both Nick and Stan. He placed his hand on Stan's shoulder and displayed a phony smile. His Southern dialect was obvious. "Hi, ol' buddy," he greeted, "How ya doin'? Are ya goin' into this-here courtroom to testify? You be sure an' tell th' truth now...ya hear?" His tone of voice was dripping with sarcasm. He took another step and turned to face Stan. He sneered and said, "By th' way, Stan...I noticed that ya got yaself a new car! A Ford, ain't it? Ya take good care of that-there car, ol' buddy...Ya hear?" He cackled with laughter.

Stan and Nick entered the atrium of the building and mingled with the crowd of people. They made their way to the main entrance and peeped into the large courtroom. The room was overflowing with people, mostly men. While a few men wore suits, some were casually dressed in the summer attire of tee shirts with slacks or jeans, while others wore faded bibbed overalls. The few women in attendance were mostly elderly. They sat idly in their wooden benches and fanned themselves, for the heat in the courtroom was sweltering.

It was too early to begin the legal proceedings; as a result, the large room was extremely noisy from the constant chatter of voices. When they looked toward the front of the large room, they saw Stan's father and Peter Wilson in the front row. An officer of the court appeared and ushered Nick and Stan to seats beside them.

In order to be heard over the noisy din, Stan spoke loudly when he told his father of the fire that had recently destroyed

143

their former hiding place. Lester Mullins was shocked when he responded. "That horrible sin was committed by that gang of renegades—The Klan! I'm afraid that my house will be next, when they discover that all of us are living there!"

Stan reassuringly placed his hand on his father's shoulder and smiled. "Dad, I don't think they know we are living there yet. But to be on the safe side, maybe we should move."

"I might station some guards around my house—or maybe we *should* change locations. What do you think, son?" Stan's father was deeply concerned.

"Dad, don't worry about it for now. I've got some ideas about our best course of action that I'll discuss with you later."

Peter Wilson looked up with sleepy eyes. The odor of alcohol was obvious when he spoke. "Hell, don't worry about any of that crap! I told you that I'd protect all of you!" Lester Mullins looked at him with an expression of doubt.

At 10:a.m. the jury filed into the courtroom and took their seats in the jury box. Immediately afterward, The Honorable Fred Daniels emerged from a nearby door and took a seat behind his bench. He was a bearded, overweight man who was wearing bifocals. When he called the meeting to order, an immediate hush fell over the courtroom. Sitting together in a nearby group were thirteen defendants who were represented by two lawyers, Oliver Smith and William Howell. As a unit, they stood when the judge gave the instructions and cited the charges, which had now been reduced to manslaughter. He acknowledged and accepted their lawyers' pleas of *not guilty*. The Klan members and their lawyers returned to their seats.

Nick carefully inspected the group of defendants. Because Stan had been an active member of the Klan, he was familiar with each member of the group; however, with the exception of Cowboy Galyon, Bird Dog Johnson, and Skip Hickman, whom he had recently met, Nick knew none of them. When they saw Nick staring at them, a few of the defendants sneered at him. At a moment when the judge was distracted, one of them displayed an obscene gesture.

144

When the noise in the courtroom gradually increased, the judge restored order when he tapped his gavel on the bench and immediately called the court to order. The all-male jury members peered out over the courtroom in anticipation. Some were challenged to determine whether or not they were in any way involved in the case. The judge then addressed the prosecuting attorney, Timothy Steele. "Mr. Steele, the court is now ready to hear your opening statement."

The attorney was a slim man who looked younger than his age of forty-two. He stood and faced the jury. "Gentlemen of the jury, my name is Timothy Steele, and I will be prosecuting this case. I'm going to keep my opening statement very brief. This case is going to be easily proven. We have two credible witnesses to the crime of murder who have no reason to lie. Whenever you hear their account of this heinous murder, you'll be sure to return a verdict of guilty. Thank you." He then returned to his seat beside Nick and Stan.

Judge Daniels thanked him. He then addressed the defense attorneys. Oliver Smith and William Howell. "Which of you would like to deliver the opening statement?"

Attorney Oliver Smith was middle aged. A rapidly balding man, he was short and obese. He stood and said, "Your honor, I respectfully request that you dismiss this case."

"On what grounds, sir?"

"On the grounds that the man accused of the murder isn't even present. Also, Stan Mullins is himself a former Klan member. I question his motive for testifying against his peers. Also, we are not even sure that a murder ever took place. And even if it did, none of the defendants had any part in it."

"Request denied," said the judge. The spectators stirred in their seats, and reacted with slight grumbles. With a tap of his gavel the judge restored order. "Do you have an opening statement, sir?" asked the judge.

"No sir—not at this time," answered the defense attorney.

Timothy Steel, the prosecuting attorney quickly stood and said, "Your honor, I would like to call Stan Mullins to the stand as a witness."

As instructed by the judge, Stan walked to the witness stand. He was nervous and sweating profusely when he took a seat. After stating his name and age, he was sworn in by the prosecuting attorney. He nervously awaited the first question.

The lawyer slowly paced in front of him. He finally turned and asked Stan, "Mr. Mullins, I understand that you were at a Klan meeting when you witnessed a double-murder. Why did you happen to be present at the scene of the crime?"

"At the time I was a member of the Klan, sir."

"And you are no longer a member?"

"No sir. I stopped being a member when I realized that they were capable of committing murder."

"Mr. Mullins, give this court your account of what you witnessed." Stan proceeded to give a detailed account of everything he witnessed on that night: the phone call from a fellow Klan member informing him that the group was going to whip a Negro at the meeting, his surprise that the Negro was his friend, Rufus, and his horrible shock when the Klan leader, Mike Bronson shot both Rufus and Preacher Temple.

The prosecuting attorney asked, "Why were the Ku Klux members intending to whip Rufus?"

"They claimed that he had molested a little white girl. But I know that wasn't true, because…"

"Objection!" the defense protested. "That statement is only the opinion of the witness."

"Objection sustained," said the judge.

The prosecutor continued, "But why was the preacher killed? In spite of the injustice of killing the black man, I at least understand the Klan's justification of it. But why the preacher?"

"Well, it was like this: The preacher came out of his hiding place and yanked the hood from the Klan leade's head, exposing his identity. He knew that the preacher would tell the entire town about it. So he shot him, and then he felt that he had no other choice but to also shoot Rufus."

"And the man who shot them—what is his name?"

"His name is Mike Bronson. He was a county deputy."

146

"Well, where is he? Did he just suddenly vanish into thin air? Why isn't he in this courtroom being tried for murder?"

"He just disappeared." Stan explained. "No one has seen him again since he committed the murders."

"Are you sure the killer was this guy—Mike Bronson?"

"Yes sir. I'm sure of it."

The lawyer turned to face the judge. "I have no further questions, your honor." The judge excused Stan with a reminder that he could be recalled in the future. Stan left the witness stand and took a seat beside his companions. With his handkerchief, he wiped the sweat from his face.

The prosecuting attorney remained standing. "The prosecution calls Nick Parilli." Nick walked to the witness stand, where he gave his name and age before he was sworn in. He took a seat in the chair and prepared himself for the barrage of questions.

The lawyer looked directly into Nick's eyes. "Mr. Parilli, I'm going to begin by asking you the same question that I asked Mr. Mullins. I understand that you claim to have witnessed a double-murder at a Klan meeting last year. Why were you at a Klan meeting? Were you also a member?"

"No sir," Nick answered, "I went there with a preacher in an attempt to stop the Klan from whipping a Negro man who was my friend." Nick told of the Klan's abduction of Rufus, and about joining forces with the preacher in the search and discovery of the Klan's meeting place. He continued the story by telling how he and the preacher had hidden to avoid being discovered. He then corroborated Stan's account of the finale of the brutal story: the whipping of Rufus, the preacher's intercession, the removal of the Klan leader's hood, and Mike Bronson's murder of the two men.

The attorney asked, "What made you so interested in this miscarriage of justice? Why did you go on this mission of mercy?"

"Because these people were my friends, sir."

"I have no more questions, your honor," said the lawyer.

147

The judge replied, "The witness is excused." Nick stepped down and returned to his original seat beside his friends.

It was now time for the defense. At the judge's request, Oliver Smith, the defense attorney stood as Stan Mullins again returned to the stand; this time for his cross examination. After being sworn in, Stan again took his seat to give his testimony.

The attorney was an arrogant man. For a long while, he said nothing as he paced back and forth in front of the witness. It appeared that he was relishing the delay, as if he were taking pleasure from Stan's anxiety. With a look of sarcasm, he turned and asked, "In your statement to the prosecuting attorney, you claimed to have witnessed a double-murder."

"Yes sir," Stan responded.

"Really?" His smile was mocking. "Most people don't even believe a murder was committed. They think it's just a rumor. And who was the man that you claim murdered these two unfortunate people?"

"His name is Mike Bronson. He was also a county deputy at the time."

"Well, where is this man? If he committed murder, then he should have shown up for the trial!" He turned to face the judge. "Your honor, if this claim turns out to be true, then this *Mike Bronson* should be tried and convicted in absentia!"

"I'm aware of that, counselor," replied the judge. "We haven't yet located this man, but he is under indictment."

The lawyer resumed his interrogation. "Mr. Mullins, you didn't answer my question! Do you know where this *murderer* can be found?" His term, 'murderer' reflected sarcasm.

Stan was caught in a dilemma: If he disclosed the fact that Bronson had been killed by Caleb, the young grandson of Rufus, he knew the lad could be charged with murder; however, he was afraid to tell an outright lie. As a result he only dodged the complete truth. *After all, why should he volunteer information?* He finally compromised, "Sir, I don't really know where Bronson can be found at this very moment.

148

He just suddenly disappeared." Technically, Stan was truthful; for he had no idea where the body of Bronson was located.

The lawyer sneered at Stan. "So you were a member of the Klan, were you? How many other organization have you belonged to? Were you as loyal to them as you were to the Klan? Or did you also betray them?"

The prosecuting attorney stood. "Objection, your honor. That's not a legitimate question. How could the witness possibly answer that?"

"Objection sustained," droned the judge. He turned to face the defending lawyer. "Counselor, try to keep your questions relevant."

"Well, I'll ask my question in a different way," he said. "What motivated you to resign from the Klan and decide to testify against them?"

"Because they are partly responsible for a murder!"

"Partly responsible? I fail to see where they had any part in it. You said that this guy, *Mike Bronson* murdered these two men! Did the Klan members know he was going to do that? I think not!"

"I don't know!" said Stan, "But they were accomplices to murder. That makes them responsible!"

The defense attorney smiled. "You're wrong about that, Mr. Mullins. And it's going to be proven in this courtroom! Your honor, I have no further questions."

When Nick was called to the stand and again sworn in, he dreaded enduring the irritating attitude of the lawyer. He was nervous and his face was soaked in sweat.

The defense attorney began with sarcasm. He smiled and said, "Well, Mr. Parilli, I understand that you're a *Korean War hero.* We fellow Americans appreciate your service to our country." Nick could see where this interrogation was headed.

"I was never a hero, sir, but I tried to do my best." Nick answered.

"Tell me, Parilli…I understand that you also witnessed a double-murder. Would you explain how that came about?"

Without leaving out a single detail, Nick corroborated Stan's story by describing the entire incident to him. When he told of Preacher Temple leaving his hiding place and yanking the disguising hood from the Klan leader, the defense attorney asked, "And what did you do?"

"I stayed hidden. I realized that exposing myself would be suicide! The preacher did a foolish thing."

"So you stayed *hidden?* That's not exactly what you would expect from a *war hero!"* The lawyer sneered.

The prosecuting attorney stood. "Objection, your honor! He has no legitimate reason to question the courage of the witness!"

The judge begged to differ. "Objection overruled," he said. He turned to face Nick. "Why did you stay hidden, soldier? Why didn't you reveal yourself and try to reason with the Klan members?"

"I've already explained that, judge. It would have been suicide. Besides, I didn't know that the preacher would jerk off the hood and expose the killer's identity! When he did that, I knew he was a dead man!"

The obese lawyer resumed his questioning. "Mr. Parilli, I can tell from your accent that you are from somewhere in the north. Where are you originally from?"

"I'm from Chicago, sir."

"Well, I'm beginning to better understand your attitude about racial issues. Here in the South, Negroes can often be a problem to many white folks. Sometimes they are guilty of molesting white women."

"Yeah, and also sometimes white people molest Negroes," Nick answered. The defense attorney turned to face the judge. "Judge Daniels, I believe this witness is deliberately trying to be arrogant!"

The judge admonished Nick. "Mr. Parilli, If you don't start being respectful in your answers, I'm going to cite you for contempt of court!"

Nick responded, "I didn't mean to show disrespect, judge. I was just trying to be honest."

The obese lawyer resumed his questioning. "Well, let's elaborate on that subject a little more," he said. "When Stan Mullins said that your Negro friend was innocent of molesting the little white girl...Do you agree?"

"Of course I agree! My friend Rufus was one of the gentlest men I ever knew!"

"But that's just your opinion, Mr. Parilli! How do you know that the assertion wasn't true? If it was, then the Klan would feel justified in their actions!"

"Are you saying that the Klan was justified in *murdering two men?* That's baloney!" Nick was becoming irritated.

The lawyer became extremely angry. "Listen, *hero!* I ask the questions in this courtroom! Your job is to answer!" He protested Nick's remark to the judge, who immediately gave Nick another warning.

The overweight lawyer was now fuming with anger, and primed for the kill. "Listen, you! I've just finished checking your U.S. Army records! I found you were court-martialed and reduced in rank to private for insubordination to an officer while in battle! And after serving some time in a military stockade, you stayed drunk for about a week in an army barracks! *Hero?* Hell, you're a disgrace to your uniform!" He turned toward the judge. "Your honor, I have no more question for this excuse for a man!" From the rear of the courtroom came the subdued sound of spectators clapping their hands. It became obvious that many people sympathized with the Klan.

The judge banged his gavel. "Order in the court!" he bellowed. Nick became infuriated. He had a difficult time restraining himself from violence.

Judge Daniels reminded Nick that he might be recalled as a witness. He squinted through his thick bifocals at his watch. It was after 4:00 p.m. He pushed back his chair and addressed the attorneys and the entire courtroom. "This court is hereby adjourned until at 10:00 a.m. on the day after tomorrow, when the prosecution will interrogate the defendants. But until then,

151

this court is in recess." He ended the session with a loud bang of his gavel.

Nick left the courtroom in frustration, for he began to fear that this case might be a lost cause; however, Stan was more optimistic. When he noticed Nick's obvious disappointment, he draped his arm around him. "Nicky, I know how you feel, pal. But this case is far from over. You and I will be called back to the witness stand, and the defendants haven't testified yet. But now is the time when the Klan is going to feel more threatened by our testimony. We'll need to be even more cautious."

They joined Lester Mullins and the private eye, Peter Wilson on the steps of the courthouse as they left the building. In the yard outside, Klan member Skip Hickman again appeared beside Stan and Nick. His crooked grin exposed his teeth when he said, "Why there's ol' Stan! I bet yer proud of that new Ford! When did ya buy that classy vehicle? Don't be drivin' it aroun' town! Ain't no tellin' what could happen to it! Some crazy nut might force it off th' road!"

Nick became livid with anger. He viciously slapped the man across the face. "Get away from us, you son of a bitch!"

As several bystanders curiously stared, Skip Hickman rubbed his face and backed away. "You're gonna pay for that, you bastard!" He hurriedly made his way through the crowd. When Nick attempted to chase him, he was restrained by Stan.

Stan's father and Peter Wilson watched the Klan member as he fled the scene. The private eye said, "Man! You've got quite a temper! And right here in front of the courthouse! I guess you know that guy could have you arrested!"

"I don't care!" Nick angrily said, "I've had just about all of the crap I can take for today!" Lester Mullins only smiled.

When they reached their vehicles, Peter Wilson's car was parked beside Stan's new Ford. Stan said, "Nicky, do you mind driving my car to Dad's house? I'll ride with Peter in his car. I want to talk to both Dad and Peter about something."

"Sure, Stan. I'll meet you at your father's home." The men got into their vehicles and drove toward the Mullins residence. Lester Mullins sat in the front seat beside Peter Wilson, who was driving, while Stan relaxed in the back. They had only traveled for a few miles when Stan introduced a delicate subject. "Pete, I don't want you to be offended, but I need to talk to you about something."

"What's on your mind, Stan?" He was curious.

"I'll just be blunt with you. I'm a little disappointed in the way you've handled the investigation."

"Disappointed? What are you unhappy about?"

"I feel that you misrepresented yourself to my father. You claimed to be a private detective, but so far, you haven't even brought in a single clue about who might have murdered my uncle. And another thing…You 've been drinking a lot."

Peter seemed to be remorseful. "Stan, I realize that I've been boozing quite a bit, but I'm going through a rough time right now. My wife, Helen just filed for divorce. You'll see some improvement when I get accustomed to the divorce."

"Well, when are you going to dig up something?"

"I've already dug up something. I've recently done some investigative work. I *do* have something to report."

"Such as…?"

"Such as some news about Little Billy Sneed. I went to see him a couple of days ago. You and your father told me that he's poor. *A street person*, you called him. Well, I've got news for you! He's far from being a street person! Hell, he's living in a fancy apartment in an exclusive section of town! I wish I could afford a place that nice!"

Stan's father immediately became interested. "Where do you think he got the money, Pete?"

Peter only shrugged. "Hell, I suppose somebody is paying him off!"

"Paying him off?" asked Stan's father.

"Yeah. Somebody's paying him off to keep quiet about something. And since he lives in such a swanky place, that *something* must be pretty big!"

153

"What else have you found out about the other suspects, Pete?" Stan asked.

"I'm not sure, but I'm suspicious of a couple of them. Anyway, I want to talk to you about something else. Since my wife sued me for divorce, I've been under a lot of stress. That's why I sometimes drink too much. As a result, I haven't done a very good job. I'd like to ask a favor."

Stan's father asked, "What favor?"

"I'd like to take a temporary leave of absence. Since my life is in such turmoil, I need some time off to get my wits together. I can't concentrate well enough to be investigating complex criminal activities."

"How much time do you need, Pete?" Lester asked.

"A couple of weeks should be enough, and then I'll resume my investigations. Would that be permissible?"

"What about the money I'm paying you, Pete? I agreed to pay you five-hundred dollars a week plus your other expenses until this murder is solved."

"Just don't pay me until I'm back on the job." Pete said.

Stan had been patiently listening to the conversation. He suddenly made a suggestion. "Let me propose a deal that might work for all of us. Where are you staying, Pete?"

"For now, I'm living in a hotel room in Cedar Valley. I own a home in Chicago where my wife is currently living, but she is divorcing me. I came to Tennessee to be near my aging mother. I think that's one reason my wife is pissed-off at me."

"Okay, here's a solution to all of our problems," said Stan. "Pete, you should forget about your investigation for now. Instead, just concentrate on offering protection for our family. We're not even able to go anywhere in our vehicles without being harassed. On the other hand, you have a bullet-proof car, and you are carrying a loaded weapon. Each time we go anywhere, we should ride in your car. Also, my father can continue to pay you. Just concentrate on protecting us."

"But I can't be with your family twenty-four hours a day. Sometimes you people go places at night when I'm asleep in my hotel room." Pete said.

"If it's okay with Dad, you can move in with us. When this case is solved, you will no longer be employed by my father."

Peter Wilson sighed with relief. "If it's okay with your father, you've got a deal! But you realize, of course, that when I'm not available, you'll just have to drive on your own."

Lester Mullins agreed with the proposal. He reached across the front seat and shook hands with the private eye, and then turned to face his son. "Stan, you've recently become a more responsible man. This is the first time you've ever shown an interest in helping me make decisions."

"Dad, this is the first time I've ever had the guts to do it."

At 5:30 p.m. they arrived at the Mullins residence. When they went inside, Nick had already arrived. Kathy quickly ran to meet Stan and hugged him while the others took seats in the living room. Lauren's mother sat quietly in her wheelchair where she entertained herself by playing with her earrings and repeatedly folding and unfolding a sheet of paper. Lester Mullins knelt in front of her wheelchair. He smiled at her and playfully ruffled her hair.

When everyone gathered in the living room, most of the talk was about today's courtroom activity. The discussion of the behavior of the sarcastic defense attorney continued to irritate Nick.

After the wives prepared the evening meal, Peter Wilson shared dinner with the group before leaving for his downtown hotel room. His final words were, "Lester, I'll move all my belongings into your house sometime tomorrow."

Chapter 16

Early on the following morning, Peter Wilson brought his meager belongings to the Mullins residence. He agreed to provide protection and stay until both murder cases were solved. While Nick, Lauren and her mother had remained at the Mullins home, Peter Wilson had escorted Stan and Kathy to the store to shop for groceries.

Shortly after 11 a.m. on the same morning, Lester Mullins walked into the office of Sheriff Kirkland. He again met the sheriff, who introduced him to the T.B.I. agent, Lieutenant Morton. After shaking hands with both men, Lester chose a chair facing the agent, while the sheriff sat behind his desk. The agent was a handsome, well-dressed man wearing a dark suit. Stan's father had been eager to discuss his brother's murder with the agent; as a result, he leaned forward in his chair and initiated the conversation. "Lieutenant, I'm certainly glad that you're helping us. I really want to put my brother's death behind me as quickly as possible. I can promise you that I will fully cooperate, and help you in any way I can."

The agent responded. "Mr. Mullins, I can understand your concern and anxiety; however, I can't guarantee that this case will be solved quickly. But I'll give it my best shot, sir."

"That's all that I can ask of you, lieutenant. A few days ago, I hired another man who I thought might be of help to you, but since my family has been harassed and threatened, and attempts have been made on their lives, I decided to just use this man for protection. He's armed and the glass in his car is bullet-proof. Of course, the death of my brother is totally different from the case currently being tried in court."

The agent nodded his head. "Yeah, I've had some long discussions with Sheriff Kirkland about that murder case. It involves the Ku Klux Klan, doesn't it? Well, this case may also be connected to the murder of your brother. Has it occurred to you that the Klan members who were also members of the county police force had a strong motive to kill your brother? According to Sheriff Kirkland, some of them were involved in criminal activities with Sheriff Mullins, and after he turned over a new leaf, he was threatening to expose those activities."

"Yes sir. That thought has occurred to me. In fact, I'm almost convinced of it. You can imagine the strain my entire family has been enduring! We've had to deal with two separate murder cases. And during this entire time, some of these Klan members have been trying to kill my relatives."

"That must have been tough," said the agent. He removed a pen and writing pad from his pocket. "Mr. Mullins, can you give me some information about your brother's murder?"

Sheriff Kirkland had remained quiet, listening to the discussion. He finally said, "Lieutenant Morton, although my resources are somewhat limited, I may be of some help in this case." He reached into his desk drawer and removed some paperwork. "Mr. Mullins has thoroughly discussed his brother's murder with me. He gave me a list of people that he thought might have some connection to the crime. The information is included in these papers." He reached across his desk and handed the packet of papers to the agent.

Lieutenant Morton began to study the information. He finally spoke. "This guy *Billy Sneed*. He seems to know something about all of these other suspects. According to this information, he was a jailhouse snitch for Sheriff Mullins. I can probably begin my investigation by starting with him. How can I contact him? Do you have his address?"

"No, but the sheriff can get it for you. But I'll warn you in advance, you can't believe a word he says," Lester answered.

"Do you have a strong suspicion of a specific person who might have wanted to kill him, Mr. Mullins? As a former mayor, you probably know some of the sheriff's associates."

"Yes, I do. You were right in your suspicion that maybe an ex-member of the police force might have killed him. I believe his killer was a guy who is known as 'Cowboy' Galyon. He was a deputy sheriff during my brother's time in office. He once even threatened to kill my brother. I don't know exactly where he lives, but it's somewhere here in town."

Sheriff Kirkland said, "I can get all of those addresses for you, Lieutenant."

The agent sat for a while, studying the information on the paper. He finally said, "Well, this is a start. Sheriff Kirkland, I'm going to depend on both you and Mr. Mullins to work closely with me during this investigation. In the meantime, I'll keep both of you posted on any new development in the case." He slowly stood and shook hands with both men before leaving the sheriff's office.

For a while, Lester Mullins and the sheriff kept their seats and continued to discuss the meeting. "What did you think of the T.B.I. agent, Mr. Mullins?" asked the sheriff. "Maybe we're finally getting somewhere."

"I sure hope so. I'd like to see this matter resolved and move on with my life. In addition to worrying about solving the murder of my brother, I have to deal with the threats of the Klan members." He stood and shook hands with Sheriff Kirkland before leaving the office.

When Lester arrived at his home, Peter Wilson had left his skimpy belongings in one of the spare bedrooms. He had completed his chore of taking Stan and Kathy to the market, and had later driven into Cedar Valley to handle a personal matter. While Lauren and Nick were in the kitchen preparing for an early dinner, Kathy was in one of the bathrooms taking a shower, and Lauren's mother, Bonnie Rose was asleep in her wheelchair. Stan was in an angry mood. He continued to peek at his watch as he nervously paced the floor. Suddenly, he stopped pacing. "Where is that guy, anyway?"

Stan's father took a seat in a chair and asked, "What guy?"

"Pete Wilson! After he took us grocery shopping and dropped us off at home, he left here like a whirlwind! He claimed to have some urgent business in town, and that he'd be back by four o'clock! But it's already past four-thirty!" He again peered at his watch.

"So what are you upset about?" asked his father.

"I'm upset because he was supposed to take Kathy and me into Knoxville! I was intending to take her to dinner and a movie! I'm tired of seclusion! Didn't we hire the guy to offer us protection by taking us places in his car? If he didn't want to spend the evening with us, he could have made two trips!"

"Stan, don't worry. He might have experienced some unexpected problem. Anyway, why don't you just forget about eating out and have dinner with us? He might be back by then, and he can drive you to the movies."

"But it will be getting late. I wanted to get back home early. Nick and I have a busy day tomorrow. We need to discuss some things and get ready for our court testimony on the following day!" He again looked at his watch and turned toward the bathroom. "Kathy! Are you almost ready?"

"Just about, Stan!" she replied.

Stan's father asked, "Do you intend to drive to Knoxville in your own car? Don't you think that's too dangerous— especially, right in the middle of this murder trial?"

"Dad, it's only about a twenty minute drive to Knoxville! And I'm not waiting any longer for that guy!"

When Kathy walked into the living room she displayed her usual vibrant beauty. "I'm ready. Let's go, honey!"

In spite of his father's protests, Stan drove his new Ford down the long driveway and turned toward Knoxville.

Stan was in a romantic mood. He smiled at Kathy as he switched on the radio and leisurely lit a cigarette. She rolled down her window to dissipate the smoke. The air from outside the car burnished her blonde hair as she found some country music on the radio. They both felt a rare sense of freedom, for this was the first time in several days that they had been alone together to embark on a trip to some place—any place. The rhythm of the music captivated him, as he began to tap his left foot to the beat of it. They shared a moment of happiness, for they had been granted a brief reprieve from the fearful events that had recently dominated their lives.

Stan's decision to drive his own vehicle had deeply worried his father; however, he began to feel that perhaps he had been led to exercise too much caution. After all, Knoxville was only twenty minutes away, and this was only a one-time event.

They enjoyed an expensive dinner at Regas Restaurant; and afterward, a movie at the Tennessee Theater, where they saw, *Gone with the Wind* for the second time.

It was early twilight when they began the short drive to the Mullins home. When the vehicle entered the suburbs of Cedar Valley, the broad expanse of road was brightly-lit by a row of evenly-spaced street lights that illuminated the street. Ahead of them was a dark, steep hillside where a multitude of houses displayed scattered, irregular points of light from inside their living rooms and porches.

Suddenly, from a wooded area on the hillside, Stan saw a bright flash of light that was almost instantaneously followed by a loud explosion from the windshield of the car. Kathy screamed, as Stan instantly pulled the car over to the curb and skidded to a stop. When he switched on the interior light, he quickly saw the reason for her scream: Her right side displayed a gaping hole that was gushing blood. He instantly realized that she had been shot by a sniper from the hillside.

Stan was panicky. Without hesitation he sped toward *Park West Hospital.* In his anxiety and haste, he drove recklessly, sometimes honking his horn, and pushing ahead of other cars. He finally parked the car in front of the emergency room.

Blood was still gushing from her side. Stan quickly checked her pulse and found, to his relief, that she was still alive. He rushed into the hospital to the registration desk and quickly received aid. In a matter of minutes, paramedics had placed her on a stretcher and wheeled her into an operating room. Although it seemed like an eternity to Stan, it was only a matter of minutes until two surgeons were attending to her.

As Stan anxiously stood in the hallway, he lowered his head and began to bitterly cry; however his emotional outburst of sadness became replaced by a seething anger. *Who in the hell do these people think they are?* he asked himself. *I swear to God these bastards will pay for this!*

He immediately called his father. Minutes seemed like hours, as he paced the floor in the waiting room. Finally, Lester Mullins arrived with Nick and Lauren. Bonnie Rose had remained at home in her wheelchair with Pete Wilson, who had finally returned to the Mullins home.

Stan's father hurried to his son and embraced him with a vigorous hug. "How is she doing, son? Is she still in surgery?"

"Yeah, Dad…I don't know what to expect." Lester Mullins sat down beside him. Both Nick and Lauren hugged him and sat across from him as Lauren began to cry.

Stan was overcome with guilt. "Dad, Kathy took a bullet that was obviously meant for me. I was a fool to drive my car against your advice. Just look what this mistake has cost!"

"Son, you must forgive yourself. We all make mistakes every day. Also, Peter Wilson can't protect us all the time. Sometimes we'll just have to take a chance and drive our own cars. You made a mistake, but we can't undo the past." After taking his son's hand, he bowed his head and prayed.

The group stayed in the waiting room through the night until it blended into early morning. While Lauren occasionally catnapped, Lester Mullins and Nick remained awake with Stan. By mid-morning, Lauren was exhausted. Lester Mullins stayed with his son while Nick drove Lauren home.

161

By mid-morning, a surgeon appeared in the waiting room with his report. Both Stan and his father stood to receive the news. When he noticed that Stan was the younger man, the doctor immediately walked to him and shook his hand. His expression was grim. "Are you the husband, sir?"

"Yes sir. I'm Stan Mullins, and this man is my father, Lester. How is my wife doing? Is she going to be Okay?"

"My name is Dr. Wiggins. Your wife suffered a punctured lung, Mr. Mullins. We were able to remove the bullet, but because of the damage to the lung, we had to remove the lower lobe of her right lung. Because of the severe bleeding, she has had a blood transfusion. We have her on oxygen at the present time."

Stan was filled with anxiety. "Is she going to live?"

The doctor placed his hand on Stan's shoulder. "It's too early to make a thorough prognosis, sir. But her vital signs are good, and she's breathing much better. I'm sorry for your misfortune."

"May we visit with her doctor?"

"Yes, you may both visit with her, but she is currently asleep. It may be several hours before she's awake and alert. After you visit with her, you and your father may wish to go home and get some rest. I'm very sorry, sir." He shook hands with both men and hurried away.

Chapter 17

Our emotions are often puzzling, for sometimes there is only a thin veneer of separation between the feelings of grief and anger. The emotions experienced by Stan when the horrible incident occurred had filled him with sadness and guilt, which are often major components of grief. As he reflected on the tragedy, his original grief was replaced by a seething anger—and finally, hatred. When he recalled the many times that he and his family had endured the cruelty of his enemies, he made a silent vow to somehow seek revenge.

The Lester Mullins household was in emotional disarray. While Lauren's mother stayed at home with Peter Wilson, Nick, Lauren, and Stan's father took alternating shifts in their visitation of Kathy. On the day after surgery, Stan spent most of his daytime hours at her bedside, for she was slow in becoming fully awake and her recovery was delayed. Stan only left her room when she was undergoing some unusual procedure, or when she was being bathed. When Kathy's condition began to gradually improve, he sometimes left her room to sit in the waiting area, or to stroll the hospital halls. His emotions were morbid, for his mind became a strange mixture of sadness, hatred, and boredom.

For several days, the Mullins household continued their regular visits to the hospital. Because of the tragedy, the trial of the Klan members was postponed; as a result, Nick and Stan were unable to appear in court to give their testimony. It would be resumed only whenever all participants could be present to testify.

Kathy began to gradually improve. Although she still required oxygen, she no longer needed blood transfusions, and the injury to her lung was slowly healing. She gradually became more lucid, and finally near normal in her emotions. She even made occasional requests to leave her bed. Stan became re-invigorated. However, her long hours of anesthesia during and after the surgery had affected her thinking, for she had no memory of her evening celebration with Stan, nor of the ambush that followed; however, her doctor believed that her loss of memory was only temporary.

As Kathy slowly improved, Stan still spent most of the long days with her, while visits from the others gradually became less frequent. Her memory of recent events gradually began to return and she was beginning to walk without help. Stan began to visit her less often as he began to spend more of his time at the Mullins home.

Stan and Nick was seated in the living room with Peter Wilson, while Lauren was in the kitchen, preparing lunch. Lester Mullins had become more concerned about Lauren's mother, Bonnie Rose. Fearing that her constant isolation would hasten her dementia, he had taken her to the city park. By introducing her to a different environment, he hoped to brighten her spirit and increase her awareness of reality.

Stan partly blamed Peter Wilson for Kathy's catastrophe. He was still irritated toward him for his failure to protect them when he and Kathy had driven to Knoxville. When they sat in facing seats, Stan confronted him. "Pete, I'm a little pissed at you! You're partly responsible for that terrible thing that happened to Kathy! Where in the world were you? You were supposed to drive us into Knoxville!"

164

Pete became defensive. "Damn it Stan! I can't always be available every time somebody in this group needs a ride! Sometimes I have emergencies, and places I need to go!"

"Well, that's what my father hired you for," said Stan, "You agreed to be our protector and driver. It wouldn't have taken you long, because it's only about a twenty-minute drive to Knoxville. To avoid spending the evening with us, you could have made two trips."

"Look, Stan," he replied, "I'll protect you when I'm available, but sometimes all of you will just have to take your chances and drive your own cars. And another thing—I'm getting sick of just hanging out here at this house, with nothing else to do except entertain Bonnie Rose!"

Nick said, "You know, he's right, Stan. He gets bored. And he can't be everywhere at once."

Pete stood. "Stan, since Lester took Lauren's mother to the park, you won't be needing me to stay here and protect her. Do I have your permission to get away from here for a while?" His tone was sarcastic.

"Yeah, go ahead Pete. Just try to be back for dinner at six o'clock." Stan's suggestion sounded like a command. He sneered at Pete and dropped the subject. As Pete drove away in his car, Stan turned to Nick and said, "You know, Nick, Pete gripes about staying here to protect Lauren's mother, but I think he actually enjoys it. I think that he might be jealous of Dad for taking her to the park. Maybe taking care of Bonnie Rose is Pete's most valuable contribution to us. At least he's good at something!"

Nick laughed. "Stan, I think I detected some prejudice and sarcasm in your remark! Hell, man…give the guy a little bit of credit! Let's face it, the man has a terribly boring job."

Stan's mood became more positive. Although he was still bitter about the sniper's attack on Kathy, her gradual improvement had lifted his spirits. As a result, he began to feel better about the possible outcome of the Klan trial. "Nicky, I think we need to talk about our next appearance in court. When we left there after our first session, we felt that getting a conviction might be unlikely. But now I feel more optimistic about it. We need to change our tactics, pal."

"In what way, Stan?" asked Nick.

"Do you remember the negative way the Klan's defense attorney characterized both of us? He made me appear to be a traitor! And he made you look like a damned coward! Well, this time when we testify, the prosecuting attorney needs to paint a more positive picture of us—bring out our good points. Our attorney should try to impress the jury with our good qualities."

Nick asked, "How do we accomplish that, Stan?"

"I need to emphasize it to the prosecuting attorney."

"That's a great idea, Stan. But that's not going to stop that chicken-shit defense attorney from again making both of us look like hell to the jury."

"Come on, Nicky! He's already made us look like hell! What more could he say that's bad about either of us? How could he make us appear any worse?

"I think you've suggested a good approach, Stan. I could sure use a little optimism about the case. When we left the courtroom after our last session, I felt like we were losing the case. And after that fat-assed defense attorney gave me hell, I felt like kicking the crap out of him!"

Stan cautioned him. "Nicky, that's another thing that could lose the case for us! *Your anger!* You can't afford to lose your head!"

"I'll try to stay calm. But I can only take so much crap!"

Lauren was wearing an apron when she entered the living room. She smiled at both Nick and Stan. "Hi guys!" she said, "Lunch is almost ready. Stan, it was sure nice of your father to take my mother to the park on this beautiful morning! It will be so good for her. She's been stuck inside for days."

Stan returned her smile. "Dad just thought it would be good for her. I think they'll both be safe there. After all, it's just down the street, and nobody in the Klan has any kind of grudge against either of them." He looked at his watch. "They should be back soon."

"But where is Pete Wilson? Why didn't he go with them? Isn't that why your father hired him?"

"Pete left a little while ago. I think Dad kinda wanted to have some privacy, and get away from Pete for a little while." Stan said. "I think that Pete wanted to take her. Also, I think he's getting tired of his role as our *protector*."

The ringing doorbell captured their attention. When Stan opened the front door he saw his father, who was pushing Bonnie Rose in her wheelchair. "We're home!" he yelled. "Lauren, your mother had a great time!" He turned to Bonnie Rose, "Didn't you, homey?" She nodded her head and smiled. It was the first time in several days that any of them had detected any emotion or noticed a smile from her.

Lauren hurried to her mother. She greeted her with a kiss and hugged her. "Wasn't that fun, Mother?" Bonnie Rose again smiled and nodded her head.

Lester said, "Next week I'm going to take her to the zoo— Right Bonnie Rose?" She again nodded and smiled.

Lauren was in a good mood. "Well, you came home at the perfect time. Lunch is ready!"

Lauren carried lunch to her mother in the living room, and then served the others at the kitchen table. The mood at the table was cheerful, for much of their conversation was about Kathy, and her gradual but steady improvement. After lunch, the men took seats in the living room while Lauren did the kitchen chores. Lauren's mother sat in her wheelchair, fussily toying with the remainder of her lunch.

Lester Mullins spoke to his son, "Stan, when sharing lunch we were talking about Kathy. I'm really happy that that she is doing well. Have you thanked God for your good fortune?"

"Dad, I've actually prayed for her on several occasions, but I doubt if it accomplished anything. I don't even know why I prayed. I guess when we get scared enough, we turn to anything, or anybody who might be able to help us—even if we really know it won't have any effect."

"But God sometimes intervenes, Son. Just like Lazarus, in the bible, sometimes He spares people from death!"

167

"Yeah, but sometimes He doesn't," Stan said. "One night while I was at the hospital praying for Kathy, an innocent little baby died just down the hall. If God is so merciful, why did He let that happen?"

"Who knows the ways of the Lord, Stan? Maybe he felt that that baby would be happier in heaven!"

Nick had been listening to the conversation in complete silence. He was hesitant to intrude on a discussion so personal.

Stan only shrugged. "Dad, I'm proud of you for your beliefs, and I'm sure you're sincere. I'm an unbeliever, but I would give anything to believe that! Oh, if it could only be true! "He slowly stood and walked out of the room.

Stan's father turned to face Nick. "Where do you stand in regard to your faith Nick? Are you like Stan? An unbeliever?"

The personal inquiry took Nick by surprise. He realized that some Southern people were inquisitive; however he found himself totally unprepared to answer such a blunt question.

"Mr. Mullins, I really don't know how to answer that. I suppose I'm a believer. By faith I'm a catholic. I once had my confirmation."

"Does that mean you've been *saved?* Is it the same ritual?"

"I suppose so, sir. I have never given it much thought. Why do you ask?" Nick felt awkward.

"I'll tell you why I asked that question, Nick. It's the most profound question that mankind has ever had to answer. And our eternal life depends on it."

"Well, I guess you could say that I'm sort of a believer, Mr. Mullins."

"*Sort of?* Our faith in God must be *total!* I worry about Stan. I can almost understand why he doesn't believe. After my religious experience I assured him that all of our lives would be better. But things have gotten worse. They are filled with trials and tribulation. We are constantly being threatened by our enemies, and we need protection in order to simply exist. That's why *now* is the time to trust God, for only He can deliver us from evil!"

"Yeah, maybe God could help us. But so would a gun!"

168

"I can understand your bitterness, Nick. I'm sorry that your return to Cedar Valley has turned out to be so full of hate and mayhem. But someday, the situation will get better." His expression was sad.

"I'll tell you when things will get better, Mt. Mullins. Whenever those Klan members are dead or rotting in jail!"

Stan's father answered the ringing telephone. After a brief exchange of words, he quickly hung up. "Nicky, that was Sheriff Kirkland on the phone. He wants me to come down to his office right away."

"Mr. Mullins, aren't you sometimes afraid?"

"Afraid of what, Nick?"

"Maybe some of the Klan members will try to seek revenge on you. What if they start recognizing your car? You keep driving your car around everywhere! Shouldn't you get Pete Wilson to take you?"

"Nick, the Klan has no grudge against me. I've done nothing to anger them. Besides, I believe God will keep me safe from harm."

"But what if the Klan realizes that we've moved in with you, and we're now living here? Wouldn't they come after you then? They might even try to do harm to your house. Remember, they burned that little shack where we used to be hiding."

"Obviously, they are not yet aware that you're staying with me. I don't believe the Klan has established an organized plan of attack on our group. I believe it's only a few individual members; after all, their attacks are only random. Most of the time we can even drive around in our own cars. If they were consistent in their attacks, we might able to fortify ourselves. Our problem is that we never know when to expect their attacks on us." He smiled at Nick before he left the house and drove away.

Stan walked back into the living room and took a seat. He asked Nick, "Did Dad give you a religious lecture?"

"Yeah, sort of. But he really means well, Stan."

"Yeah, I realize that. I admire my father, but sometimes his lectures get on my nerves. Besides religion, what did you and Dad talk about?"

"He talked mostly about how all of us have had to endure such abuse from the Klan members, and how life has been a living hell for all of us!"

"Yeah, these last few days have been the toughest times of my entire life, Nicky." Stan said.

"Cheer up, Stan! Kathy is getting better, and the trial will soon be over. Maybe the Klan will be convicted. No matter what the jury decides, we'll soon be completely free of constantly worrying about their dirty tricks."

"How do you figure that, Nicky? Those bastards are as mean as hell! They don't seem to have a conscience!"

"Well, if they're convicted, we won't be seeing them, because they'll all be in jail. And if they're acquitted, they'll all go free—so they'll no longer see us as a threat to them."

"Damn!" Stan said. "I sure hope they're not acquitted! I hope they're all convicted and sentenced to prison!"

"But that means that *you'll* also be sentenced to prison, Stan—because you were a member of the Klan!"

Stan began to consider the consequences. "Nicky I don't want to go to prison, but it will be worth it if we can convict the Klan! It's essential that our testimonies are well-received by the jurors. I want those bastards in jail!"

Nick felt sorry for him. "Stan, if the Klan members were convicted and you went to prison, what effect would it have on Kathy—and on your father?"

"I suppose that Kathy could weather the storm, but I'm not sure how my father would react." Stan said.

"You know Stan…I'm beginning to become emotionally attached to your dad. He's like a second father to me."

"Thanks, Nicky. I appreciate your feelings. Dad's a great guy. But I'm getting a little tired of the moral lectures he's always giving me."

Nick only smiled. "Hell, Stan, that's the way most fathers act toward their sons. Don't sweat it, man!"

When Lester Mullins walked into the office of Sheriff Kirkland, both the sheriff and the T.B.I. agent, Lieutenant Morton were waiting for him. He shook hands with them and sat in a chair facing the lieutenant. The Sheriff occupied his usual seat behind his desk. The agent began the conversation. "Mr. Mullins, since our last meeting I've done a considerable amount of investigation about the death of your brother, and I believe this is going to be a relatively easy case. I think I've already found the murderer."

With aroused interest, Stan's father instantly sat erectly in his chair. "Who is it? What's the man's name?"

"His name is Arthur Bowman. He's the brother of Sheriff Mullins' former maid. He had a grudge against your brother."

Lester Mullins sighed with relief. "You know, that doesn't surprise me! How did you track him down?"

"I questioned several of the suspects. Those ex-deputies known as 'Cowboy' Galyon, and 'Bird Dog' Johnson had motives, but not as strong as the motive of Bowman. Also, they were straightforward in their answers, while Arthur Bowman was evasive. I also interrogated some of the part-time deputies, but they had solid alibis. They had proof that they were out of town at the time."

"How did you obtain the information that enabled you to question these suspects, lieutenant?"

"I talked to that guy, *'Little' Billy Sneed.*, that 'jailhouse snitch', as you referred to him. But he didn't suspect Arthur Bowman. He seemed to believe that Galyon was the killer."

"How did you ever locate him?" asked Stan's father. "He usually just lives on the street."

"He doesn't live on the street anymore. He lives in a nice apartment. But he still dresses like a slob."

Sheriff Kirkland asked, "What's next, lieutenant? Should I arrest Arthur Bowman on suspicion of murder?"

'Yes, I think you should proceed with making the arrest. If he's innocent, he'll have his chance in court."

Stan's father asked, "Are you pretty sure about this guy's guilt, lieutenant? I'd really like to put this case behind me."

"Yes, sir. I'd bet on it. This guy had a stronger motive than any of the other suspects. He was really holding a terrible grudge against Sheriff Mullins, and his answers were very evasive when I questioned him."

Stan's father seemed relieved. "Well, I'll have to admit that you've made great progress. I feel much better about this case since you entered the investigation."

The agent stood. "Mr. Mullins, I just wanted to give you a report. I told you that Sheriff Kirkland and I would keep you informed about our progress. We'll continue to do so." He shook hands with both men and left the office.

Chapter 18

Both Nick and Stan reentered the courtroom with renewed confidence. In an attempt to erase the negative perception the jury had developed of their characters, Stan had recently talked with the prosecuting attorney, Timothy Steele. He requested that the attorney ask questions emphasizing their favorable traits when they gave their testimony. The courtroom was again overflowing with local people when the trial continued. Nick and Stan were accompanied by Stan's father. Pete Wilson, who was sick with the flu, had stayed at the Mullins home with Lauren and her mother.

At precisely 10:00 a.m. the judge, The Honorable Fred Daniels entered the courtroom and took a seat behind the bench. The jury also filed in and took their places in the jury box Out of curiosity, Nick glanced at the row of seats occupied by the defendants. They appeared to be unconcerned, and even bored. Some were whispering to each other while one of them was trimming his fingernails.

With a tap of his gavel, the judge stopped the noisy commotion and called for order in the courtroom. He then addressed the prosecuting attorney. "Counselor, the court is now ready to hear further testimony from the witnesses."

"Yes, your honor. I recall Stan Mullins as a witness for the prosecution." Stan stood and walked to the witness chair, where he was immediately sworn in. He was much more confident than he had been several days ago when delivering his previous testimony.

The prosecuting attorney began his line of questions on a positive note. "Mr. Mullins, you've already given testimony that you witnessed a double-murder that was committed by the defendants. Your testimony was quite convincing, I might add. When you testified a few days ago, the defense attorney tried to attack your character, instead of focusing on the things you witnessed. Rather than asking you to offer more incriminating testimony, I would like to make your story more believable by restoring your credibility to the court."

"Thank you," Stan answered.

"I understand that you come from a well-respected family, Mr. Mullins. Wasn't your father the mayor of this town?"

"Yes sir," Stan answered.

"And I notice that you have a college degree, and held a responsible position when you worked for your father as the manager of his home construction business."

"That's true, sir."

"You appear to be an honorable and respected man, Mr. Mullins. The only blemish that I can detect is your decision to become a member of the Ku Klux Klan. What made you decide to join that group?"

"At first I thought they were good for the community, but after they resorted to murder, I saw them for what they really are! It was the biggest mistake of my life, sir."

The prosecutor quickly modified Stan's answer. "Yes, it was a mistake, but you quickly corrected that mistake when you resigned. Anyone can make mistakes in his life! And why did you resign?"

"I resigned because I felt guilty after they committed the two murders." Stan seemed regretful.

"In other words, you had a change of heart! You felt compassion for the victims! That speaks well of you."

"Objection! Your honor. Counsel is leading the witness!" said Oliver Smith, the defense attorney. "Also, the court doesn't know, or even care, why the witness resigned from the Klan! And we question the assertion that he had compassion for the victims!"

"Objection sustained," ruled the judge.

"Well, let me approach that from a different perspective!" said the prosecuting attorney. "Mr. Mullins, you had enough compassion for the victims to risk going to prison with the other Klan members! I'd call that *compassion!*"

The defense attorney returned to his seat as Timothy Steele announced, "I have no further questions for this witness, your honor."

"The witness is excused." The judge seemed bored.

Timothy Steele had remained standing. "The prosecution recalls Nick Parilli." Nick stood and walked to the witness stand and took a seat, where he was immediately sworn in. Although he still had a few reservations about the outcome of the trial, he was reasonably optimistic.

The attorney smiled at Nick. "Mr. Parilli, your former testimony to this court was logical and believable. Therefore, I'm going to question you in the same way that I did your friend, Stan Mullins. Since the defense painted your reputation with a rather dirty brush, I'm going to attempt to restore your reputation and credibility to the court."

Nick only grinned. "After the hatchet job that lawyer did on me, I'm afraid you've got a difficult job ahead of you, sir." Some of the spectators chuckled.

"Well, let's see if we can give this courtroom a different picture of you, Mr. Parilli! I understand that you fought in the Korean War... Is that true?"

"Yes sir." Nick replied.

"Did you win any honors, or awards? I understand that you were awarded the *Bronze Star* for your bravery in battle. Is that true?"

"Yes sir. But what I did wasn't that heroic."

"Nick, why did you perform this act of bravery?"

"Sir, we often don't know why we do things."

"We do these things because we're *brave*, Nick. We are willing to sacrifice ourselves for others! I understand that you always tried to better yourself. After your discharge from the army... didn't you enroll in college on the G.I. Bill? And I understand that, in order to finance your schooling, you were willing to work at a lowly labor job."

"Yes sir," Nick answered.

"And what were you studying in college, Nick? What were you wanting to become in your life?"

"I was studying to become a lawyer, sir."

"So you believe in justice and fairness? That's quite a resume! Nick, tell me something. Why did you sneak into that Klan meeting, anyway? Didn't you realize the danger you'd be facing?"

"Well, at that moment I didn't think about the danger. I just didn't want them to horsewhip my Negro friend."

"Mr. Parilli, you are surely a compassionate man. I think the jury will consider this when they analyze the credibility of your testimony to this court." He slowly turned toward the judge. "Your honor, I have no further questions for this witness."

"The witness is excused," droned the judge.

Nick left the witness stand and walked back to his former seat.

The trial continued with the cross-examination by the defense. At the judge's request, Oliver Smith, the defense attorney stood in front of the witness, Stan Mullins when he returned to the stand. After being sworn in, Stan again took his seat in preparation of giving his testimony. He dreaded the ordeal he faced, for he remembered the arrogance of the obese defense attorney. In spite of his distaste of his interrogator, he felt optimistic about the outcome of the trial. The defense attorney hesitated before beginning. He finally turned to face Stan and smiled. "Well, here we are back again," he said, with a sarcastic grin. "Have you recently joined and *betrayed* any other organizations, Mr. Mullins?"

176

"I object your honor," said Timothy Steele. "The defense attorney is just taunting the witness."

"Objection sustained," answered the judge.

The obese attorney continued, "Mr. Mullins, did it ever occur to you that most of the twelve jurors don't even believe that a double-murder was ever committed?"

"No sir. Why would they not believe it when nobody can find either of these men? What happened to them?"

"Well, it's likely that the alcoholic preacher just left this area, and moved away somewhere. After all, he was just a *street person*. And as far as that black man is concerned, he probably just left this part of the country. There have been many runaway black men in the South. Nobody has missed these men. If they were murdered, where are their graves?"

"But what motive would I have to make up a lie? Why else would I feel compelled to leave the Klan?"

"Apparently, you had some kind of hidden motive. Who knows the reasoning of people *who have no loyalty?* And how convenient it is that we don't even have a murderer!" He shook his head and turned away from Stan. "Your honor, I have no further questions for this witness."

"The witness is excused," said the judge.

It was now time for Nick to endure the 'hot seat.' He strode to the witness stand and was sworn in before taking a seat. The defense attorney, Oliver Smith sneered as he stood in front of Nick. "Well, Mr. Parilli, I'm going to use the same tactic as the prosecution. I'm just going to briefly touch on the things we've already covered, such as your insubordination to your commanding officer in the midst of a battle, your court-martial, and your army jail-time. Instead, I'm going to focus on your reputation, and your character. The prosecution wanted the court to be aware of your *true character*. Well, let's elaborate on that a little more." He moved closer, so that their faces nearly touched. "You told the court that your preacher friend revealed himself to the Klan. Is that true?"

"Yes, He came out of his hiding place and confronted the Klan leader." Nick answered.

"And what did you do? You stayed hidden, didn't you?"

"Your honor, I object!" said the prosecution. "That incident has already been covered, and adequately explained."

"Objection sustained. Move on, counselor." The judge was growing impatient.

"Yes, your honor," he answered. He again looked at Nick. "Okay, let's move on, Mr. Parilli. Let's see now…A few years ago you tried to better yourself by entering some Yankee college. But you ended up as a college dropout. Why did you quit school?"

"I went into the army," Nick answered.

The lawyer sneered. "Oh, yeah! I almost forgot! And you were a *war hero* who won a bronze star, right?"

"I just tried to do my duty until I could finally get out of the army." Nick was becoming angry.

"You didn't like the army?"

"Not particularly."

"What did you think of the Korean War, Parilli?"

"To be quite honest, I thought it was a bunch of crap! The war was unwinnable!"

"Then you weren't very *patriotic*, were you?"

Nick grew even angrier. "Why are we discussing this, sir? What does this have to do with the case?"

"Objection!" protested the prosecution. "Your honor, I don't understand the relevance of this line of questioning!"

"Objection overruled!" said the judge. "I believe most of these questions are certainly relevant. They help establish the credibility and character of the witness!" He looked at the defense attorney. "You may proceed, counselor."

"Thank you, your honor!" The attorney became even more candid. "Parilli, you say that you want to be considered a principled man! But in recent years, you haven't behaved in a way to enhance your reputation. You not only were a college dropout, but since you came to Cedar Valley your choice of friends has been questionable!"

Nick glared at him. "What's wrong with my choice of friends? All of them are good people!"

"*Good people*? Let's evaluate just how good they are! First of all, one of your best friends was a black man who was accused of molesting a little white girl. And another of your close friends was that itinerant drunken preacher!"

"But it was never proven that Rufus ever molested anybody! And the preacher was a righteous man! Both of them were gentlemen!"

The attorney grinned. "*Gentlemen*? What's *gentle* about a black man fondling a white girl and a preacher that can't even stay sober? Your bad judgment gets even worse, Parilli! It's been proven that you're a jailbird! Last year's police records show that you assaulted two police officers, and that you were arrested twice—once for drinking illegal whiskey."

"But I didn't drink any of that whiskey! The deputies poured it all over me to make me smell like booze! And..."

"You always have an excuse, don't you Parilli? I've done a lot of checking up on you! Let me just sum up all your *good qualities:* You're an unpatriotic, drunken brawler who has bums for friends. You tried to elevate your status by marrying the daughter of the former sheriff, but that only resulted in the sheriff telling you to *get the hell out of town!*"

Nick was now seething with rage, for he felt like attacking the defense attorney. He somehow held his temper and asked, "Sir, are you almost finished questioning me?"

"I'll let you know when I'm finished, Parilli! I only have one more question for you: Sometimes a liberal Yankee feels that he can correct some of the so-called racial prejudice of the South. Did some Yankee do-gooder pay you to come to the South and be a rabble-rouser? Maybe this so-called murder never actually happened!"

Nick could no longer suppress his raging anger. "You're damned right it happened! And I resent your..."

The attorney interrupted, "I have no further questions for this witness, your honor!"

"The witness is excused," said the judge.

179

Nick left the stand and returned to his seat beside Stan and his father. Stan could easily detect the depressed mood of his friend when he gave him a reassuring hug. Nick only stared at the floor in disappointment.

The interrogation of the defendants was very brief and almost comical. One Klan member at a time took the stand, with each of them repeating almost verbatim the exact words supplied to them by the defense attorneys. Many of them spoke with an ignorant dialect: *'Yep, we burnt a cross and whupped a nigger for stealin' chickens that night; but he wasn't this guy, Rufus...it was a different nigger. And they wasn't no murder took place, neither. And we didn't see no strangers at th' Klan meetin'....Just members of th' group. An' we all went home early.'*

Although the prosecuting attorney did his best to convict the Klansmen, his efforts were in vain; for the cross-examination of the defendants produced an identical reply from each defendant. The entire procedure had been well-rehearsed, for each Klan member quoted a monotonous monologue, only the repetitious words of the previous defendant. The judge often used his gavel to restore order, for the testimony of the defendants often brought peals of laughter and frequent hand-clapping from the group of local people in attendance.

Both Nick and Stan realized that, for them, the trial was over. Their further participation would only consist of sitting and waiting. The judge sent the jurors to their room to deliberate. Except for the reading of the verdict, all that remained of the trial would now take place inside the jury room. Either a guilty verdict or complete exoneration of the defendants would be decided by the simple procedures of deliberation, discussion, and the casting of votes.

The trial was one of the shortest in the history of the county, for the jury deliberated for less than an hour before reaching a verdict: The grand finale occurred when the jurors returned to the courtroom. The jury foreman handed the written verdict to Judge Fred Daniels, who acknowledged the result. The foreman then stood before the court and read the verdict: *Not Guilty.* The courtroom erupted in cheers.

To most of the citizens of Cedar Valley, the verdict was a victory, but to both Stan and Nick, the decision was a profound miscarriage of justice. However, this travesty had one redeeming feature: With the acquittal of the Klan members, Stan had also been spared, for a manslaughter conviction could have resulted in years in prison for him.

In an attempt to lift his spirits, Nick pointed this out to him; however, Stan was deeply disappointed in the jury's verdict. He had ambivalent feelings about his good fortune, for his sense of relief was mixed with a deep feeling of guilt over the deaths of Rufus and the preacher. He considered the unfairness of the verdict as he realized that he and the Klan members had gotten away with their complicity to murder.

Chapter 19

On the morning after the trial had ended, the family group was settled into the living room of the Mullins home. While Pete Wilson was still sleeping in one of the bedrooms, Lester was kneeling in front of the wheelchair in an attempt to entertain and comfort Bonnie Rose. Lauren was distraught when she walked to the couch and took a seat between Nick and Stan, for the Lester Mullins household was almost totally absorbed in despondency. Both Lauren and Stan's father made many futile attempts to revive the sagging sprits of Nick and Stan. While Nick still struggled with his anger toward the defense attorney, Stan was more upset about the outcome of the trial, for he suffered from a gnawing sense of guilt. Although the *not guilty* verdict had saved him from prison, it had also suddenly condemned him to a world of emotional suffering.

However, when Nick began to view the outcome of the trial, he thought of the brighter aspects of the unjust verdict. He smiled and said, "Stan, maybe you should think of the good things that came from that verdict. First of all, you weren't convicted of anything, so you're free! And since the Klan has been declared innocent they will no longer feel threatened by any of us! All of our entire family is free!"

Stan's expression remained gloomy. It seemed that his sadness grew worse. "I'll never be free, Nicky. Not until I see those Klan members either dead or in prison!"

"Stan, get over it! You did your best! You were even willing to go to prison to do the right thing!"

"That's the whole point, Nicky," Stan said, "I risked my freedom in order to atone for my sin. But I was denied my vindication. I desperately needed to know that Rufus and the preacher didn't die in vain, and that their lives were worth something! A conviction would have reassured me of that! Don't you see?"

"Of course I see! But we're dealing with *reality*, Stan! And that reality is that the Klan members were acquitted. Learn to live with it!"

Stan's face expressed extreme anger. "Since you're talking about *reality*, Nicky, let me give you *more reality!* You said that since the Klan has been acquitted, it sets us free. Well, those bastards had better start worrying about their own freedom! For weeks our family has been threatened with death! That sniper tried to murder Kathy! We've been *the hunted*! But I intend to reverse that trend! Beginning at this very moment, the former *hunted* are going to be become the *hunters!*"

Nick was surprised. "Do you mean that we should try to ambush them, Stan? I don't know… Our family is no longer in danger. Maybe we should just let well enough alone."

"Do you mean that you're not going to avenge some of those things they did to us? That's not the Nicky I remember!"

"Stan, let's look at the practical aspect of this. Retaliation could land us in jail." Nick explained. "But I'll admit that the Klan getting off scot-free presents another problem: One of them might be guilty of murdering your uncle."

"I don't think so," Stan said. "None of the Klan members were being tried for that crime. That's a separate case that the T.B.I. is handling. Maybe they can come up with something. You know, Nicky, we may never locate the murderer of my uncle."

Lester Mullins disagreed. "I don't think the murderer of my brother was a Klan member...At least not according to Lieutenant Morton of the T.B.I. He suspects another person."

For the first time, Lauren spoke "Who does he suspect?"

"He believes that Arthur Bowman killed him. If you'll remember, he's the brother of your dad's former maid. You know, Lauren, she was like a mother to you."

Lauren asked, "Does Willie Mae know about this?"

"I don't know. But he's recently been arrested and charged with murder." He sighed with relief. "I believe my brother's murder has been solved!"

"But why does the T.B.I. agent think he's guilty?" Lauren asked.

Lester Mullins picked up the ringing telephone. "Excuse me, Lauren," he said. He then spoke into the phone. "Hello? Yes, this is Lester Mullins. How may I help you?" He listened for a long while. His face paled when he continued. "Did you say that you're calling from *Park West Hospital?* Ma'am, you should speak to my son, Stan about that." With a grim expression, he handed the telephone to Stan.

Stan talked briefly to the woman on the phone and finally hung up the telephone. His face registered shock. "I've got to hurry to the hospital! Kathy has taken a turn for the worse!"

Stan temporarily left the others behind. Within minutes, he was hurriedly driving toward *Park West Hospital*. His mind was in turmoil. The phone call had caught him completely by surprise, for he had begun to believe that Kathy's condition was rapidly improving.

He pulled his vehicle into an empty space and hurriedly ran up the steps into the hall that led to Kathy's room. When he entered, he noticed a doctor and a nurse hovering over her bed. She was unconscious and again receiving oxygen, and an IV was attached to her arm. When the doctor noticed his entry into the room, he turned to face Stan and immediately shook his hand. "Mr. Mullins, my name is Dr. Stafford. Last night your wife began to experience difficulty in her breathing. We discovered that she has an infection in her right lung."

"How bad is the infection, Doctor Stafford? Do you think she has a good chance to recover from this?"

"We haven't yet made that determination. It's a bit early to speculate, but it's definitely a backset to her recovery."

Stan was devastated. "But Doctor...I thought she was steadily improving!"

"She was, Mr. Mullins, and if we can cure this infection, she'll continue to improve. We're giving her antibiotics, and I feel that she will quickly respond. Just think positive. I can assure you that she will receive the best of care." Both the doctor and the nurse turned to leave.

"May I stay in the room with her?" Stan asked.

"Of course," the doctor replied. "But we gave her some medication to make her sleep, so she may not be awake for a while." The doctor and his nurse closed the door behind them.

For hours Stan remained by her bedside. During that time another nurse entered the room and informed him that his father and Nick had arrived and were now in the waiting room. Stan began to have morbid thoughts: *What will I do if she dies*, he wondered. With nowhere else to turn for help, he lowered his head and prayed.

Stan continued to sit by her bedside for more than an hour. When she still hadn't awakened, he finally left the room and walked to the waiting room to welcome his father and Nick. Upon first seeing him, they both stepped forward and hugged him. Both men offered condolences before taking their seats beside him.

Stan looked at his father. "How can I manage to endure it if she dies, Dad?"

"Son, you need to pray for her. God often delivers us from these kinds of sad circumstances."

"Dad, I've already prayed for her. I've tried prayer on other occasions, but it doesn't seem to work for me."

"God sometimes answers our prayers in different ways, Stan." his father said. "Just continue to pray."

Nick asked, "What do the doctors say about her, Stan" Do they believe she'll pull through?"

185

"They talk encouraging, but they don't know anything for sure. She now has an infection in her lung, and she's again on oxygen." Stan said.

"Just try to keep the faith, Son," said Lester. "I have a feeling that she's going to pull through this crisis."

Stan bowed his head. "Oh God, please don't let her die!"

Nick placed his arm around his friend. "Stan, Lauren wanted to come with us, but she thought it best if she stayed home with her mother. She said to tell you that she is saying a prayer for Kathy."

Stan said, "Thank you, Nicky."

The three men spent hours in the waiting room. It was a time in which a repeated mention of Kathy was deliberately avoided. They discussed many things that loomed ahead in the future. In an effort to cheer Stan, Nick mentioned that the recent acquittal of the Klan members had freed them from harassment and attempts on their lives because their enemies no longer felt threatened. They also discussed the drastic change that would soon take place in their living arrangement. Since they would no longer have to hide from the Klan, there would be no need to live in the Lester Mullins home. Nick offered a suggestion to Stan's father. "Mr. Mullins, I know that you would be glad for us to stay with you, but there's no longer a necessity for it. I guess that Lauren, her mother and I will move back into the home of your brother—Sheriff Mullins old home-place. Since we no longer have to hide from the Klan, we'll be safe there now."

Lester Mullins was saddened. "Yes, I suppose that makes sense." He turned to Stan. "Son, I suppose you'll continue to live with me…Right?"

"I guess so, Dad. I won't have any choice. If Kathy pulls through, she's gonna need a place to recuperate. By the way, Dad…What about Pete Wilson? We won't be needing his protection any longer. Are you going to dismiss his services?"

"I'm glad you mentioned that, Stan. I just learned that Pete is trying to place his aging mother into a local nursing home.

If he succeeds, he says he's returning to his former home in Chicago. Until he has her placed in a home he'll be needing a place to stay. He can stay with me if he chooses. Or he may prefer to stay with Nick and Lauren."

"'He's welcome to stay with us, Mr. Mullins," said Nick.

Stan suddenly stood. "I'm still pissed about that sniper shooting Kathy. That shot was meant for me, you know!"

Nick said, "We realize that Stan. But at some point, we just have to let go of our hatred. We've been at war with these guys for a long time. Maybe it's time to end it."

"But what if Kathy dies? What then?" Stan asked.

"Then we should find out who the sniper was, and have him arrested. Let the court handle it."

Because of his extreme anger, Stan no longer attempted to hide profanity from his father. *"Let the court handle it?* Damn it Nicky, you saw how that damned rigged jury handled our recent case! Hell, they acquitted the bastards! And you said that I should first identify the sniper! I already know who it was! Remember Skip Hickman, the guy you slapped after our testimony? If you'll remember, he recognized my new car! How else would he identify my car, so he could shoot at it?"

Nick felt sympathy for Stan. "Stan, I can understand how you feel. But at some point this violence needs to end. We need to let the law punish the perpetrator!"

"Nicky, I'm beginning to become a bit disgusted with your obsession with adhering to the letter of the law! You've always been this way! It's time to realize that sometimes we make our own justice!"

Doctor Stafford walked into the waiting room and went directly to Stan. "Mr. Mullins, your wife is on her way to surgery. She's still asleep, so there's no need for you to visit with her. Our staff will keep you notified of our progress and of any changes in her."

Stan was shocked. "But why is she being taken to surgery? I thought you said the antibiotics would heal her infection!"

"Sir, we certainly hoped so, but her infection is worse, and she is having a difficult time with her breathing. Also, we haven't been able to awaken her. We'll keep you informed."

Stan suddenly stood. "Where is she now?"

"She is just now being taken down the hall toward the surgery room. Would you like to see her for a moment?"

Stan was panicky. "Oh, yes! Please let me see her!"

Lester and Nick followed Stan into the hallway. The movable operating table was being pushed down the hall just ahead of them. Out of respect for Stan's private moment with his wife, Stan's father and Nick turned back toward the waiting room. The attendant stopped pushing the table and stepped aside with the doctor as Stan hovered over her. She seemed to be sleeping peacefully. He cuddled her slender body and whispered something into her ear before tenderly kissing her. He watched as Kathy was pushed into the surgery room. After the door was closed, Stan broke into tears as he walked back down the hall toward the room where his father and Nick were waiting for him.

For a long while they all remained silent after Stan re-entered the room, for Stan's tears had created an awkwardness between them. They all took seats together. In an attempt to console his son, Lester Mullins hugged him and tried to reassure him with comforting words. "Son, please just put your trust in God and he will heal Kathy. You're lucky, because she will return to you. But I'm much less fortunate, because your mother is gone from my life but will never return to me. This is a cross I'll always have to bear."

The war of words between Nick and Stan was temporarily postponed, for it had been buried beneath the traumatic event of Kathy's upcoming surgery. For the remainder of the long day, Lester Mullins and Nick stayed with Stan in the waiting room of the hospital, awaiting some hopeful news about Kathy's surgery. As twilight approached, Nick remained with Stan while Lester again hugged his son and told him goodbye. He had decided to return home and stay with Bonnie Rose, giving Lauren an opportunity to join Nick and Stan.

Twilight had gradually faded to darkness when Lauren arrived at the hospital. She immediately hugged both Nick and Stan and asked about Kathy. They were fraught with worry as they sat together in the waiting room. To distract their minds from worry, they talked of many events of the past, and the time when Stan and Kathy had first met. Sometimes during the long hours of reminiscing, Stan would stop talking, and hang his head in sadness.

Later in the evening Dr. Stafford entered their room. Stan quickly stood and asked, "How did the surgery go, doctor? Is she going to be okay?"

"The surgery went reasonably well, Mr. Mullins. Your wife is now in her room and is breathing much better. Her lung had collapsed, so we had to get it repaired. She is still under the influence of anesthesia, so it will be a while until she is fully awake. I wouldn't advise visiting her just yet, for she can't communicate with anyone, and she needs her rest."

"How is her chance of complete recovery?" Stan asked.

"Complete recovery? Mr. Mullins, we're really not ready to discuss that yet. I'm just hoping she lives."

Stan was shocked. "Do you mean she could possibly die? How would you classify her condition?"

"I'm sorry, Sir, but her condition is listed as critical." He looked at Stan with sympathy before he turned and left the waiting room.

By midnight they were tired and emotionally drained. But their exhaustion was trivial when compared to the heartbreak they suffered when the doctor re-entered the room. He looked at Stan with sympathy when he told him the sad news: "I'm sorry, Mr. Mullins, but your wife just passed away."

Chapter 20

After the death of Kathy, Stan became silent and withdrawn, sometimes behaving as if he were in a trance. He was like a man possessed with a demon, for his mind became dominated by a maniacal fixation on revenge. His initial sadness became replaced by a seething hatred.

The funeral was immediate, and only a private affair. Since Stan hadn't placed the information in the obituary section of the local newspaper, only a few people knew of her death. Consequently, it was only a small, dismal ceremony in which Stan simply went through the motions when being offered comfort. Only a few people were in attendance. During the burial ceremony at the gravesite, he was even more reclusive. With no desire to associate with people, he sought solitude. Although Kathy had numerous friends, the small gathering denied her many final farewells.

Following the funeral, it was nearing twilight when Stan joined his family group at the Lester Mullins home where a family mourning was in process. Lauren prepared a light dinner, but only Lester and Pete Wilson nibbled sparingly on the food. Nick realized that Stan wished to be alone, so he and Lauren took a seat on the couch, while Stan became more withdrawn and retreated to the bedroom. The mood in the household became a mixture of despair and unbelief, for the sudden death of Kathy had been a complete surprise.

After a brief dinner in the kitchen, Stan's father followed Pete Wilson into the living room where they sat on the couch facing Nick and Lauren. "I hate to bring it up at a time like this," Lester said, "but there are a few things that we all need to discuss."

Nick said, "Yeah, I know, Mr. Mullins. Maybe we should involve Stan in our discussion. He's back in the bedroom. Do you want me to call for him?"

"No, Nick, I don't want to burden him with simple things right now. Let's let him be alone in his grieving. Stan will conform to whatever we decide. First of all, we need to discuss where we'll all be living. Of course you are all welcome to stay here, but since we no longer need to hide from the Klan, there's no reason for all of us to live here at my house. Obviously, Stan will stay here with me. Nick, you and Lauren may wish to move back into my brother's house—I think Lauren would like that."

"That would be fine, with us, Mr. Mullins," Nick said.

Lester turned to Pete Wilson. "Did you ever get your mother placed in a local nursing home, Pete?"

"Yes, all but finishing a little paperwork. I'd like to stay somewhere here in Cedar Valley until my mother is admitted. Then I'll be going back to Chicago."

Stan's father said, "Well, Pete, you're welcome to stay here for free with Stan and me. Or you might prefer living with Nick and Lauren...The choice is yours."

"Thanks, Lester," said Pete, "I appreciate it."

Lester smiled. "I'm really going to miss all of you."

Lauren was sad. "Mr. Mullins, you've been so good to us. I really feel like you're a second father to Nick and me."

"Thank you, Lauren. By the way, what are your long-range plans? Are you and Nick going back to Louisiana?"

Nick said, "Yes, we're definitely going back, but first I may have to get a job here until I can accumulate a little money. Lauren and I are getting a little low on funds."

Lester asked, "Is Lauren going to sell my brother's house? After his death, the house would obviously go to Bonnie Rose, but because of her mental condition, I'm sure it will automatically become the property of Lauren. It will bring quite a bit of money, you know."

"Yeah, I guess she'll sell it eventually. But first Lauren and I are going to take her mother back to Louisiana with us."

"Nick, get the house appraised and I might buy it. It will make a great investment."

"Yeah, it will eventually sell for a big sum of money. But Lauren and I need money *now!*"

"Stan's father said, "I anticipated that. I know that both you and Stan must be running short on money. I'll help you."

"But you've already helped us enough, Mr. Mullins. I don't want to take your money as a gift. The only way I would accept money from you is in the form of a loan. I want to pay you back."

Lester said, "Okay, if it would make you feel better, we'll call it a loan. Nick, this has been a tough time for all of us. Maybe we can again have peace. With the arrest of Arthur Bowman, I believe they've captured my brother's killer. Maybe we can all start living normal lives again. I think our troubles are all behind us."

Everyone looked up when Stan came out of the bedroom and nervously paced the floor. His father became concerned about his anxiety. "Stan, we've been discussing a few things that you should be aware of. It seems that this war we've had with the Klan members is over. Also, it appears that they've caught my brother's killer. We need to stop any further retaliation. I think the others are moving into my brother's house, and I assumed that you were going to live with me."

Stan seemed to be in a state of confusion. "Whatever you say, Dad." He stopped pacing. Without further explanation, he said, "I've gotta get out of here for a while." He walked to the door and left the house, leaving the others bewildered.

On the following day, the move to the home of Sheriff Mullins was a simple undertaking. Nick, Lauren, and Pete Wilson gathered up their few items of clothing and drove with Bonnie Rose the short distance to their new home. Stan had been gone for the entire night, and even into the early afternoon hours of the following day he still hadn't returned. His father was terribly worried about him. That evening, Lester Mullins was completely devastated when, without notice, Stan returned home long enough to gather his belongings and move out of his house to an unknown location.

Upon their return to Sheriff Mullins' former residence, Nick and Lauren were disheartened by the deterioration of the surrounding grounds. The grassy area of the yard had grown into a patch of weeds, and the shrubbery needed pruning; also, the interior of the house was dust-covered and smelled musty. The next couple of days were spent in cleaning the place. Nick hired a grounds-keeper to improve the yard, while he and Pete Wilson helped Lauren clean and refresh the interior. Lauren's mother seemed more content, for she was happy to again be living in the home that vaguely brought back memories.

One evening when Lauren's mother was dining in her wheelchair beside them, Nick and Lauren were sharing dinner with Pete Wilson. Nick began to worry about Stan's mysterious disappearance. He asked Lauren, "Where do you think Stan has gone? I've called his father a couple of times and he is really worried. Do you think he'll finally return?"

"I don't know, Nicky. At the moment Stan is extremely depressed about the sudden death of Kathy. I hope he'll finally be able to put this terrible event behind him."

Nick said, "He seems to be in a fog. I wish he'd go home."

Lauren changed the subject. "Nick, we can't continue to worry about things we can do nothing about. We're finally free from all the stress we've endured! I need to get away for a while and enjoy our freedom!"

"That's a good suggestion, Lauren. Where would you like to go? I'm sure that Pete would stay here and watch over your mother...Right Pete?"

"Sure, I don't mind. Feel free to go wherever you please. I need to stay and do some things here at home. Besides, Lauren, your mother and I are becoming big buddies!"

Lauren became excited. "Let's go back to the lake where we enjoyed the Mimosa Festival last year! I think they're going to celebrate it again this weekend! Nicky, that's where we had our first real date! Remember?"

Nick said, "Lauren, I don't mind taking a couple of days to relax and enjoy ourselves, but beginning next week, I'll need to find some kind of job. We need the money. Remember, you and I will be returning to Louisiana in autumn."

"But didn't Uncle Lester promise to let both you and Stan have some money?" Lauren asked.

"Yeah, but that's only a loan, Lauren. I promised to pay him back."

Lauren laughed. "You're the same old *honest Nicky!*"

On Saturday morning, Lauren and Nick left their new home and drove Lauren's car to the Mimosa Festival. For the first time in weeks they behaved like excited teenagers, for their newfound freedom had returned them to a carefree mood. Nick drove Lauren's car through a maze of vehicles and parked in a grassy field by the lakeside.

The couple engaged in several activities of this time of renewed freedom. The day was bright and sunny, and the blue sky was unblemished by a single cloud. Memories of their first date returned to them as they relived last year's event. Only a few cars were parked in the field, for it was still too early for the festival to begin. From the lake the monotonous drone of a motorboat reflected the mood of the lazy summer day.

By mid-morning people began to arrive in droves. As in last year's event, food stands were scattered through the park offering all kinds of refreshments. The tantalizing aroma of

194

cooking foods reminded Nick of last year's festival, and the unexpected joy he had experienced with Lauren.

On the lake, a motorboat towed a water skier between the lazy sailboats; and on the nearby shore at least a dozen children were frolicking among the slides, swings and a large sandbox. Preparations were being made for a multitude of recreational activities, and under the protective umbrella of a large oak, a string band was warming up, and a barbershop quartet was practicing in a shady clearing near the lake. For the less energetic or adventurous, several park benches were situated beneath the shade of several mimosa trees near the lakeshore, where parents could enjoy a brief respite from attending to their energetic children. From a loudspeaker, strains of country music echoed through the park area.

Nick and Lauren strolled down to the lakeside, where they fed the gathering of swimming ducks the crumbs from the cheese crackers they had recently bought; and later in the day, they engaged in games with other couples. At twilight, they remembered their participation in last year's square dance; as a result, they joined the group and danced until late in the evening, when the group finally disbanded.

After the dance ended, they again strolled to the lakeside. Darkness had brought cooler air. A soft breeze from the east stirred the surface of the lake, pushing miniature breakers ahead of it, gently caressing the shore. The brilliant moon had risen higher in the sky, and cast a shimmering path across the surface of the water, and a stronger breeze ushered in the fishy aroma of the lake. When Nick again held her in his arms and kissed her, vivid memories returned. A year ago, it was a similar moment beside the lake when he realized that he had fallen in love with Lauren. Their lakeside rendezvous was a liberating experience that gave them a renewed view of life.

On their homeward journey Nick decided to search the want ads for a job opportunity, so they drove into Cedar Valley to buy a newspaper. As Nick continued to drive, Lauren leafed through the paper. The headlines shocked her: *Local man shot to death.* The continued story stated that no one knew the identity of the shooter. The murdered man was Skip Hickman, the Klan member that Stan suspected in Kathy's death—the man that Stan had vowed to kill.

When Lauren read the news to Nick, he immediately slowed the vehicle. "Lauren, that's the guy who threatened Stan during the trial! Stan swore he was going to kill him! If he carried out his threat, he's started this damned war all over again! The Klan is sure to retaliate!"

She said, "Nicky, don't jump to conclusions! Stan may not even be involved in that awful killing! Maybe it's only a coincidence."

But Nick knew better. He understood Stan well enough to remember his insatiable thirst for vengeance. The liberating dream that had lured them into memories of the past had suddenly evolved into a nightmare.

Chapter 21

Early the next morning Nick was awakened by the ring of the doorbell. He was exhausted as he slowly rose from the bed, for he hadn't slept well. Because of the headlines in the local newspaper, his night had been mostly sleepless. He slipped on his robe and opened the front door. He wasn't at all surprised when he saw Stan's father standing on the front porch. He rubbed the sleepiness from his eyes, "Hi, Mr. Mullins, come in. I've been expecting you."

When Lester Mullins stepped inside he was holding a newspaper in his hand. "Have you seen the headlines in the local newspaper, Nick?" His hand trembled as he held the paper. "According to the news, one of the Klan members has been murdered!"

"Yeah, I read it last night. I didn't get much sleep because I thought about it for most of the night."

Nick continued to stand as Stan's father slowly took a seat in one of the recliners. He unfolded the newspaper and pointed to the headlines. "According to the paper, the Klan member's name was Skip Hickman! Isn't he the guy that Stan swore he was going to kill?"

Nick sat on the couch. "Yes, that's the same man."

"Well, do you think Stan killed him? He was acting strange when I last saw him! He seemed to be full of hate." Lester was obviously in despair.

Nick shrugged. "Mr. Mullins, it's possible that Stan didn't kill him. Maybe it's only a coincidence. I notice that the police don't have any suspects in the case. The shooting happened in an isolated part of town, and whoever killed him apparently just sped away in an unidentified vehicle."

"Nick, I pray to God that Stan hasn't started to get revenge against those guys. I just hope he hasn't started on a killing rampage!"

Both men looked when Lauren entered. She pushed her mother to a comfortable area and immediately walked to Stan's father. She leaned over and hugged him. "Hi, Uncle Lester," she greeted. She saw the newspaper in his hand. "I'll bet you came here because you're worried about Stan."

He smiled at her. "Yes, Lauren. Do you think that Stan had anything to do with this killing?"

She reassuringly hugged him. "Probably not, Uncle Lester. It could have been anybody. After all, Klan members make many enemies."

With an expression of anger, Lester said, "If Stan did this terrible thing, I'm sorry for the victim's family. But I'm even more regretful about the consequences for us, because this means retaliation from the Klan. *The War continues!*" He left his seat and walked to the wheelchair. He then leaned forward and hugged Lauren's mother. "I need to be going," he said.

Nick stood. "Where are you going, Mr. Mullins? Stay and have some coffee with us."

Lester looked at his watch. "No, thank you, Nick. I'm going to snoop around town and see if I can find out more information about that murder. Somebody surely knows more about it than that newspaper's report. Also, I need to find out the whereabouts of Stan. Somebody surely knows where he is staying. He hasn't been home for more than two days now."

After again hugging Lauren's mother, He said his goodbyes to the others and left the house.

Pete Wilson walked into the living room. He was tucking his shirt tail into his pants. As he entered the room, he rubbed his eyes and yawned. "Got any coffee brewin' Lauren?"

Lauren only sighed. "No, I just now got out of bed, Mr. Wilson. But I'll get some coffee started." She left for the kitchen.

Pete looked at Nick. "Good Morning, Nick," he said, "When I went to bed last night I overheard you and Lauren as you sat in the living room. You were talking about a murder somewhere here in town." He took a seat on the couch.

Nick explained the report of the shooting to him as Pete attentively listened. "Wasn't that Stan's dad who just left?"

"Yeah, that was Mr. Mullins. He's really worried about Stan. Poor guy! Hell, he's about to go nuts!"

"Does he think Stan had anything to do with killing that Klan member?" Pete asked. "What do you think, Nick?"

"Yeah. As much as I hate to admit it, I believe Stan is the guilty party. I know how vengeful he can be."

"Well, I'll be damned!" said Pete. "I knew he was as stubborn as hell, but I never even thought he was capable of murder!" Pete clumsily pulled up his pants as he stood. "Listen, Nick, after I have some coffee I'm going into Cedar Valley and attend to a few things. Tell Lauren not to make any breakfast for me. I'll just eat in town." He walked into the kitchen for his morning coffee.

After Peter Wilson left the house, Lauren wheeled her mother into the kitchen where she served breakfast to her as she joined Nick for their morning meal. Their breakfast was mostly consumed in silence as they both reminisced about their contradicting moods of the previous day: The pleasant memories of their former courtship was in direct opposition to the horrible news awaiting them at home. Lauren's eyes became moist when she thought of the contrast.

Peter Wilson had been gone for a couple of hours. Lauren was cleaning up the kitchen while Nick was sitting on the living room couch searching through the want ads in the local newspaper for some kind of employment. When the phone rang, Nick immediately answered. The caller was Pete Wilson. "Nick, you may not believe this, but somebody just killed another Klan member! He was shot in the head!"

Nick was shocked. "Who was killed, Pete? What was the man's name?"

"The guy's last name is Johnson. Most people referred to him as 'Bird Dog' Johnson. He was once a county deputy for Sheriff Mullins."

"When and where did this happen?" Nick asked.

"It happened early this morning at a beer joint in Loudon, Nick. A place by the name of, *The Red Top Tavern.*"

"How did it happen, Pete? Did anyone witness it? Does anyone know the identity of the shooter?"

"No. Nobody has any idea who shot him. It happened in the parking lot. The place was almost empty, so not many cars were parked there. Whoever shot him just got the hell out of there in a hurry!"

"Where did you hear about this?"

"Hell, Nick, it's all over town! The newspaper still hasn't had time to write a story about it. Do you believe that Stan did this killing?"

"Yeah, I do, Pete! But I want you to keep quiet about it, okay? Don't breathe a word about this to anybody! Stan's in deep trouble! I'm afraid he's on a rampage! I wonder how many Klan members he intends to kill?"

"Hell, Nick, I don't know. I just hope Stan never gets mad at me about anything!"

When Nick hung up the telephone, he immediately called Lauren back into the living room. When he explained the telephone discussion with Pete Wilson, she was not only stunned, but also heartbroken. "Nicky, what are we going to do about this? It seems that Stan has gone crazy!" She began to cry. "This terrible news is going to kill his father! Do you think the police will arrest Stan? "

"Lauren, it's only a matter of time until Stan is arrested and charged with murder. Sheriff Kirkland has recently hired a couple of competent deputies. Stan is on a mission! He may keep killing Klan members until he is caught."

"I wonder what made him single out 'Bird Dog' Johnson as his next victim?" Lauren asked.

Nick pondered the reasoning behind Stan's choice of victim. After considerable thought, the answer became apparent: Johnson was one of the key suspects in the murder of Sheriff Mullins; also, Nick remembered Stan's hatred of him when 'Bird Dog' had behaved so cowardly during their fight at *The Red Top Tavern.*

"Lauren, I wonder where Stan is hiding?" Nick asked. "He must have rented a room somewhere! Surely he realizes that the police will suspect him of these killings! They know that he wants revenge because some of the Klan members have been constantly harassing us, and were found *not guilty* in the murders of Rufus and the preacher!"

"Nicky, did it ever occur to you that Stan may not be guilty of these killings?" she asked.

"You keep saying that, Lauren! That's just some of your wishful thinking. Stan is guilty! I know how vengeful he is."

"What do you think will happen to him, Nicky?"

"He'll continue to kill Klan members until they're all dead, or until he's arrested." Nick said.

Lauren continued to cry. "Nicky, I believed that all of this hatred was behind us! If Stan did this, I'm afraid that he has started it all over again!"

"I know that, Lauren! I'm worried that some of these Klan victims have relatives or close friends who might retaliate against us! Also, they might suspect that Stan is living here in this house with us! Damn! I'll be afraid to leave you and your mother alone!"

Chapter 22

Several days passed and still no one had heard a word about the whereabouts of Stan. Because he was so worried about him, Lester Mullins had visited with Nick and Lauren on numerous occasions and had made many phone calls. Also, the police were suspicious of Stan. Sheriff Kirkland had visited with Nick in his search for him, but he quickly realized that Nick knew nothing of his whereabouts. So far, the police had gotten nowhere in their investigation.

Nick was completely puzzled about Stan's behavior. He wondered where he could be hiding, and why he hadn't made an effort to contact him. It was as if he had evaporated into thin air. Nick spent much of his idle time worrying, and pacing the floor, for he felt a desperate need to talk with Stan. Much of his time was a combination of anxiety and boredom.

The days became uneventful. Nick was bored, Stan was still missing, and the murder investigation was at a standstill. As a result, Nick decided to move on with his life. While seated on the couch in the living room, he began searching through the want ads in the newspaper. When he called for Lauren, she came from the kitchen and took a seat beside him. "I've decided to look for a job," he said. "I'm getting bored."

"She was surprised. "But Nicky…You don't need a job right now. Uncle Lester agreed to let you have money if you need it. Besides, we'll be going back to Louisiana soon."

"Yeah, but I intend to pay him back. Lauren, I don't expect a free ride from Stan's father. Anyway, I'm about to go *stir-crazy*. But maybe our stressful situation is gradually returning to normal, because it appears that Stan has stopped his murderous rampage."

"But it's possible that Stan didn't kill anybody, Nicky. Think positive! Maybe he's just gone off by himself to brood over losing Kathy." Lauren said.

Nick said, "God, I hope you're right, Lauren."

"Have you found any job possibilities in the want ads?" she asked.

He pointed to an advertisement. "Here's a part-time opening at *The Royal Café* for a waiter. But it's a night job. That's the only one I found except for a couple of construction jobs. I hate to take a job when Stan's situation is still so unresolved, but Lauren, we need to get on with our lives."

Pete Wilson steered Lauren's mother into the living room and parked her wheelchair beside the couch. He smiled and said, "Lauren, your mother and I have recently become big buddies. Let me show you what she can do." He placed a crayon between her fingers. In a wobbly fashion, she drew a few crude smudges on the pad in front of her. Pete laughed and pointed at the smear of color. "Who says this ol' gal doesn't have talent? Why, she might even become an artist!"

Nick said, "Pete, Lauren and I really appreciate the fact that you're entertaining Lauren's mother. I can see that you've become emotionally attached to her."

Pete sighed. "Yeah, I guess so, Nick. Playing little games with her gives me something to do. Sitting around all day doing nothing can drive a man nuts! I guess I'll try to find a job pretty soon. I finally got my mother into a nursing home. I guess I'll stay near her for about a month and then I'll be returning to Chicago." He grinned. "I think my wife, Helen has decided to forget about our divorce."

"That's great news, Pete! I'm glad for you. What kind of job are you looking for?"

Pete appeared to be embarrassed. "Nick, if you promise you won't get mad at me, I've got a confession to make."

"What kind of confession, Pete? Who did you murder?"

"Well, I didn't murder anybody, but I did something pretty bad. I pretended to be somebody that I'm not." He fumbled for words. "I told Lester Mullins that I was a private investigator, but I never held that kind of job."

Nick became curious. "What kind of job did you have in the past?"

Pete looked away in shame. "I was a used car salesman."

"Really? Have you ever held a job that required doing any kind of police work??"

"Yeah…I was telling you guys the truth about being a Chicago policeman in the past."

"What were your main duties as a Chicago policeman? Were you involved in solving crimes?"

"Well, not really. I was mostly a traffic cop."

Nick was puzzled. "Then why did you pretend to be a private eye, Pete?"

"I've just always had a burning desire to be a private detective. I guess it was just a dream of mine that would never become a reality. My unrealistic dreams were the main cause of my wife wanting a divorce. I'm sorry, Nick."

"Pete, how did you ever get the credentials that identified you as being a private eye? You sure had me fooled!"

"If you know the right people you can obtain any kind of phony credentials. That part was easy."

Nick frowned at him. "You sure pulled the wool over our eyes, Pete! What about your expertise with a gun, and the bulletproof glass in your vehicle? Were they just scams, too?"

"That claim of bulletproof glass was a bunch of crap. Most people don't even know what it looks like. But my expertise with a gun is authentic! I'm a crack shot with a pistol! And I worked as a bodyguard for more than a year for a man in Chicago. So I wasn't lying when I said I could protect your

204

family. I'm sorry about any trouble I caused, Nick. I just felt like confessing this to you."

"I wonder why Lester Mullins didn't look into your background more carefully?" Nick was still puzzled.

"I guess he was just gullible, But Stan saw through my guise pretty quick. He's sometimes a pretty observant guy."

Nick laughed. "I guess I'm also gullible, Pete. I believed your story, too."

"You know, Nick, sometimes you're too trusting for your own good. It's a dishonest world out there!"

Nick only chuckled. "Well, Pete, you sure pulled a fast one on our family. But don't continue to feel guilty about it. What made you decide to confess this to me?"

"I began to feel guilty. I felt that I needed to confess to somebody."

"But why me?"

"Because I felt safe with you. If I confessed to Lester Mullins, he would have preached me a sermon. And if I confessed to Stan, he probably would have killed me. It became pretty obvious that I wasn't authentic to you guys when I started making mistakes. And I'll admit that I wasn't very skilled when it involved investigating people. Also, when my wife threatened divorce I became too frustrated to think very clearly."

"Pete, I'm encouraged to hear about your former job as a bodyguard, and your skill with a gun. Maybe the Klan won't bother us anymore, but if they do, it's possible that someday we might still need some protection from you."

Shortly before dark on the following day, Nick prepared to apply for an evening job as a waiter at *The Royal Café*. When he drove into town he wondered if he could contact any of Stan's friends in order to learn of his whereabouts. In search of a familiar face, he spent almost an hour visiting the poolrooms and bowling alleys in the area; however, after questioning a couple of Stan's acquaintances he ultimately abandoned the search.

Because the downtown area was small, he quickly located the restaurant. It was an outdated establishment with a dim neon sign in the window. Nick parked in front and entered.

Inside the dimly-lit interior only a few customers were seated in booths. Since he could see no employee or manager in the dining area, Nick made his way to the kitchen where he saw a middle-aged, heavy-set man preparing food. When Nick introduced himself, the man cleaned his hands on his apron and turned to face him. "Can I help you sir?"

"Well…Maybe." He shook the man's hand. "Are you the owner of this restaurant?"

"Yes, sir."

"Well, I'm looking for a job. I saw your ad in the local paper. I understand that you need a waiter."

While the employer began asking the usual questions, Nick overheard a noisy disturbance coming from the front of the café. With curiosity, he followed the owner into the dining area. A few of the customers were staring out the front window while a couple of others had left the restaurant and gazed into the distance from the street.

"Man! That must be a terrible fire!" said a customer, "It's lighting up the whole sky!" Nick heard the screaming wail of sirens as he followed the restaurant owner to the sidewalk where they inspected the bright horizon. It suddenly occurred to Nick that the brilliant glow was coming from the exact direction of the Mullins home.

He quickly left the restaurant and ran to Lauren's car. In less than three minutes he was within a couple of blocks from the burning house. When he came closer to the home, Nick's heart was racing as he got his first glimpse of the raging fire. It was the Mullins home. *Oh God, please let everyone in the house be safe!* he silently prayed.

A column of jet-black smoke towered upward, rising high into the sky. When he turned the final corner, the burning house was in full view, revealing a horrifying scene of complete mayhem. Because of the frantic activity surrounding the fire, Nick had to park his car a block away. Several vehicles and dozens of people surrounded the house from at least a hundred feet away from the fire. The intense heat made a closer position impossible.

The hungry flames had burned completely through the roof, leaping skyward to great heights. Windows exploded, sounding like shotgun blasts as the intense internal heat sent shards of glass flying into the yard. Two fire trucks spewed thousands of gallons of water into the hellish inferno, but with little effect. As the fire grew more intense, it became obvious that it would ultimately consume the entire house.

Nick left the car and ran toward the fire, wending his way through the crowd of onlookers, looking at their faces, in a frantic search for Lauren and her mother. As he reached the front edge of the ring of people, he was suddenly restrained by two firemen. Although he was still a considerable distance from the fire, the heat was almost unbearable. The firemen warned, "Get back! Get back!" as Nick struggled to free himself from their grasp.

"Some of my family is in there!" Nick screamed.

"Don't get any closer!" shouted one of the firemen, "We looked earlier, but we didn't see any evidence of anyone who might have escaped the fire. Keep searching! You might find your relatives somewhere among the crowd! But it's useless to try to go any closer! Nobody could possibly be alive in there!"

Nick broke free and ran toward the burning house, but the unendurable heat drove him back. *The fireman was right,* he thought. *Nobody could be alive amid such hellish heat.*

Nick was becoming panicky when a man among the crowd noticed him frantically scurrying around. The man called to him, "Is this your home?"

"Yes! I'm searching for my wife! She was inside the house when it caught fire!"

"I think you've found her, mister!" he said, "She's lying over there on the ground! She seems to be doing reasonably well, but she's pretty badly burned!"

Nick rushed to her side and knelt beside her. He took her in his arms and cried bitterly as he cuddled her close to him.

In an obvious state of shock, she was clad only in her panties and bra, for the fire had burned away her clothing; also, her body displayed several severe burns. Her state of awareness fluctuated, and she bordered on delirium. As her voice broke into incoherent sobs, she tried to explain the disaster to Nick. In a disjointed monologue, she related her last hour of horror.

Nick was finally able to comprehend the terrible truth: Both Lauren's mother and Pete Wilson had died in the fire.

Chapter 23

The aftermath of the disastrous fire brought many changes to the lives of Nick and Lauren. She was immediately taken to the emergency room of *Park West Hospital*. After she was admitted, Nick spent the majority of his time there. Although she had suffered several severe burns, her condition was listed as serious rather than critical. Also, since they no longer had a place to live, Nick found it necessary to move back into the home of Lester Mullins. Upon her release from critical care at the hospital, Lauren was expected to join him.

Both Nick and Lauren were deeply saddened by the death of Lauren's mother; in fact, her demise in the fire became a threat to Lauren's recovery. Because of her constant tears, Nick found it nearly impossible to console her. Also, the unexpected death of Pete Wilson bore heavily on Nick's mind. At first, Nick had been surprised that such an agile man had died in the fire; however, Lauren explained his final act of heroism: During his long stay with Nick and Lauren, Pete had developed a child-like penchant for playing games with Lauren's mother. When the fire suddenly burst out of control, he was entertaining her in the kitchen, while Lauren had quickly escaped out the front door. When Pete noticed the speed of the fire, he had unsuccessfully tried to push Lauren's mother to safety in her wheelchair, but the flames engulfed them before he was able to maneuver it through the door. Lauren was guilt-ridden because she had survived while her mother had perished in the inferno.

When Nick thought of Pete Wilson, he felt a deep sadness. The man was a contradiction: While it was true that Pete had been an imposter, he was like many ambitious people: He simply nourished dreams of success that were, for him, unattainable. It was indeed a twist of irony that with his confession to Nick of his dishonesty, he displayed a profound honesty that exonerated him.

The funeral for Lauren's mother was held at Smith's Mortuary. Because of Sheriff Mullins' former popularity, many mourners attended; however, Lauren's confinement to the hospital was even more traumatic because the funeral was delayed until she was able to leave the hospital. Pete Wilson's remains were shipped to Chicago for burial.

Immediately after the fire, Nick had been puzzled about its rapid pace. Prior to the fire, he had only spent a short span of time in the town before he discovered the tragedy. *How did it expand so rapidly that it completely engulfed the house in only a matter of minutes?* he wondered.

The puzzling question was answered when he received a police report from Sheriff Kirkland. A thorough investigation by the police confirmed that the fire was a case of arson. After the fire, several empty cans that smelled of gasoline were discovered in the yard beside the Mullins home. The fire had been deliberately set.

Upon this discovery, Nick became enraged, for some outlaw group had deliberately caused injury to his wife and killed his wife's mother. In addition, the fire had claimed the life of Pete Wilson. He began to have a more profound understanding of the hatred displayed by Stan.

After Nick took Lauren to the home of Lester Mullins he began to spend many long hours at her bedside. The recent fire had left Lauren with a deep feeling of guilt, for she had earlier entrusted the care of her mother to Pete Wilson, while she was lazily napping on the living room couch. She became consumed by a selfish feeling, for she feared that she had neglected her own mother. Nick found it very difficult to absolve her of self-imposed guilt.

Lauren's physical condition improved, but her emotional wounds remained. After her return home, her mental state became unpredictable, for her mood of peace and contentment could quickly change to a disposition of sadness.

Nick began to wonder if she needed treatment from a psychiatrist. Lester Mullins often attempted to brighten her spirit, but his cheerful talks of pleasant moments seemed meaningless to her. Lester was also in need of encouragement, for he had still heard nothing in regard to the whereabouts of Stan. The mood of the household became dismal.

As the days passed, Nick began to feel even angrier about the recent fire. He began to understand the vengeful attitude of Stan. But his craving for revenge was far less demanding than his desire for peace. Retaliation would lead to a continuation of hostilities, which could result in *all-out war* with his enemies. He and Lauren had too much at stake to risk the suffering involved in attaining such hostile retribution.

The ringing telephone aroused Nick from his sleep. Lauren was snoring as she lay beside him. He checked the time: 7:00 a.m. *Who would be calling at this early hour?* he wondered. Ordinarily, he allowed Stan's father to answer the phone; however, Nick remembered that Lester had made an early trip into town. He reached to the nightstand and picked up the telephone.

Nick was caught by surprise when he heard the voice of Stan. 'Hello? Who am I speaking to? Is this Dad?"

"Damn, Stan! It's about time we heard from you! This is Nick! Your father had to go into town for something! Where have you been? Your dad and I have been worried sick about you! What have you been doing?"

211

"Hi, Nicky. I'm glad I'm talking to you instead of Dad. I'm not quite ready to listen to one of his sermons. I just heard through the grapevine about your house burning down. I just wanted to express my sadness. That's a tough break, pal. And I'm sure you can identify the responsible party!"

"Of course I realize *why* it was done, but I don't know exactly who did it."

"You know damned well who did it! It was the Klan!"

"Yeah, but I can't identify any *specific people* who might have done it, Stan."

"Nicky, you don't need to know the exact names of the people who torched your home! Hell, if you kill all of them, you've found and punished the guilty bastards!"

"So it was *you* who killed the two Klan members! I was hoping that you weren't involved! Damn, Stan! What do you plan to do?"

"I plan to continue the things I'm doing. I'm hiding where the police can't find me."

"Stan, do you realize that your retaliation is the action that caused our house to burn? Why do you insist on keeping this war going? When will it end?"

"It will end when all of those bastards are dead! Nicky, there's a tremendous difference in the way you and I see things! You've always believed in obtaining justice through the court system. Well, what kind of justice did we receive during the Klan trial? I guess you're pissed at me for killing those guys. Evidently, you think I'm responsible for the fire. Nicky, I just did what I had to do! One of those bastards killed my wife!"

"That's true, Stan. But Kathy was killed by only *one of them*. They're not *all* guilty! Do you plan to keep on killing them until they're all dead, or until you're caught?"

"Nicky, Kathy wasn't the only victim. Those guys also were responsible for the death of Rufus and the preacher. Also, I'm sure that one of them killed my uncle, Sheriff Mullins."

212

"Stan, I'm not pissed at you. I understand. I forgive you for anything you've done. When will I see you again?"

"Nicky, my past relationship with you means more to me than anything, pal. But I'm afraid that our good times together are over. Obviously, it's only a matter of time until the police locate me. I just have one more chore to perform and my mission will be complete. Tell my dad that I'll try to contact him later"

"I'll tell him Stan. What are your future plans?"

For a moment, Stan hesitated. "Well, I don't have any long-range plans. A guy in my predicament can't plan a bright future. But for now, in order to escape being captured I intend to leave Cedar Valley forever. You'll never see me again, pal. So long, Nicky." He hung up the telephone.

"Stan! Wait a minute! Stan!" Nick yelled into the phone; however, the conversation was over. With sadness, he slowly hung up the phone. His mind became flooded with precious memories of his long association with his best friend: their college years, Stan's generosity, a close friendship in Cedar Valley, and their plans for the future. He realized that they were almost opposites in personality; however, they had shared a friendship that had transcended their differences. Nick was heartbroken to realize that this strong bond had suddenly come to an end. He stood by the phone and wept.

Nick was in a sad state of mind for the remainder of the week. *Why had Stan ended their relationship so abruptly?* he wondered. *What was his remaining chore on his mission of vengeance?*

Lauren was still in bed when Stan's father returned from his trip into town. Nick immediately told him of his earlier phone call from Stan. Lester became excited. "Where is he?" he asked. "Is he coming home?"

"He didn't tell me where he was calling from," said Nick. "I'm sure he doesn't plan to come home. He doesn't want anyone to know where he is, Mr. Mullins."

Lester's face registered sadness. "Well, I guess that means he's guilty of murder. Why else would he be hiding?"

"Yes, Stan admitted the killings to me, "Stan said.

"Did you try to get him to surrender to the police?"

"No sir. Stan would never do that. He feels justified in his actions. I believe he's glad he killed them."

"But maybe if he surrendered, the court might go easy on him! Just look at all the things we all endured before he finally took action! I think the case might be dismissed!"

"Yeah, maybe so, Mr. Mullins. But I don't believe that Stan would ever give up to the authorities."

"Did he say that he'll call back again? I need to talk some sense into his head!"

"Yes, he told me he'd call you," Nick said. "He said he was leaving Cedar Valley."

"He's leaving? For how long?"

"He said he was leaving this area permanently. He even told me goodbye."

"My God! Does that mean I'll never see him again? Surely he doesn't mean that!"

In an effort to comfort him, Nick said, "I think he meant it, but I still I think he'll come back someday."

"Where do you stand on all of this, Nick? Is Stan justified in committing murder?"

"Mr. Mullins, I feel like killing them myself, but murder can never be justified. If we keep killing, where will it end?"

"Nick, if you receive another call from him when I'm not here, would you please try to talk him into surrendering to the police?"

"I'll try, but I don't think he'll ever give up." When the conversation was over. Stan's father wiped tears from his eyes and returned to his study.

Although the mood of the household remained sad, the daily routine returned to near normal. Since Lauren's mood swings had begun to stabilize, she resumed her responsibilities of preparing meals and housekeeping, for staying occupied with chores had become her coping mechanism. Nick had

214

abandoned any attempt to seek employment, and Lester Mullins spent much of his time either isolating himself in his study or attempting to console Lauren.

On an early Sunday morning, Stan's father suddenly displayed a drastic mood swing. He invited Nick and Lauren into the living room where they took seats facing him. He was already dressed in his most fashionable Sunday suit when he began his appeal to them. "I need to talk to both of you about something," he said. "All of us have allowed circumstances to dictate our attitudes. Well, I've had enough of it! We need to start thinking positive! Nick, look at all of the great things in our lives! First of all, if Stan will come home and turn himself in to the police, I think the courts will go easy on him. Also, I know that you and Lauren feel that you suffered a great loss when your home burned. But your loss was only *sentimental*. You didn't really experience a *financial* loss!"

Lauren asked, "What do you mean, Uncle Lester?"

"Well think about it. All you've really lost are *memories!* Lauren, you and Nick will collect enough insurance on that mansion to support you for years! When I was in town yesterday, I checked with the insurance company. My brother had that house insured for a fortune!"

"Mr. Mullins, that's great news. But I'm too worried about other things to celebrate." Nick said.

Well, that's not all of the good news, Nicky! Lauren is getting much better! And with their arrest of Arthur Bowman, the police has solved the murder of my brother! Just think! We can all begin our journey toward recovery now!"

"I guess I should be happy about the good things that have happened, and I'm overjoyed about Lauren's improvement. But I'm still sad about the death of Lauren's mother...and the way Pete Wilson died."

"Nick, Lauren's mother was completely miserable while she was alive. According to the scriptures, she is really in a better place now. Be happy for her! But I agree with you about Pete Wilson. That's sad. You know, he was really a pretty nice fellow."

215

"Mr. Mullins, Pete was a nice guy, but he was also a phony. He was never a private detective."

"What do you mean, Nick?"

"He confessed to me that he was a used car salesman. The only affiliation he ever had with the police was as a traffic cop in Chicago. Maybe you should have checked his credentials more closely."

"Well, I'll be danged! He sure had me fooled! But it all turned out okay, because Pete did a pretty good job as a bodyguard for our family, and the T.B.I. agent solved the murder of my brother. But it sure saddened me to learn of Pete's death."

"Yeah, I still miss the guy," said Nick.

Stan's father suddenly stood. "Well, that brings me to the reason I invited you into the living room to hear my little appeal. I want both of you to attend church with me today! With God's help, we all can begin our lives anew!"

Nick was hesitant. "Mr. Mullins, thanks for the invitation, but I don't believe that Lauren feels like attending church this morning. I think she might wish to stay at home and rest. I want you to know that I really appreciate the way you tried to lift Lauren's spirits, and the gentleness you extended to her mother. I also admire your positive attitude about the future. We'll try to attend church with you next week."

"That sounds good to me, Nick." He prepared to leave.

"Aren't you going to stay for breakfast?" Nick asked. "Lauren was planning to cook something for us. Weren't you honey?" She smiled and nodded her head.

"No, I'll have breakfast in town," he answered. He started for the door and abruptly stopped. He turned to face them and said, "I'm going to hold you to that promise you made."

Nick asked, "What promise?"

"Your promise to attend church with me next week, Nick."

Chapter 24

When he heard the loud knock on his front door, House Cat Jennings rolled over in his bed and turned on his bedside lamp. A glance at his wristwatch revealed the time: *9:15 a.m.* He silently cursed as he slowly crawled out of bed, for his night had been mostly sleepless. His jittery nerves had kept him lying awake for most of the night. He had finally dozed off at near daylight, only to be abruptly awakened by the loud knocking on his door.

Who in th' hell could be calling on me at this early time? he wondered. He dreaded the remainder of the day, for it would involve more suffering from his withdrawal symptoms. He had only stopped taking his daily dosage of opiates a couple of days earlier, and each hour of the day brought more shaking and nausea.

Because of his slight fever, he suffered from the chills; consequently, he was dressed in woolen pajamas. Without bothering to dress himself, he threw back the heavy covers and slowly positioned himself in his wheelchair when he heard another knock at his door. "Damn it! Wait a damned minute! I'm comin'!" When he opened the door, he shielded his eyes from the morning sun. Stan Mullins stood in the doorway.

"Well I'll be damned!" he exclaimed, "If it ain't my ol' buddy Stan!" The men exchanged handshakes.

"Hi, House Cat," Stan greeted. "It's great to see you again."

"You too, ol' buddy! Come on inside." Stan only continued to stare at him. He was shocked when he first looked at his old friend, for his appearance had undergone a drastic change since their last meeting. Stan noticed the feverish temperature of his trembling handshake, and studied his emaciated appearance. His complexion was extremely pale, and he appeared to have lost a considerable amount of weight. Because Stan was hesitant to begin the conversation by mentioning his visible deterioration, he pretended to ignore the obvious.

But House Cat was perceptive. He quickly recognized Stan's expression of shock. "I know what you're thinkin,' Stan. You're noticin' how terrible I look since th' last time you seen me. Well, I've slipped quite a bit since then." He moved aside in his wheelchair. "Hell, come on inside, pal. I don't want to spend th' entire day shootin' th' shit in th' front yard."

When Stan walked into the shack he left the door open, for the heat inside the house was sweltering. While house Cat remained in his wheelchair, Stan took a seat in a nearby rocking chair. "What's happened to you, pal? Have you been sick?"

House Cat was trembling. "Hell, I'm *just now gittin' sick!* If you'll remember, th' last time you visited me, I told you about my pain from my war wounds an' how I was tryin' to kill th' pain by takin' drugs that I was buyin' from 'Little Billy' Sneed. Well, I'm sufferin' withdrawal from some of th' drugs I've been takin'. I just quit a couple of days ago, so my body ain't adjusted to th' change yet."

"Well, I'm glad you quit, House Cat. But maybe you're having withdrawal because you stopped taking the drugs too abruptly. Maybe you should have tapered off, instead."

"Stan, I ain't never been worth a shit at taperin' off anything. The only way for me is to brave it cold turkey!"

"You've been spending quite a bit of money on those drugs, haven't you?" Stan asked.

"Hell yes! I was spending half my government check on that crap. And the worse th' pain got, th' more drugs I had to take! Also, Billy Sneed kept goin' up on th' price of th' drug. I'm sufferin' now, but I've got a hell of a lot more money."

"How have you been buying these drugs from Billy? Do you drive to his house?" Stan asked.

"Yeah. He ain't got a car."

"Can you drive okay with only one leg, House Cat?"

"Yeah, as long as I strap that contraption in th' corner to my right half-leg. I have to step on th' gas with my left foot."

"What did Billy Sneed think when you quit paying him for the drugs? Did it piss him off?"

"Yeah, he got madder than hell! He even offered to sell me some of th' drug for half-price, in order to keep me hooked! I told him to stick th' drugs up his ass!"

"I'll bet that remark pissed him off." Stan said.

"Yeah. But he's mostly mad at me because I stopped payin' him! He swore to get revenge on me! But that little shit don't scare me!"

"Good for you, pal!" said Stan.

House Cat became angry. "What am I going to do, Stan? I'm caught between a rock an' a hard place! I need th' drugs to kill th' pain, but it's breakin' my ass financially to keep payin' such a ridiculous price for 'em! Billy Sneed is livin' in a fancy apartment on my money! If I could sneak into his place whenever he's gone, I'd steal th' damned drugs!"

"I don't believe I'd do that, House Cat. Take it from me, you don't want to become a wanted man!"

House Cat changed the subject. "Stan I'm glad you came to visit me because I've got a couple of questions to ask you. First of all, th' last time I saw Billy Sneed he told me that Sheriff Mullins' house burned down."

"Yeah, it sure did, House Cat. I hated to hear the awful news. Nicky and Lauren were living there at the time, and Lauren's mother and another guy died in the fire. Obviously, the Klan did it!"

"Damn, Stan! Those bastards! An' speakin' of th' Klan...A couple of guys were killed recently. I suspect they were members of th' Klan, but I don't know for sure. I remember that you hate th' Klan. Did you have anything to do with their deaths?"

Stan rocked slowly in his chair and calmly answered, "Sure, House Cat. As a matter of fact, I killed both of them."

House Cat was stunned. "You *killed* them? Does anybody else know this?"

"Yeah. I guess everybody in Cedar Valley knows it. The police department is also looking for me."

"What do you intend to do, Stan? Are you goin' to surrender and depend on th' mercy of th' court? By the way, Stan, where have you been hidin'?"

"Just anywhere I could lay my head, House Cat. Obviously, I couldn't go to Dad's house. I rented a room in Sweetwater for a few days, and I also stayed in Loudon. I was wondering if I could stay here for a few days."

House Cat sat up in his wheelchair in a feigned indignant manner. "Stay here? Are you kiddin'? Do you expect me to get arrested for aidin' an' abettin' a criminal? You've gotta be shittin' me!" He then burst into laughter, and spoke seriously. "Hell, Stan, stay here as long as you wish. I wish you would kill every one of those cowardly bastards! I heard about that raw deal you got at that farce they called a trial! How long would you like to stay here?"

"For only a few days, House Cat. The local police are after me. To keep from rotting in prison, I'll soon be leaving Cedar Valley for good."

"Where's your good friend, Nick these days, Stan? Does he know you killed those Klansmen?"

"Yeah, he knows. I called him and told him goodbye. I'll probably never see him again. Damn! That was a tough decision to make! Also, before I leave, I'll need to call Dad and tell him goodbye."

"How is th' investigation going about th' murder of Sheriff Mullins?" House Cat asked.

"Dad says they have caught the killer. The police recently arrested Arthur Bowman and charged him with the murder, I guess that case has been solved."

House Cat only shook his head. "Th' police arrested th' wrong man, Stan. Th' jury will never convict that guy. After he's acquitted, th' whole damned investigation will start all over again. Half th' people in th' county will become a suspect! Th' real killer is one of those damned Klansmen, probably Cowboy Galyon. I heard that he even threatened to kill Sheriff Mullins. That's th' reason I'm glad you're killing those bastards! I hope you kill 'em all! I can guarantee you that whenever th' Klan members are all dead, you'll never need to search for the killer again. You'll be solvin' two murder cases: the murders of both Rufus and Sheriff Mullins."

Stan said, "Well, I guess I'll solve both cases because I intend to kill them all!"

House Cat smiled. "Stan, that's th' only way you'll ever find peace. Also, people are beginnin' to get tired of bein' suspected of murder."

Stan asked, "House Cat, didn't you once tell me that Billy Sneed could furnish anything to a guy for a price?"

"Sure, Stan. He must have good connections, because he can furnish almost any kind of weapon. Hell, he can get guns, knives, or poison, if a man is willin' to pay th' price!"

Stan grinned. "Do you think he could provide me with some dynamite?"

"Dynamite? What do you want with dynamite, Stan?"

"Can't you guess? If I could only discover where they meet as a group, I could quickly put an end to my mission."

House Cat smiled. "Hell, Stan, I can help you with that."

"How?" Stan asked.

"Before Billy Sneed and I became enemies, he told me of a Klan member who was hooked on drugs. Billy was sellin' 'em to him. The Klan member blabbed to him about their next meetin' place."

"Where, and when?" Stan quickly became interested.

"They're meetin' at an abandoned church buildin' out in th' country. It's a September Labor Day celebration."

"Can you show me this old church building?"

"Sure, Stan. An' I can also provide you with dynamite. Hell, you don't need Billy Sneed for that! When I was in th' house construction business, I sometimes had to blast away an old house to make room for th' new structure. Dynamite is easy to get for a construction man!"

"Damn, House Cat! My little plan is coming together! Can you show me how to use the stuff?"

"Sure, Stan. You just have to be careful with it."

"Why are you so willing to volunteer your help? What's in it for you?" Stan asked.

"Pal, you'd be surprised to know what's in it for me, so I'll just keep that reason to myself. Also, th' Korean War taught me to look at life different. Why shouldn't I help you? In life, a man is forced to choose between two things: right, or wrong. Th' Korean War was *wrong*. Durin' that time I killed many men for no reason. But durin' th' war I kinda got used to killin' people. I'd kill a man in a minute if I thought he's pushin' me aroun.' But why use dynamite, Stan? You're doin' a pretty good job th' way you're killin' 'em off one at a time!"

"I'm an impatient man. The police is after me, and I don't have time to accomplish my goal by performing one task at a time. House Cat, did you ever watch a dramatic play?"

"I can't say that I have, Stan. Why?"

"The elimination of the Klan in Cedar Valley is much like a dramatic play. It is a story that consists of three acts: Act 1 was when I killed Klan member Skip Hickman; Act 2 was my killing of Bird Dog Johnson; and Act 3 is the most important, for it will be the grand finale. I have only one remaining chore, and I'd like to finish this play with one final act."

Chapter 25

Conditions were gradually returning to normal in the Lester Mullins household. Lauren had improved both physically and emotionally, and Stan's father was greatly relieved because his brother's murder had apparently been solved. Although Nick continued to worry about Stan, he realized that both he and Lauren needed to move forward with their lives; as a result, he was mostly biding his time until they could return to Louisiana in autumn and resume their former lives.

Shortly after breakfast one morning, Lester retreated to his upstairs study while Nick and Lauren went outside to rearrange some of the shrubbery in the front yard. Involving herself in difficult tasks was Lauren's method of coping with the stress she had endured for so long. She was feeling particularly ambitious when she decided to attach a vertical string of roses to a trellis at the corner of the house. Although Nick volunteered to install the arrangement, Lauren, who had a greater interest in flowers, insisted on doing the job. "Nicky, men don't appreciate beautiful plants. Bring me a stepladder out of the garage and I'll string these roses up the trellis." Nick immediately obeyed. Unfortunately, when she climbed the wobbly ladder, it fell over into the yard. In the process, Lauren suffered a broken leg. While Lauren cried out in pain, Nick dashed inside and called an ambulance.

Without disturbing Stan's father in his upstairs study, Nick hurriedly called *Park West Hospital,* which sent an ambulance that arrived in less than ten minutes. Nick jumped into Lauren's car and followed the ambulance until it arrived at the hospital, where the emergency staff quickly wheeled her into a room. While he tried to console her, Lauren continued to cry out in pain. After sitting with her for a lengthy time, he finally returned to the hospital office to fill out the necessary paperwork.

When he hurriedly returned to her room, her pain had mostly subsided, for she had been given an injection of pain medication by one of the nurses. He continued to sit beside her for a long while. She began to cry. "Nicky, things were getting better until I had to pull this stupid stunt of breaking my leg. What else bad can happen to us?"

"Don't worry about it, Lauren. You'll heal in a few days."

"But we're supposed to return to Louisiana soon. I'll have to wear a cast in the classroom while I'm teaching!"

"Maybe you can hop around on one leg when you're chasing your students." His remark brought a laugh from her.

In a short while, a nurse's aide wheeled her into an operating room where she was scheduled to undergo surgery. Nick sat in the waiting room for a couple of hours before she was finally returned to her original room. Throughout the entire incident, Lester Mullins had been unaware that Nick and Lauren had even left the house. Nick immediately called him on the phone and explained the details.

Lauren was still sleeping when Nick left the hospital and returned to the Mullins home. The unexpected and stressful ordeal had consumed his energy. Stan's father joined him as they drove away for dinner in a downtown restaurant. Soon after, Nick returned to the hospital where he spent several hours talking with Lauren in her room. When she retired for the night, Nick drove back to the Mullins home and joined Stan's father.

They stayed awake until after midnight, sitting in the living room while discussing how their lives had intertwined.

Stan's father appeared to be sad. "While you and Lauren were at the hospital today, I received a call from Stan."

Nick quickly became interested. "What did he have to say? Has he decided to surrender to the police?"

"No. He only justified what he had done and told me goodbye."

"Well, was it a permanent goodbye, or does he plan to return?"

"I think it was permanent, Nick. His tone had an ominous finality about it. I don't think that any of us will ever see him again."

Nick looked at him with sympathy. "Gosh, I'm sorry to hear that, Mr. Mullins. But you've certainly been very good to Stan."

"But I haven't *always* been good to him. When he was young I was often cruel to him. I took away his confidence, and seldom gave him credit for his good qualities,"

"But you have a good relationship with him now. And I know how you feel. Stan is not my blood-kin, but I've always felt like he's my brother."

"Well, that assessment goes two ways, Nick. Since you and Lauren have moved in with me, I've come to think of both of you as my children. When I think of my sins against Stan, I'm burdened with guilt. But I can't atone for my sins, because we can't change our past. It will be a part of us forever. All we can do is to live our lives *in the now!*"

"That's a good way of seeing things, sir." Nick said.

"Nick, when you return to the hospital to see Lauren, I'd like to go with you. And by the way, I promised I'd let you have money for expenses, but because of all the confusion in our lives, I've almost forgotten it. When your fire insurance pays off, you can pay me back." He opened his billfold and counted out a generous amount of money. Nick realized that the discussion resembled a father and son conversation.

225

Nick and Lester Mullins drove separate cars when they had breakfast in town and went to room 201 in the hospital to visit with Lauren. She was in much better spirits.

"How's my little sweetheart this morning?" asked Lester, as he leaned over the bed and kissed her on her cheek.

"I'm doing better this morning, Uncle Lester! And who's that handsome guy you brought in with you?" When Nick kissed her, she hugged him tightly.

"Well, I can see that you're in a better mood this morning, honey!" Nick said. "I brought your Uncle Lester with me so he can cheer you up, but I can see you're in better spirits than either of us!"

"Nicky, I began to realize just how lucky we are! We'll soon be going home to Louisiana, and we've got a whole life ahead of us! Nicky, we…"

Lester interrupted. "Lauren, you mentioned going back *home to Louisiana.* Why can't you think of Cedar Valley as your *home?"* How would you like to make your home with me? I'd love to have both you and Nick staying with me!"

"But Uncle Lester…Nick is going to college there and I've got a great teaching job. We could never give up those things!"

"But Nick could get his college education here, and I'm sure you could find a good teaching job! I've already lost my wife Mary Jane, and it appears that I've also lost Stan. I'm a lonely man, Lauren! And I have this big house…"

"Have you heard from Stan, Uncle Lester?"

"Yes. He called and told me goodbye."

"But I'm sure he'll come back! He loves you and Nicky too much to stay away permanently!"

"Come back to *what,* Lauren? Years in prison?"

"But you said that maybe the jury might be lenient with him, and maybe they might consider the killings justified!"

Stan's father lowered his head in despair. "That was just wishful thinking on my part. You should have seen the way the local citizens reacted at the Klan trial when the jury rendered a '*not guilty*' verdict. Cedar Valley loves the Klan."

"Gosh, I didn't realize that, Uncle Lester! Do you think that Stan might have to go to prison?"

"Go to prison? If Stan confessed to the murders, he might even receive the death penalty!"

"Surely the jury wouldn't do that to him! No wonder he won't turn himself in to the police!!" Lauren began to cry.

Stan's father changed the subject. "Well, Lauren, it's pretty obvious that you and Nick won't consider staying in Cedar Valley and living with me. I guess I'll just continue to live alone. Think it over. If you change your mind, just let me know." He looked at his watch. "Gosh, it's getting later than I thought. I need to be going. Hurry up and get well, Lauren."

After a few more minutes of casual conversation, he hugged Lauren and returned to his home.

Chapter 26

The winds of retribution had long been gathering. The dark clouds of hatred that had forever hovered over Cedar Valley forewarned an approaching violent storm. Although the morning was sunny, Stan could sense the turbulent winds that would soon set in motion the tempest that was yet to come.

It was barely daylight when he parked his car behind the abandoned church building, making sure that it couldn't be seen from the road. Three oaken picnic tables were in the yard, graying with age, and teeming with termites. The abandoned Church of God was situated in a dark and gloomy woodland, where a thick layer of rotting brown leaves covered the forest floor. The once-white weatherboard siding on the building had faded to an ashen gray, and the tin roof that supported the bell tower was now bronzed with rust.

Stan entered the interior of the small chapel. The musty odor inside exuded an aroma of antiquity; and when he walked, the creaks from the planked floor intruded on the eerie silence of the room. He saw the row of wooden pews and the broken stained glass windows. When he peered at the empty choir loft, his imaginative mind could almost hear the piano as it accompanied a small group of hymn-singers.

In spite of the harrowing burden that lay before him, Stan remained stoically calm, for he was totally dedicated to this final solution. He glanced at his wristwatch and noted the time: *6:18 a.m.* He estimated that the Klan members would begin to arrive shortly before noon, which would allow him four or five hours to accomplish the task. He carried in his pocket the names of the Klan members that he had earlier listed. When he had belonged to the group during the prior year, it had contained sixteen members; and recently, Skip Hickman had joined; however, Klan leader Mike Bronson and Sheriff Mullins were was now dead, and Stan had recently eliminated both Skip Hickman and Bird Dog Johnson. Unless other men had joined without his knowledge, he calculated that thirteen members remained in the group. Since the Labor Day holiday was so popular in the area, Stan was almost certain that all members would attend the Klan picnic.

He walked to his station wagon and carefully removed a coil of wiring, a box of blasting caps, and a container with several sticks of dynamite. While carrying the roll of wire in a bib attached to his waist, he then divided the explosives into five equal portions. He left one of them in his vehicle, and carried the remaining four to opposite corners of the church. The absence of outside underpinning beneath the floor exposed the entire underside of the building. Stan was pleased, for this open space would make his gruesome task simpler.

He stooped down and peeked into the darkness beneath the floor, withdrew a flashlight from his pocket and slid the allotted amount of dynamite into a corner beneath the floor. When he crawled into the dark area, the air was dank and moldy, and much of the area was infested with cobwebs. The beam of his flashlight revealed the spiders on the underside of the floor, and the roaches crawling in the dirt. A mouse darted away from him and crawled into a nearby hole in the rotting wood. He wiped the cobwebs from his face and strategically placed the explosives near the corner of the structure before connecting the blasting cap and the end of the wire. He then crawled from beneath the antiquated chapel.

229

Because of his unfamiliarity with explosives, he carefully followed the rehearsed instructions that House Cat had given him. He continued the task when he repeated the process by placing the explosives under the remaining three corners of the building.

Returning to his vehicle, he removed a large battery and a detonator, the combined devices that would send the electrical charge to the dynamite. He carried the plunger and unrolled the coil of wire as he retreated for several yards into a safe alcove in the surrounding forest before attaching the wires.

He again noted the time: *10:30 a.m.* The Klan members should soon be arriving. For nearly an hour he sat on the forest floor among the thick foliage and saw-briars until he recognized two Klan members park their vehicles. When they stepped out of their cars he recognized Cowboy Galyon and one of the long-term members, Jimmy Kirby. They greeted each other before carrying picnic baskets to the tables in the church yard and spreading cloths on the rotting tables. When they took seats beside each other and began talking, Stan was too far away from them to hear their conversation. Apparently, the Klan members intended to have an outdoor picnic. Stan quickly became distraught; for he had previously assumed that the Klan would conduct their meeting inside the chapel. An outdoor picnic would eliminate his plan to kill the members by dynamiting the building.

The day was hot and humid. Stan wiped the sweat from his face and continued to patiently sit among the bramble in the woodland as he pondered his predicament. He counted the members as they arrived. By 1:00 p.m. all thirteen of them were seated at the picnic tables in the church yard. He began to worry, for he feared that they would all ultimately leave without ever moving inside the building.

When he heard a distant faint rumble of thunder from the west, Stan was surprised, for rain hadn't been predicted. He felt the gentle gusts of a cooling breeze as he looked toward the western sky and noticed the increasing darkness. The breezy gusts slowly increased to gale-force winds as the sky became as black as ink. Lightning flashed as bottles and napkins blew off the picnic tables. The Klan members quickly scurried toward the front door of the small chapel.

Suddenly, a downpour of frigid rain began to drench the forest and the surrounding area. The wind was now blowing the rain horizontally, bending the surrounding trees, and the front double-doors of the small church vibrated in the howling tempest. When Stan realized that all the members were inside the temple, he quickly pushed the plunger that detonated the explosives.

The enormous explosion was deafening, and shook the entire woodland like an earthquake. The roof of the building was gone, and nearby trees were almost uprooted and bent horizontally. The church building that had once existed had now been replaced by a blazing inferno; and immediately afterward, the black smoke was quickly being dissipated by the fierce wind.

Stan was now soaking wet from the storm; however, he failed to notice, for his physical awareness was of less importance than his emotional sensations. He felt totally recompensed. The debt that had for so long been owed to him by the Klan had now been paid in full. When the smoke began to clear from the carnage, he walked among the dead remains of his former enemies. While he was able to recognize some of them from his remembrance of their clothing, identification of their faces was impossible, for they only reflected grotesque caricatures of living men.

The acrid odor of smoke continued to linger, and the rain was now falling in torrents as the raging tempest intensified. The increasing wind was accompanied by flashing bolts of lightning and booming thunder; however, Stan was oblivious to the angry storm as he calmly walked to his car. He removed the dynamite he had previously left in his car and placed it under the hood. Following the earlier instructions of his friend, House Cat, Stan installed the necessary components inside the engine of his vehicle. His final chore was almost complete. All that remained was a simple assignment that required a small amount of work but much determination.

Before he entered the car, he pulled off his wet shirt, and squeezed the wetness onto the forest floor. When he looked across the hillside and saw the lights come on in a distant farmhouse, he realized that the occupants had heard the explosion and would soon report it to the authorities. After entering the car, he looked outside and noticed the water flooding the church yard as the storm continued to rage. His instincts caused him to wonder if he would be able to drive away through the water; but on second thought, he realized that it really didn't matter, for he wouldn't be driving anyway.

The Klan members had paid the price for the murder of Rufus and Preacher Temple; however, Stan realized that he was equally guilty of the crime. Therefore, he felt that he was deserving of the same punishment.

When preparing for his deadly mission, Stan had brought with him a portable radio. After entering the car he sat idly for a while, for he was resolved and unhurried. He searched his radio until he located a station that featured country music. For several minutes he listened to the soothing voice of Eddie Arnold, realizing that whenever the song ended, all that remained to complete the gruesome task was a simple turn of the car key.

When the country song ended he turned the key. In so doing, he fulfilled his former promise to Nick: He left the town of Cedar Valley forever.

Chapter 27

The storm was raging when Nick drove away toward *Park West Hospital* to visit Lauren. Although it was early in the evening, the sky was dark and only brightened by the frequent flashes of lightning that lit the landscape, and the wind had increased to become a howling tempest. The steady roll of thunder was suddenly overshadowed by a sudden flash of light and an explosive blast that shook the earth. *Wow!* thought Nick. *A huge bolt of lightning must have struck a nearby tree!*

Because the windows had fogged, he temporarily stopped the car and swabbed the windshield. Since driving had become more difficult, he sat for a long while, When he finally continued to drive toward the hospital he heard the wail of sirens in the distance. An ambulance and a fire truck were followed by a police car when they sped down the dark street and turned into an isolated road toward the countryside. Nick became curious. *Maybe that loud bolt of lightning struck a house,* he thought. Since he was in no hurry, he decided to follow. He continued to trail the police car for a couple of miles into an area of scattered houses and farmland.

When he rounded a curve on the mountainous road, he saw the smoking ruins of the chapel amid the surrounding forest. He began to realize that some catastrophe had occurred. The emergency vehicles had parked at the site and the fire truck was beginning to spray water on the burning building.

Since Nick was the first person to arrive at the scene, no one from the emergency crew had seen him. The rain was heavily falling when he parked his vehicle on the road shoulder. He grabbed his umbrella, and trotted toward the smoldering ruins. The remaining structure of the chapel was now clearly revealed by the large searchlight from the fire truck. However, it was the beam of light that exposed the remnants of the nearby vehicle that captured Nick's attention. The roof of the car had been completely blown away by a powerful blast, and only the nearby dead body revealed the driver. But it was when he saw the gold color of the car and the license plate number that he was certain that the vehicle belonged to Stan. When Nick saw the empty cars parked beside the old chapel, he realized that the Klan members had gathered inside the flaming building. He now had a complete understanding of the mayhem that had occurred.

When other cars began to park on the road shoulders, the curious onlookers were warned to keep their distance from the smoldering ruins. Nick walked to a nearby ditch and threw up. He didn't bother to view the remains of either Stan or the Klan members. He simply closed his umbrella, re-entered his car and drove away.

On his continuing drive to the hospital, the storm began to subside. Nick began to cry. He had so many unanswered questions that only Stan could answer. *Why had he decided to kill the Klan members in such a heinous manner? Where had he obtained the knowledge to discharge explosives? Did he have an accomplice? Why had he decided to end his life? What effect would this terrible deed have on his father? How could he discard the memories that they had shared together?*

Nick was in a state of shock as he drove onward. He wondered how he could ever explain this terrible event to

Lauren, and even more difficult, to Stan's father. It saddened him to realize that the pleasant times with Stan were forever gone; however, he could still cherish the happy memories. But memories are not reality. They are only images of the mind, only phantoms from the past that embodied a million ghosts that would forever remain in his mind and heart.

The rain had diminished when Nick finally arrived at the hospital parking lot. He left the car and strode into the front entrance of the building. As he walked toward Lauren's room, he dreaded explaining the prior events of the evening to her. On his walk across the lobby he passed the entrance to the emergency room. When he looked toward the open double-doors of the entrance he saw two attendants hurriedly rolling a stretcher that carried a patient toward the operating room. He was amazed to discover that the patient was Billy Sneed.

Billy was wearing a blood-soaked shirt. He was barely conscious and his eyes were filled with fear. He suddenly looked at Nick, and with a gasping breath said, "I need to talk to you, ol' buddy!"

As the aides continued to transport him down the hall, Nick followed alongside him and asked, "What happened to you, Billy?"

One of the attendants quickly reprimanded Nick. "Look, mister! This man is on his way to surgery! He's been shot several times. You can visit him later!" Nick stopped following the stretcher as the men delivered Billy toward the surgery room.

Nick caught the elevator to room 201 and slowly walked to Lauren's hospital room. Before stepping inside, he gathered his courage, for this wasn't just an ordinary visit, but an event of shocking revelation. *How can I ever report such news?* he wondered. He opened the door and stepped into the room.

Lauren was lying in her bed watching television. Upon his entry, she looked up and smiled; however her pleasant expression quickly changed when she saw Nick's ashen face. "What's wrong, Nicky? Did something bad happen?"

235

Nick forced a smile and said, "Yeah, Lauren…But before I tell you about it, I want to find out how you're doing." He walked to her bedside and kissed her.

He asked, "When will you be leaving the hospital?"

"I'm supposed to go home tomorrow," she said.

"Good. Why did they keep you so long, honey?"

"I had a setback after they set my broken leg. I had a temperature for a while, but it's better now." She studied his demeanor. "Something's wrong! Tell me what it is, Nicky!"

Nick looked sadly at her when he sat at the corner of her bed and explained the terrible events that had recently occurred. With a shocked expression, she began to moan. She then buried her head in her pillow and began to bitterly cry. When she finally regained her composure, she pulled him to her. She hugged him tightly and began to ask questions. "Are you sure that Stan killed the Klan members with explosives?"

"Yeah, Lauren. It took me a while to figure out what happened, but it became obvious when I realized that all of the Klan members died inside the building and their vehicles were parked in the church yard. It was obvious that someone had detonated a bomb."

"You said that Stan committed suicide. How do you know that one of the Klan members didn't kill him?" Lauren asked.

"Because I knew that Stan wanted to kill all of them. Also, his car was the only vehicle that was destroyed. Obviously, he detonated a bomb that leveled the old church building and then blew himself up in his car."

"I wonder where Stan got the explosives, Nicky. Do you think that someone else helped him do this terrible thing?"

"I don't know, Lauren. Also, I'm puzzled about how he knew how to detonate a bomb!"

Lauren again began to cry. "How are you ever going to tell Stan's father about this, Nicky?"

Nick again lowered his head in despair. "God only knows, Lauren. This is going to be one of the toughest things I've ever had to do! And speaking of Stan's father…He still wants us to stay here in Cedar Valley and live with him because he's so lonely. I know that we could never do it, but I sure hate to refuse him. Poor guy. He's really going to be even lonelier when I tell him about Stan's death and the way he died. I sure hate to abandon him at such a terrible time."

"I know it, Nicky. Maybe we should invite him to live with us in Louisiana! What do you think?"

"He'd be welcome, Lauren, but I don't think he'd never leave Cedar Valley"

As Lauren became more adjusted to the shock of the recent catastrophe, she and Nick continued their conversation about memories of Stan, and how he had left such an indelible impression on both of their lives. Because he felt that Lauren had endured enough trauma he decided not to tell her of his encounter with Billy Sneed in the hallway of the hospital. After hugging her and assuring her of his return on the following day, he left the room and caught the elevator to the first floor.

Because he felt an urgent need to talk to Billy Sneed, Nick immediately hurried to the nearby nurse's station beside the emergency room and spoke to the head nurse. He was told that Billy had recently undergone surgery and had been taken to the critical care unit in room 107. His condition was listed as critical. However, she informed Nick that Billy Sneed was allowed no visitors except for hospital personnel. Nick walked away in disappointment.

He decided that in order to enter the critical care unit, he needed to dress like one of the employees. When he began to walk down the hallway toward the hospital exit he noticed a closet between hospital rooms. In curiosity, he opened the closet door and switched on the light. On the shelves he saw freshly laundered stacks of hospital clothing. He sorted through the stacks until he found a medical doctor's lab coat. Nick slipped on the white coat, turned off the light, and stepped back into the hallway.

He briskly walked back down the hallway toward the nurse's station. When the head nurse noticed his white lab coat, she waved to him without even looking up; as a result, he passed the nurse's station into the critical care unit with little notice. Nick made his way down the hallway until he reached room number 107. He looked up and down the hallway before opening the door and entering the room. Billy Sneed was alone in the room, lying on his back in his hospital bed.

Nick walked to the bedside and looked down into Billy's fearful eyes. The rumpled sheet and thin blanket that covered him defined the outline of his shriveled body. The tube in his nose supplied the oxygen from the tank by his bedside, and his scrawny arms were inundated with needles attached to the container fastened to the stand by his bed. Apparently, the surgeon knew that Billy was on his death bed. It appeared that he had been placed in the recovery room only to die.

Although Nick had never liked the man, he began to feel a deep pity for him. Using a paper towel from the table top, he reached down and wiped the sweat from the dying man's face. "How are you doing, Billy?" Nick asked.

"I'm dyin', man!" Billy whispered. Nick leaned over the bed to better hear him. Billy understood that his time was short, but he wanted to make sure that Nick received his message before he died.

Billy was almost delirious with pain medication and he could only speak in whispers. "I'm dyin,' ol' buddy...But before I go...I got a secret...I wanted to tell ya." His voice began to fade away as Nick bent even closer until his ear was almost pressed against Billy's lips. His voice was only a whisper, and barely audible. It was a labored effort that required a lengthy time in the revelation of it. With his final breath he revealed his deathbed secret.

Chapter 28

When Nick left the hospital, the violent storm returned and grew stronger. It was a befitting occurrence, for it reflected the emotional turbulence within him. It was almost as if the tempest was in angry protest of the hatred and growing unrest that had for so long infected Cedar Valley. The drive was precarious. The streets had begun to flood and the windshield wipers struggled to swab away the rain.

During the drive toward the home of Lester Mullins, he cautiously steered the vehicle through the flooding streets and flashes of lightning. Nick was in no hurry, for he needed time to collect his thoughts, and ponder the terrible task that lay before him. He wondered how he would ever summon the courage to tell Mr. Mullins about the death of his son, and the horrible way he had died.

Traffic was sparse on the dark streets, for most residents had avoided the unexpected deluge. Nick slowly made his way through the flooding streets until he arrived at his destination. He pulled into the driveway, picked up his umbrella, and dashed out of his car. When he entered the rear door of the garage, a crack of thunder accompanied by a bright flash of lightning lit the landscape and struck a nearby tree.

Nick shook out his umbrella and walked slowly through the pitch-black interior of the garage. He brushed against Lester Mullins' vehicle and noticed that it was wet. Obviously, Stan's father had also driven somewhere in the storm. When he opened the door to the downstairs hallway, he detected a dim light coming from one of the upstairs rooms. He entered the hallway and began to walk up the stairs, noticing that the lamplight was coming from Lester Mullins' study.

Stan's father quickly looked up when Nick walked into the dim-lit room. Lester was seated behind his desk while looking over some paperwork, which he quickly lay aside when he saw Nick enter the room. "Well, hello, Nick. How is Lauren doing? When does she get to come home?"

Nick was almost overcome by a feeling of awkwardness as he tried to maintain his composure. "Lauren is doing fine, sir. She can come home tomorrow."

Lester. Mullins smiled. "That's great news, Nick! I'll bet you had a rough time driving in that storm. Did it almost wash you away? I stayed home all evening because I hate storms."

"Yeah, Mr. Mullins, it's really storming hard out there," Nick answered.

"Nick, you're one of my best friends. You're like a son to me. Why don't we do away with all this formality? Why don't you just call me Lester?"

"Well, okay, Lester. I can do that."

"Nick, I've been worrying about Stan. I wonder where he is staying. I wish I could just hear something from him!"

The mention of Stan caused Nick to dread his task even more; however, he was not yet ready to reveal the truth about Stan to Lester. "Mr. Mullins...er, Lester, I received some news about him in town earlier today. But before I tell you about it, I need to discuss something else with you."

Lester's eyes reflected extreme interest. "Oh? What's on your mind, Nick?"

In his mind, Nick began to search for a way to begin the discussion. He finally decided to simply speak honestly, and from his heart. "Sir, I've been asking myself a puzzling question all day: *Who is this man, Lester Mullins?* Just who are you, Lester? There seems to be *two of you!*"

Lester stared at Nick. "What do you mean, Nick? Why are you asking me a question like that?"

In spite of the sadness in his heart, Nick began to regain his courage. "Okay, sir…Let me put it another way: Are you the Lester who showed so much tenderness to Lauren's mother, and the man who has been so generous to everyone else in your family? Or are you the Lester who killed his own brother, and lied about it?"

Lester Mullins seemed to be in shock. His face grew pale when he answered, "Nick! My God! Where did you get such an idea, son?"

"I realized the truth when I was visiting Lauren in the hospital. The ambulance brought in Billy Sneed after he had been shot several times. Before his death, he told me a secret. I didn't doubt it because it was a death-bed confession."

"Are you accusing me of shooting him? Why would I do such a thing?"

"According to Billy, you shot him because he had been extorting a great deal of money from you. You were paying him to keep quiet about your killing of your brother. Billy was fishing that morning at the river and witnessed the killing after you followed your brother there!"

"But you don't have any actual proof that I killed him, Nick! You know how Billy Sneed lied about so many things!"

"I believed him, Lester. People don't lie when they're dying. Anyway, after I talked with Billy, several things began to add up in my mind. I began to put two and two together."

"What things could you put together that prove that I murdered my own brother?" Lester was filled with anxiety.

"Several things. First of all is your motive: You knew that Sheriff Mullins was the only person who actually knew for sure that you were involved in dishonesty during your term as city mayor. He was a partner in your dishonesty."

241

"Nick, many people knew of my crimes! You were in jail a couple of times! Don't you remember how some of the prisoners knew about my bootlegging?"

"Yeah, Lester, but that was just gossip from a bunch of jailbirds! None of our law-abiding citizens even knew about their gossipy accusations! Most church-goers in Cedar Valley still think of both you and Sheriff Mullins as being upright citizens! You realized that your brother was the only man who could reveal your dishonesty. Without a confession from him, you'd never be suspected. And since he had made up his mind to confess everything, it would incriminate you!"

Lester Mullins began to realize that Nick was convinced of his guilt. As a result, he began to face the reality of his situation. "Well, Nick, I guess you've made your point. What other things gave me away?"

"One of the things that made me suspicious was your attitude about Billy Sneed. Every time investigators wanted to question him, you tried to steer them away from him because you knew he had the goods on you. You realized that if you stopped paying him blackmail or if someone offered him more money than he was extorting out of you, he'd rat on you. Also, you claimed that you didn't leave the house tonight, but when I entered your garage I noticed that your car was wet from the storm. You drove to Billy Sneed's apartment and shot him tonight! You even hired an incompetent private eye because you knew that he would never be smart enough to gather any evidence against you. Also, there were a few things that didn't exactly point to your guilt or innocence. But some of your attitudes were suspicious."

"Such as?" Lester was now totally dejected; however, he was curious about Nick's analysis.

"Well, Lester, after you killed your brother, you developed a morbid fascination with death. You seemed to try to justify killing your brother by saying that he is better off dead, because he is happier, and with God. You said the same thing about Lauren's mother when you said that she had always been unhappy, and finally found her happiness in heaven."

242

Lester became resigned to his guilt. "Okay, Nick. It seems that you've nailed me. What do you plan to do about it?"

Nick took no delight in punishing Stan's father, for he realized that his final retribution would be heartbreaking—the moment that he learned of his son's terrible death. "Lester, I swear to you, I honestly don't know what to do."

"Nick, Stan told me all about you. He once told me that you always tried to adhere to the letter of the law. But I want you to think about something, Nick. When I killed my brother, only two people knew it: Sheriff Mullins and Billy Sneed. But since they're both dead, you and I are the only people in the world who know about it. We could move on and have happy lives if you'd just forget it. You can see I'm a changed man, Nick. If I could relive my life, I'd never kill my brother. In fact, if I only had the power, I'd bring him back to life. But none of us can change the past. I've lived these last few months in regret. I've really suffered over this."

"You have a big problem, Lester." Nick said, "You tried to atone for your sins with your imagined conversion experience and your good deeds to others. But conversion requires confession of our sins. You never really confessed."

"That's where you're wrong, Nick. I confess my sins to God every day."

"But not to *the public,* sir. You hid from your sins with lies, and misleading statements."

Lester earnestly stared into Nick's eyes. His voice had now adopted a pleading tone. "Nick, you don't *always* adhere to the letter of the law. I remember when Stan told me about the way you withheld information when little Caleb killed Mike Bronson. You didn't even report the crime. Couldn't you find it in your heart to do the same for me?"

"Aren't you forgetting something? Arthur Bowman has been accused of the murder of your brother. He is languishing in jail awaiting his trial. What do you intend to do about him?"

"Nick, I'd never let him suffer for a crime I committed. As a last resort, I fully intend to confess to the murder."

Nick was dubious. *"When* were you going to confess, Lester? After he was convicted and already had a noose around his neck?"

Lester became totally frustrated. "Nick, I'm just living my life one day at a time. I'll deal with that problem when it's necessary!" He threw up his hands in despair. "God, please deliver me from this! I can't stand any more bad news at the moment!"

Nick deeply dreaded the terrible chore that awaited him; however, he realized that now was the time to reveal the heartbreaking news to Stan's father. "Lester, I'm very sorry to give you this kind of news, and I want you to know that I share your pain. Get a grip on yourself, sir! The story I'm about to tell you is very bad!" As Nick related the story to him, he witnessed the change in Lester's expression, for it began with anxiety and ended in horror. In order to spare him unnecessary pain, he withheld some of the most horrid details.

When Nick had concluded the gruesome story, Stan's father sat for a long while and simply stared at him. Finally, he reached into his desk drawer, removed a pistol, and slowly placed it on his desktop.

Nick was shocked. "Lester, do you intend to shoot me to keep me quiet about the murder?"

Lester Mullins only stared straight ahead. "It no longer makes any difference to me what you do or say, Nick!"

Suddenly, the dim light in the room disappeared when a simultaneous boom of thunder and a flash of lightning plunged the room into utter darkness. A couple of seconds later, Nick saw another flash of light and heard a second boom. At first he feared that Stan's father had taken a shot at him in the darkness; however, when the lights returned, Nick saw the horrible truth: With his hand still holding the smoking pistol, Stan's father lay forward on his desk with a hole in the side of his head.

Chapter 29

The violent storm had finally ended. The morning was sunny and warm on the day that Lauren was released from *Park West Hospital.* After Lester Mullins' body had been taken to the mortuary, Nick accompanied Lauren to Lester's home where they both grieved the deaths of Stan and his father. Two days later, they prepared for the two funerals that were scheduled for later in the day at Smith's Mortuary. At each of the funerals Lauren repeatedly wept as the Baptist Pastor spoke kind words of both men, particularly of Lester Mullins, for he was a highly-respected person in the town of Cedar Valley. Citizens of the community were mystified that suicide had claimed the lives of both men, for most of the people were totally unaware of the causes.

Nick and Lauren faced several responsibilities in their preparation of their return to Louisiana. First on the agenda was telling Sheriff Kirkland of Lester Mullins' confession of the murder of his brother; thus insuring the release of Arthur Bowman, who had been languishing in jail under the suspicion of murder. Then they secured the settlement of Lauren's inheritance of the insurance money from her home that had been recently destroyed by fire. Their final obligation was settling the account and cancelling the lease of the Lester

Mullins residence. Consequently, they contacted a local lawyer to handle the details of both financial situations.

Nick and Lauren were now ready to leave for Louisiana. When remembering that their journey together had begun in this small community, they were saddened to realize that it was highly unlikely that either of them would ever again see Cedar Valley, Tennessee. Their memories of this little town stimulated mixed memories, for their best and worst experiences had occurred here. With melancholy feelings, they leisurely packed their clothing and drove away.

Epilogue

During early Autumn of 1955, Nick increased the speed of the Buick as they travelled southward toward Louisiana. When he remembered the deaths of Stan and his father, his mind was filled with sadness. Beside him, Lauren stared straight ahead, almost as if she were in a trance. He thought about the aftermath of the terrible events that had unfolded since he had moved to the South. Radical changes had taken place. Several people for whom he had held a deep affection were now dead; also, many of his enemies had been killed.

He wondered if his move to the South has brought about this tremendous upheaval that has taken place. He began to realize that for every risk man takes, for every positive change he makes, there is a price to be exacted; for the lives of all people, like the links of a chain, are bound together. To toss even a tiny pebble into undisturbed water has a rippling effect on the entire surface; for all choices have consequences: Moral conclusions are composed of two elements: causes and results.

But who can predict the aftermath of man's choices? Life is a roll of the dice, for every act in life is a trade-off. Nick might have avoided bringing about these terrible occurrences if he had stayed in Chicago; but if he had done so, Cedar Valley would still be a bed of corruption…and he would not have found Lauren.

In spite of his terrible method, Stan had eliminated the evil Klan in Cedar Valley; but did the end justify the means? And even if it did—how long would it last? How long would it be until another Klan group had organized and were once again whipping, or murdering a black man?

Nick considered Stan's vengeful retaliation. Some would consider him a murderer, others a crusader—perhaps, even a hero. However, regardless of whatever label he bears, Nick only knows that a certain brand of justice had been attained, if only temporarily.

In a civilian society, Stan's actions would be judged as murder; however, as a military man in the war Nick had killed men for reasons far less justifiable than the motives for which Stan had killed. Who decides when killing is justified? Does a government's sanction of killing in war dictate the conditions under which it is acceptable for men to kill other men?

By eliminating the Klan in Cedar Valley, Stan had not significantly changed the South. With his misguided methods he had only been able to carve a tiny niche in a monumental mountain. But it occurred to Nick that even tiny niches would ultimately whittle away the mountain, causing it to crumble. However, if they are to be permanent, these niches must be carved by countless courageous people who are dedicated to using legal and peaceful methods to attain justice.

He had traveled to the South to find peace and fairness; instead, he had found only a fleeting illusion of peace and a mockery of fairness. But to nurture hopes of finding a state of perpetual serenity, regardless of where one journeys, is only to cling to a fantasy; for like the years in the unrelenting flow of time, life is made up of changing seasons. To everything there is a season, and a time for every purpose under the heaven. The season for revenge has passed. It is no longer a time to kill, nor a time for temporary healing; but it is a time for self-examination and permanent change. Nick realized that the South must retreat from violence, bind up wounds, regenerate spirits, and move forward on the long journey toward a season of reformation.

However, a retreat from violence doesn't mean a withdrawal from the battle against repression. Permanent healing means more than a temporary reconciliation brought about by a free pardon for past injustices; for the process of healing is sometimes a long and arduous journey. It requires a repression of prejudice, a righting of wrongs, and recovery from affliction. Healing the malignance that infects the South will be a lengthy transformation. Before healing can take place, there must be reparation. It is not yet a time to make peace, but a time to pause and reflect; and to gird up loins in preparation for the inevitable war to come; for past events have taught Nick that reconciliation cannot be attained without justice. The mortal enemy of justice is prejudice; and the parents of prejudice are poverty and ignorance. Nick decided that his mission in life is to take up arms against these enemies.

But his battle against this mortal enemy must be non-violent, fruitful and complete. He has begun to realize that violence is counter-productive; for it only begets more violence and ultimately tends to strengthen the enemy's resolve and only leads to a temporary illusion of success. True reconciliation will be attained only through a slow evolution of peaceful but relentless resistance brought about by education, establishing and enforcing laws, and a willingness to change.

During the fifties, the South was rife with institutionalized racism and repression. Nick could sense an approaching revolution; for an insatiable hunger for dignity, equality, and respect reside within the human heart. He remembered the words once spoken by Woodrow Wilson: 'The seed of revolution is in repression.' Nick felt that a time was coming when good men will rise up and stamp out the repression in the South. As he looked ahead to the remainder of the 20th Century, he silently vowed to be a part of that revolution.

Nick glanced at Lauren, who was hanging her head in sadness. From past experience, he realized that life is not predictable and serene like a smooth flowing river, but rather an undulating stretch of rapids, a roller coaster of ups and downs. After each golden day, the setting sun often introduces the despairing blackness of night.

But the sun also rises. In the past, during times of depression, both Nick and Lauren had always been able to glean a ray of sunshine from the darkness. In their minds they searched for a small gem of hope with which they might be able to comfort each other.

Lauren turned her head toward him. "Nicky, I can't believe all these terrible things have happened. I believe that this is the darkest moment of my life."

Nick gently patted her on the knee. "Things will get better, Lauren. Just give it time."

Her cheeks flushed and a faint smile graced her lips as she looked up at Nick. "By the way, honey…this might not be the best time to tell you—but we're going to have a baby."

Nick grinned. "See? Haven't I always told you? The darkest hour of the night comes just before the dawn!"

ABOUT THE AUTHOR

Don Pardue grew up in a small town in East Tennessee. After completing a tour of duty in the U.S. Air Force during the Korean War, he received his education at Tennessee Wesleyan College, Atlanta Art Institute, and the University of Tennessee, where he earned a BFA degree and later taught courses in graphic design.

He is the author of six novels: *Blossoms of Winter*, *Tom, Dick, and Harriet*, *Maiden Harvest*, *Random Reflections*, *Southern Sanctuary,* and *Southern Storm.*

During his career he worked as creative director for a Knoxville design studio. He is now retired and spends his free time painting and writing in Lenoir City, Tennessee.

Don is a charter member of the Authors Guild of Tennessee.

Praise for Don Pardue
for his sequel of *Southern Sanctuary:*

"Don Pardue is one of our great Southern writers. His work is comparable to that of William Faulkner, Flannery O'Conner, and Willie Morris."
    -Robert Cranny, author of *The Storm* and *The White Deer*

Don Pardue's books

Blossoms of Winter
Tom, Dick, and Harriet
Maiden Harvest
Random Reflections
Southern Sanctuary
And
Southern Storm

Are available
through

www.amazon.com
or
www.neilans.com

Also available as e-Books
through

www.amazon.com

Made in the USA
Charleston, SC
26 August 2016